The Temporary DETECTIVE

For Chris,

JOANNE SYDNEY LESSNER

Best wishes
XO!

Dulcet Press

Also by Joanne Sydney Lessner

Pandora's Bottle

ISBN: 0615605818
ISBN-13: 978-0615605814

Printed in the United States of America
Cover design by Linda Pierro

Published by Dulcet Press
New York
www.dulcetpress.com
info@dulcetpress.com

For my parents, who have always believed in me

ONE

"I'M SORRY, BUT THERE'S NOTHING I CAN DO FOR YOU."

Isobel Spice regarded the powerfully built, dark-skinned man behind the desk, who looked like he'd be happier thundering down a football field than dispensing temporary office jobs to aspiring actors. Or, in Isobel's case, withholding them. This was supposed to be the easy part. She had arrived in New York on the first of October perfectly prepared to claw her way into acting auditions, but not into an office survival job, too.

Isobel picked up the brass nameplate on the man's desk. He'd obviously given it the once-over with his sleeve that morning. She could see the streaks.

"James Cooke. Good stage name."

James snatched the nameplate from her and set it down. "You have no office experience."

"Of course I don't. I just graduated from college," Isobel said patiently. Having reenacted this scene at seven other temp agencies, all of which had turned her away, she knew her lines.

"Look, I'm sure you're very bright—"

"I'm smart, I'm reliable, I'm available, and, no, I've never worked in an office before, but I've been in many in my lifetime. Doctor's offices, professor's offices, the principal's office—" She flashed a disarming smile. "That was just once, in sixth grade. But I pick things up quickly, and you can't tell me that all your employees with years of experience are any better than I am. If they were, they'd have real jobs!"

James stared back stonily. "People temp for all kinds of reasons."

Isobel sighed. "I know that. I came to New York to pursue my acting career. I need to eat, I need to live, and I have no upper body strength. The one time I tried to wait tables, I dropped five boiled lobsters on a nun."

James glanced past her shoulder at the open door, then leaned forward, his left cuff pulling back to reveal a gold watch with half the gold scraped off.

"Listen, I've only been here a week," he said in a low voice. "The boss has strict guidelines about who we take on, and I can't jeopardize...I mean...you understand."

Isobel returned his whisper spiritedly. "Of course. But you understand too, then, don't you? I mean, how did you get this job?"

He sat back, bristling. "I've been in the recruiting business for five years."

Isobel threw her arms wide. "Then what are you worried about? You have experience! You won't have a problem getting another job."

James pushed away from his desk, but his chair bounced off a metal filing cabinet and sent him rolling back to her. He stood with a grumble and gestured toward the door.

"I can recommend other agencies that are flexible about taking people with less experience."

Isobel tried to stem a rising tide of panic. She was pretty sure she'd been to all of them, and they weren't flexible enough. Temp Zone was her last hope. If he didn't take her on, she didn't know what she'd do.

"If you give me a chance, I promise you won't regret it!"

A resonant guffaw escaped, unchecked, from James's gut. "Whenever somebody says that, I usually wind up regretting it double. I'm sorry, Miss Spice, but I can't send you out."

"I prefer Ms. Spice. Otherwise it sounds like you've put in too much coriander." She swiveled her chair and crossed her ankles daintily, recalling her favorite choreographer's observation that it was more flattering to the leg than crossing at the knee. But despite her attempt to be offhand, her heart was racing as she tried to figure out how to get James Cooke to change his mind. Unfortunately, his broad jaw was set in a determined refusal to be charmed by her. There was nothing left but the direct appeal.

"Can't you just give me a break? This isn't brain surgery!"

James walked over to the small, dusty window, craning his neck against his overly starched collar. Isobel took his discomfort as a hopeful sign and crossed the fingers of one hand inside the other.

He turned to face her again. "How many phone lines could you handle?"

"Four." She saw him frown. "Five—six! And I type fifty words a minute."

"Most of our temps type over seventy-five. Software?"

"Mac and PC, Word, Excel, PowerPoint…"

"Photoshop? InDesign?"

She was tempted to lie, but thought better of it. Even PowerPoint was a stretch.

"I could learn."

"The thing is—"

The metallic jangle of the telephone interrupted them. They stared at it, as it rang a second time.

"Aren't you going to get that?" Isobel challenged.

"Temp Zone, James Cooke speaking."

He sat down again and listened for a few seconds. Then he glanced at Isobel and quickly turned his back on her. "Mm hmmm," he said into the phone.

She leaped up, circled behind the desk, and thrust her face in his. "I can do it!"

James put his hand over the mouthpiece and whispered furiously, "You don't even know what *it* is!"

Isobel shook her chestnut brown ponytail so vigorously that it smacked her in the face. "I don't care!"

James waved her off. "This morning? By when?" He

glanced at his fake gold watch. "I don't have anyone..."

Isobel didn't know what the job was, but she knew she had to have it. This wasn't simply a temp job at stake; it was her whole New York experience. She felt as if she were facing a cosmic test. If she landed this assignment, the rest would fall into place: her own apartment, her first professional acting job, new friends, and, with any luck, a boyfriend. Whatever this job was, it was a barometer of her future, she was sure of it.

Isobel bounced on her heels and jabbed an enthusiastic thumb at her chest, but James ignored her. Scowling, she grabbed a notepad and pen from his desk and scribbled, "You'd rather send nobody than me?" She underlined the word "nobody" twice and shoved the paper in front of him.

Beads of sweat dotted the ebony sheen of James's brow. He swallowed. "All right, I've got someone. Name is Isobel Spice. Sure...no problem. Glad I could help."

He hung up and ran a hand over his coarse, close-cropped head as if he were trying to erase whatever impulse had crumbled his resolve.

Isobel exhaled with relief and sank back into her chair. "Thank you!"

James took the top sheet from a stack of forms and briskly started filling in blanks. "Okay, they need you by ten," he said. "It's a last-minute thing...phones and light typing. Half-day until one o'clock. I'll be asking for feedback, so you'd better learn quickly." He tore off a pink copy of the form and handed it to her. "InterBank Switzerland, One Madison Avenue, seventeenth floor. Ask for Felice Edwards. She's the human resources director. And call me when you get settled."

Isobel took the paper and stood up. "James, you're a peach."

As he brushed past her to the door, she realized just how imposing his physique was.

James the giant peach, she revised.

He grasped her hand hard, but Isobel, who was proud of

her own unexpectedly firm handshake, gripped it right back.

"Thank you for taking a chance on me," she said.

He glanced around, and then put his mouth close to her ear. "I gotta ask. What happened after you dropped the lobsters on that nun?"

"They rushed her to the emergency room to treat her for burns, and then they fired me. Or maybe they fired me first, I can't remember. It was a long time ago."

She flashed him another bright smile and hurried out before he could reconsider.

JAMES COOKE RETURNED TO HIS DESK and picked up the completed employment request form for InterBank Switzerland. He rattled the paper nervously.

Half-day, phones and light typing. How hard could it be?

"James!"

He started guiltily. His boss, Ginger Wainwright, was leaning against the doorframe. An officious, brassy redhead of a certain age who dressed down in an effort to mask her obsessive personality, Ginger had a habit of sneaking up on her staff. She always claimed to be "just passing by," but she passed by an awful lot. After a week, James still wasn't used to it.

"How's it going?" Ginger asked.

"Fine. It's all good."

"The young woman who was in here earlier. Potential employee?"

He blinked away an image of Isobel's long ponytail smacking her in the face and nodded. "Could be."

"Good. Okay. I was just passing by."

"Uh, Ginger, just out of curiosity—I mean, for future reference—what do we do with candidates who are smart and well-educated, but have no practical experience?"

Ginger sniffed dismissively. "Send them to Temporama or Sally Nelson and let them get some training. Then if they're any good, we'll poach them."

"We don't ever take a chance and send them out? If they seem to have a lot on the ball, I mean."

She gave him a stern look. "We don't take chances at Temp Zone. That's why we're tops. Right?"

"Right," James answered, forcing his mouth into a deferential smile. "That's what I thought."

He listened as Ginger's heels clacked away down the hall, and her voice echoed into the office of another recruiter.

"Anna? How's it going? I was just passing by."

James got up and closed his door quietly. Then he returned to his desk and looked at the request form again.

He had a feeling he'd just made a big mistake.

TWO

ISOBEL STEPPED THROUGH THE DOORS of the tall, silver office building that housed Temp Zone and paused to inhale a noseful of diesel fumes. The scent was as pleasing to her as a whiff of Chanel. Everything about New York was exciting, even the polluted air. She was finally living the dream she had nurtured throughout her Milwaukee childhood and four years at the University of Wisconsin. She would work her way up through the ranks like generations of actors before her, starting with shoestring showcases in moldy church basements. Then she'd move on to summer stock in barns, regional productions in actual theaters, and national tours in refurbished vaudeville houses, before making her assault on Broadway from the Off side (okay, Off Off, if necessary). Now, by the grace of James Cooke, she was on her way to subsidizing this neatly plotted trajectory with her first paycheck.

James Cooke. There was a story there, she felt sure of it. But this wasn't the time to speculate about him; she had more pressing matters to contemplate. As Isobel elbowed her way down Madison Avenue, she reviewed her performance.

Use of smile: effective.

Persistence: the right amount of pluck tempered with sweetness.

But she'd made that stupid comment about going to the principal's office. And she'd told him about the lobsters.

Isobel liked to think that others found her candor charming, but she knew from experience that this was not always the case. She tried to impose a one-second delay between her brain and her mouth, but sometimes she just couldn't stop herself from blathering, especially when she was nervous. Her mother, her acting teacher, and especially her precocious younger brother, Percival, were forever telling her that she didn't need to work so hard to make a good impression, but it was not a lesson easily absorbed. Her interview with James was a good reminder that a deep breath was never a bad thing, and as she paid for her venti latte at Starbucks on Twenty-fourth Street, she resolved for the umpteenth time to restrain her rebellious tongue.

She left the coffee shop and turned the corner. Bright rays of October sunshine glinted off the art deco spires of One Madison Avenue like neon lights above a theater marquee. Isobel glanced at her watch. Almost ten o'clock. Right on time.

Here goes, she thought, and made her entrance through the revolving door.

She showed her driver's license to the guard at the front desk, signed the visitors' log, and waited patiently for an elevator, scrutinizing her reflection in the polished brass. She always dressed to emphasize her compact figure. Today she had chosen a tasteful rose-colored button-down shirt and black pants.

It never hurts to look the part, she reminded herself.

Isobel trailed a sea of suits and skirts into the elevator and allowed herself to be squashed into the corner. By the time it reached the seventeenth floor, there was only one woman left. Isobel followed her out.

"Is this InterBank Switzerland?" Isobel asked.

The woman sniffed sideways as if a bad smell had just wafted by, and pointed to a frosted pane of glass next to the heavy wooden door. If Isobel looked sideways and squinted, she could just make out the company name etched into it.

"Thanks," Isobel said, but she was addressing a flowered rear end. The woman swayed down the hall, nodding indulgent hellos on either side as if she were a duchess passing among her tenant farmers. The office, which seemed to stretch on for miles in every direction, was buzzing. There were cubicles upon cubicles in the center of the giant space, with conference rooms veering off into obscured corner areas. There didn't appear to be a receptionist, so Isobel inched her way over to the first desk on the left. A stout, bearded man was on the phone, arguing. Isobel cleared her throat softly.

"What?" he growled, covering the mouthpiece.

"I'm looking for Felice Edwards."

"Sixteenth floor."

"But I'm supposed to be temping on seventeen—"

"Felice Edwards. HR. Sixteen!" He put the receiver to his mouth again. "They gotta move me. I swear, I'm like the freakin' doorman."

Isobel returned to the hall and rang for the elevator.

This is stupid, she thought. It's only one floor down.

She followed the signs to Stairwell A and descended the two half-flights to the sixteenth floor, but when she tried the door, it was locked. Cursing her luck, she darted back upstairs to seventeen and reached for the knob.

The door had locked behind her.

She pounded on the door, but it was solid steel. She called for help, but the thick metal absorbed her cries, and after a minute, her fists ached too much to continue. There was nothing to do except try every floor until she found a door that opened.

But there was no reentry on fifteen, fourteen, thirteen or twelve. She began to panic more about getting out alive than being late. Fully expecting the door on eleven to be locked as well, she went flying through it with such force that she knocked into a delivery boy, whose paper bag burst against his chest, splattering him with scrambled egg and cheese.

"Sorry! I'm really sorry!" she cried, ignoring the stream of accusatory Spanish as she ducked into an open elevator. By the time she arrived on the sixteenth floor, it was almost ten fifteen. The gracious gold lettering and wide glass-fronted doors made it clear that this was the main reception area.

Isobel leaned against the rounded, wood-paneled front desk and steadied her voice as she addressed the receptionist, who was talking to a tall, curvaceous woman with coffee-colored skin and fabulously twisted hair.

"I'm here to see Felice Edwards."

The tall woman disengaged herself. "That's me. Are you Isobel?"

"Yes! I am so sorry I'm late."

Felice smiled. "I'm just glad you're here. Follow me."

Back in the hall, Isobel reached for the elevator button, but Felice continued toward Stairwell A, talking over her shoulder. "These elevators take forever."

Isobel opened her mouth to protest, but thought better of it. They trudged upstairs to seventeen, where Felice opened the door with a key that hung on a lanyard around her neck.

"You'll be working in Frank Lusardi's group," Felice said, as they passed the angry bearded man in the cubicle and rounded the bend to one of the distant corners. The floral-skirted duchess from the elevator stood waiting for them in an open area with three vacant desks.

"This is Paula Toule-Withers. She'll show you around." With a vaguely reassuring flutter of her fingers, Felice retreated.

Paula rapped sharply on the nearest desk. "You're late."

"I know, I'm sorry, I was—"

"We've already started our department meeting," Paula said in a voice that betrayed the remains of a posh British accent warped by years in the U.S. "Just answer the phones until we're finished. Surely, you can manage that?"

Then she, too, was gone, and as if on cue, three phone lines rang at once. Still standing with her bag slung over her shoulder, Isobel set down her coffee and started answering.

"Good morning, InterBank Switzerland, please hold."

"Good morning, InterBank Switzerland, please hold."

"Good morning, InterBank Switzerland, please hold."

She bit her lip and looked at the three blinking red lights.

Praying that nobody else would call, she picked up the first one again.

"Good morning. Can I help you?"

"Lou Volpe for Stan. He there?"

"I'm sorry, but he's in a staff meeting."

"Tell him I called."

"Can I get your num—?"

Click.

Isobel yanked open a desk drawer and rummaged around for a message pad. She pulled out a pair of maroon-handled scissors, a used-up roll of Scotch tape, a bent metal ruler, and a crusted-over bottle of Liquid Paper. Clearly, nobody had occupied this desk for some time. As she fished in her handbag, she balanced the phone on her shoulder and took the second call.

"Is Nikki in yet?" said a sexy male voice.

"She's in the staff meeting."

"Are you sure?"

"Yes," replied Isobel, with cheery confidence.

He laughed. "Don't worry, I'll call back."

Isobel frowned and picked up the third call.

"Doreen? How could you keep me waiting all this time? DOREEN?" shrilled the woman's voice through the plastic.

"Um, this is Isobel."

"Who? There's no Isobel."

"I'm temping today. Can I help you?"

"Let me help *you*!" barked the woman. "Always pick up Frank's line first. He's the Senior VP. The others are unimportant." Another line started ringing. "And don't keep people on hold more than a few seconds!"

Isobel pulled her ponytail in frustration as two more lines jingled.

"Tell Frank I called." The woman hung up.

"I would, but who the hell are you?" Isobel muttered to the silent receiver. She gave up trying to find paper and picked up the next line, hoping that remembering messages wouldn't prove any harder than memorizing lines.

But the phones kept ringing, and Isobel kept answering. She paused to catch her breath while four of the six lines blinked on hold. The fifth line rang. Isobel grabbed it and, without thinking, shouted, "What?"

There was a pause, then a familiar deep voice said, "This is James Cooke from Temp Zone. May I speak to Isobel Spice?"

She gasped and slammed down the phone.

"Shit!" She sank down in her chair. It was all over now. She couldn't handle the phones—she could barely get herself onto the seventeenth floor. The temp agencies were right to turn her away. She was in over her head.

A nasal snicker from across the way stemmed her wave of self-pity. Isobel looked up to see an unattractive, overweight woman with a squarish face settling her paisley-clad bulk at the opposite desk.

"You can let them go to voice mail, you know."

"What about these?" Isobel indicated the blinking lights.

The woman rolled her eyes. "Those you gotta answer."

Isobel dug deeper in her bag and produced a handful of wrinkled receipts. One by one she picked up the holding lines and scribbled down the messages. Two more calls came in, but she let them go to voice mail. Finally, it was quiet.

"You must be the temp," the woman's grating tones intruded. "I'm Doreen Fink. I'm sure we'll be *very* good friends," she added with a wink that made Isobel flinch.

"I took a few...several...okay, a lot of messages," Isobel said. "One was a woman for Frank, but she didn't identify herself."

"Frank is Mr. Lusardi, and if she didn't say, then it was his wife. Did she sound like a bitch?" Doreen spat. Isobel nodded. "Then it was *her*." Except that in Doreen's thick Brooklyn accent, it sounded more like "huh."

A pudgy, downcast man with a shock of thick brown hair appeared at Doreen's side and held out a sheet of yellow legal paper.

"Could you...?" His high, timid voice trailed off.

Doreen pointed to Isobel. "Give it to huh," she said. "I got enough to do."

The man cleared his throat. "Can you type this for me?"

"Sure," Isobel said, relieved to have a job she could handle. She glanced at the letter and the signature jogged her memory. Stan Henderson. The very first call.

"I took a message for you from..." She racked her brain. "Lou Volpe!" She yelled the name as if she'd just discovered a winning lottery ticket.

"Oh," Stan said dully. "What's his number?"

Isobel's heart sank. "I'm sorry. He didn't leave one."

Stan's doughy face drooped even further, and he trundled away. Isobel set his letter aside and started shuffling through her receipts, trying to decipher her scrawls. A thick pad of message notes in triplicate landed with a thump, inches from her nose, and she jumped.

"You need one of these," Doreen said, looming over her. Up close, Isobel could see that her chin was dotted with dark spots, either failed electrolysis or a bad case of blackheads, and her breath smelled like garlic.

Who eats garlic first thing in the morning? Isobel wondered.

"Um, thanks," she said, leaning away from Doreen.

"Conchita is Stan and Paula's assistant, but she won't be in until noon today, so you gotta cover for her until she gets back. I'll take care of Frank's phones and stuff."

"Okay."

"And no personal calls." A lascivious smile bent the corners of Doreen's mouth. "Unless we get to hear about how good it was last night. You got a boyfriend?"

"No."

"Too bad. Last temp we had, she had this guy who liked to do her every morning before work in the bathroom of a different Starbucks," Doreen said, practically salivating at the thought. "Then they'd talk about it on the phone all day."

Isobel moved her Starbucks cup to the other side of the desk. She needed to find something to do. Immediately.

The phones were still quiet, so she picked up Stan's letter. Then she remembered James. She shuddered involuntarily, thinking about how unprofessionally she'd handled his call. But she had promised to check in. Maybe if she altered her voice a little, he'd think he had reached someone else earlier.

"Temp Zone, James Cooke speaking."

"Hello, James," she said, trying to keep her voice high and light. "It's Isobel. I'm at InterBank Switzerland and everything's fine."

"What's wrong with you? Sounds like you've been inhaling helium."

Isobel readjusted her voice. "Nothing. I just swallowed funny."

"You didn't check in. I tried you before, but the receptionist must have transferred me to the wrong number. What's your direct line?"

Isobel looked down at the phone. All she saw were four digits: 6583. Her eyes flew to a sheet pinned to the corkboard on the wall, listing employee names and four-digit extensions. She looked frantically around for some indication of the exchange, but she couldn't find one. Doreen was nowhere to be seen.

"Can you hang on a sec?" Without waiting for an answer, she dropped the phone on the desk, where it landed with a clatter. She sprinted down the corridor and almost collided with the bearded man.

"What's the telephone exchange here?"

"212."

"No, not the area code, the first three numbers."

"What do you mean? We all just got extensions."

Isobel exhaled in frustration. "If somebody calls you directly from the outside, what do they dial?"

The man looked at her impatiently. "212-441—"

Isobel ran the length of the floor back to her desk.

"212-441-6583," she said finally to James, who could have interviewed and hired several new temps in the time he'd been waiting.

"That's odd. I could have sworn that's what the receptionist said."

Isobel giggled nervously. "Really? Well, you know, sometimes wires get crossed."

"Yeah, but it sounded like you."

"Oh, here comes the boss! Gotta run. Call you later!" She hung up, cursing herself for being so unprepared. Isobel knew she wasn't fooling James. She gave a defeated sigh; there was only so much she could do. She fired up the computer and, in between calls, examined Stan's letter.

It was riddled with bad grammar, which presented her with a moral dilemma. Should she correct it? She considered asking Doreen, who had reappeared. But after overhearing her on the phone, exclaiming, "You think *I* screwed *you* in the back?" Isobel determined that the difficulty presented by "between he and I" would be lost on her.

"Hey! Who are you?"

An attractive, slender woman with auburn, boy-short hair was depositing a bulging tote bag on the third desk.

"Isobel Spice. I'm temping."

"Nikki Francis. Nice to meet you. I don't suppose anyone called for me?"

"No. Wait! A man called, but he didn't leave a message. I said you were in the staff meeting. He seemed surprised."

Nikki laughed. "I'm sure he was. I do the department billing, part-time. I'm really an actress."

"Me, too!"

Across the room, Doreen gave a loud snort. "Another one? Jeez, this town is crawling with youse. If you're all so good, whaddaya doin' here?"

Nikki turned her back on Doreen. "Ignore her. She's a cretin."

Isobel felt her stomach unclench for the first time all

morning. "Can I ask your advice?" she whispered. Nikki nodded. "Stan Henderson's memo is full of grammatical errors. Should I correct them?"

"Go ahead. He'll never know the difference. Just don't change the meaning."

Isobel gave her a grateful smile and went back to work.

The morning passed surprisingly slowly after the initial flurry, and Isobel puttered back and forth between her desk and the small area around the corner where Frank, Stan and Paula had their offices, delivering letters for signing. She was eager to talk to Nikki some more, but whenever she attempted to start a conversation, Doreen would leer at them and say, "If you two don't stop chitchatting, I'm gonna have to put youse over my knee!"

As one o'clock approached, Isobel's stomach was growling, and she had to pee like a racehorse. She hadn't been to the bathroom all morning, and the coffee had gone straight through her. She decided to push through and hit the ladies' room on her way out, so she tidied up the last few memos and checked her watch. It was a few minutes before one. She stood up. So did Doreen.

"I'm taking lunch," Doreen announced. "You take yours when I get back."

"I'm leaving," Isobel said. "I was only hired until one."

Doreen picked up the phone and punched some numbers. "Felice? We need the temp all day. She says she's only here 'til one." Doreen waited a moment, then called across to Isobel. "Can you stay?"

"Well, there's an audition I was hoping to go to—"

"She can stay," Doreen said and hung up. Before Isobel could respond, Doreen plunged on. "You can take lunch at two. I'm off to the ladies'." And with a swing of her elephantine behind, she was gone.

Nikki smiled sympathetically at Isobel. "I hate to tell you, but if it's an open call, you'll never get in now anyway. You have to get there first thing in the morning to get a time slot."

"Oh," Isobel said. Clearly, she still had a lot to learn—on all fronts.

"Doreen shouldn't have done that, though," Nikki went on. "It's not really up to her."

Isobel brightened. "On the other hand, it will make me look good to my temp agent. I'll call him."

But before she could pick up the phone, deafening alarm bells rent the air.

"What's that?" she screamed at Nikki, who was already grabbing her bag.

"Emergency drill!" Nikki shouted back. ""Get your stuff and follow me!"

Isobel felt her heart skip a beat. "Are you sure it's a drill?" she shouted.

"Blue light!"

Isobel looked up at the wall where Nikki was pointing. Underneath the whirling red emergency light was a smaller flashing blue one with the word "Drill" taped next to it.

As soon as Isobel started to run, she realized just how desperately she had to pee. She was halfway down Stairwell A to the sixteenth floor, when she realized there was no way she'd make it to the bottom. She watched Nikki and the suit jackets recede down the steps, then raced back upstairs through the door, which, thankfully, had been propped open.

As Isobel bolted down the corridor, it dawned on her that she didn't know where the bathroom was. She tried to recall which direction Doreen had taken, but the corridors, unfamiliar and interchangeable, refused to yield a door with a female icon. Isobel dead-ended at Stairwell B and doubled back as the alarm bells continued their raucous clanging. She sprinted past her desk, where the offending Starbucks cup mocked her from atop the phone message pad, and dashed around the corner. Finally, there it was—the ladies' room.

With renewed energy, Isobel pushed open the door and flew past the vestibule with its makeup desk and long mirror. She flung open the door to the first stall.

And screamed.

THREE

ISOBEL RESTED HER FOREHEAD against the cool tile of the bathroom wall and watched the automatic sink wash down her response to what she had just seen. She was tempted to look again, to make sure she wasn't hallucinating, but the splayed feet just visible under the stall were enough to convince her.

Doreen Fink was sitting on the pot, with a pair of scissors sticking out of her meaty bosom and blood dripping down the sides of her mouth. Her eyes were glassy and unseeing, and although Isobel had never seen a dead body before, she was pretty sure Doreen had peed her last. With a jolt, Isobel remembered that she still had to go to the bathroom terribly. For a moment, she couldn't move; her hands seemed frozen to the sink. Then, feeling cold and hot at the same time, not to mention distinctly weak in the knees, she inched her way as fast as she could to the stall farthest from Doreen's, sat down, and tried to think.

She knew she should call for help, but she didn't want to be the person who found Doreen, with all the possible guilt that implied. She could simply leave and belatedly join the emergency drill, but no doubt Doreen's stall door would display two large handprints from where she had pushed it inward. Those handprints would be even harder to explain if she fled the scene of the crime, which she was well aware was a crime in itself. If only she had passed out, she wouldn't have to do a thing. She briefly considered faking it, but decided this was not the best time to be caught acting. No, going for help was the only sensible course of action.

She flushed, washed her hands, and splashed cold water on

her face. The alarm bells had finally stopped, and it wouldn't be long before people would be returning to their desks. Somebody might come into the bathroom at any minute.

Somebody did.

It was Paula Toule-Withers, who glowered at Isobel and reached for the door of the first stall.

"Don't go in there!"

Isobel's shout startled her every bit as much as it did Paula, who shrieked and jumped back, hitting her head on the tile wall.

"Holy Christ!" yelped Paula. "What is wrong with you, you stupid twit?"

Isobel had half a mind to let Paula see for herself, but the words choked themselves out anyway.

"She's dead! We need to call for help."

Paula sucked in her breath and growled, "I'm telling Felice—no more actresses!"

And with that, she pushed in the door to Doreen's stall.

Isobel wasn't sure which she found more satisfying: the fact that Paula didn't even make it to the sink, or the fact that now her fingerprints were on the stall as well.

AS ISOBEL WAITED IN THE SMALL, airless conference room with the others, she found herself annoyed by how thoroughly Doreen Fink had ruined her day. If only Doreen hadn't tricked her into staying longer, Isobel wouldn't have been around to discover her body. Then again, obnoxious as Doreen had been, it seemed unjust to blame her for her own death. Even so, Isobel couldn't help feeling manipulated. She wondered if she could bill for the extra time.

Paula Toule-Withers returned from her police interview, retrieved her things, and left without a word. Isobel looked around the table at the others. The color still hadn't returned to Stan Henderson's pudgy face, which was greenish pale against his shock of brown hair. Senior Vice President Frank

Lusardi, a dark-haired man in a well-tailored suit, was occupied with his BlackBerry and seemed to be trying to maintain his distance from the rest of the group, which was difficult, given the close quarters. Conchita Perez, a matronly Hispanic woman, was hunched over a rosary, wiping away her tears with a parade of never-ending tissues that emerged from her sweater sleeves like clowns from a Volkswagen. Isobel would have liked to compare notes with Nikki, but she had been the first person interviewed and released.

Isobel was famished. She hadn't eaten anything since breakfast, and it was already four o'clock. Finally, the young policewoman who was running interference came back and gestured for Isobel to follow her past the roped-off bathroom to an unused corner office.

"Sit down, please," said an intense, ferrety-looking man from behind the desk. "I'm Detective Harvey and this is Detective Kozinski." He nodded at the policewoman, who had terrible skin and fair hair pulled off her face with an incongruously girly headband.

Isobel sat in a straight-backed visitor's chair and folded her hands in her lap.

"State your name," commanded Detective Harvey.

"Isobel Spice."

"Address?"

"I'm staying at the Evangeline Residence for Young Women on Gramercy Park South until I find an apartment of my own. I just moved here."

"Phone number?"

Isobel rattled off her cell phone. Detective Kozinski picked up a small inkpad and a piece of white cardboard.

"We'd like to take your fingerprints for elimination purposes. If you don't mind."

Isobel blinked at the two detectives. "Do I have a choice?"

"Legally, you can refuse," Detective Harvey said.

Isobel knew her fingerprints were all over the bathroom, albeit for completely innocent and explainable reasons. Still, she didn't see any reason to call attention to them if she didn't have to.

"I'd rather not," she said.

Detective Kozinski shrugged and set the inkpad on the desk next to a bottle of Purell and a roll of paper towels. "How long have you worked here?" she asked, flipping open her notebook.

Isobel looked at her watch. "Six hours."

"Very funny," said Detective Harvey.

"No, really. I'm a temp. I was hired this morning, very last minute."

"Through which agency?"

"Temp Zone."

"Who's your rep?"

"James Cooke," Isobel said, as Detective Kozinski scribbled. "Wait! You're not going to call him, are you?" Isobel asked, horrified.

Detective Kozinski paused, pen in mid-air. "Do you have a problem with that?"

"No! I mean, yes. It's just…" Isobel picked up the Purell and smoothed down a peeling corner of the label. "This is my very first temp job and it was going so well. Doreen asked me to stay extra—"

"Doreen did?"

"Yes."

"And what did you say?"

"There was an audition I wanted to go to, but Doreen sort of bulldozed me into it. Then I realized that it would make me look good to James if they wanted me longer. I had to convince him to take a chance on me, because I've never worked in an office before. I just graduated in June, and I only moved to New York a few days ago. I really want to make a good impression on him. I don't want him to think I cause disaster wherever I go."

Detective Harvey cleared his throat. "Do you usually cause disaster wherever you go?"

"No, of course not!" This time, Isobel knew better than to mention the lobsters. "He just didn't believe me when I said I could juggle six phone lines at once."

"Had you ever met Doreen Fink before today?"

Isobel shook her head. "I'd never met any of them. I still haven't met some of them."

"What were you doing in the bathroom during the emergency drill?" Detective Harvey asked.

Isobel cocked her head. "Isn't that obvious?"

"In a murder investigation, nothing is obvious. Please tell us why you ignored the emergency drill and went to the bathroom instead."

Isobel felt her face grow warm. "Because I had a Starbucks venti bursting the seams of my bladder. I was trying to be a good do-bee and not take a break, but I couldn't hold it anymore."

"So you pushed open the door to the first stall without looking underneath to see if someone was in it?" Detective Kozinski asked.

"Why would I look?" Isobel asked. "It was an emergency drill. Nobody was supposed to be there."

The two detectives exchanged a glance, then Detective Harvey said, "We don't have any more questions for you right now, but we'd like you back here tomorrow at nine a.m."

"But I haven't been hired for tomorrow," Isobel protested. "Will I get paid?"

"Put it this way," Detective Kozinski said, as she ushered Isobel toward the door. "They're gonna need a secretary."

FOUR

JAMES COOKE GRABBED THE REMOTE from the floor, snapped off the television and began to search for his stash. He was pretty sure there was a small bottle of Jack Daniel's, the kind you get on airplanes, hidden somewhere in the kitchen for emergencies. And this might well turn out to be an emergency.

He rarely turned on the eleven o'clock news, and he couldn't decide if he was glad he had or wished he hadn't. Tonight's story about the murdered secretary at InterBank Switzerland hadn't mentioned Isobel Spice, but he couldn't help wondering if she was involved somehow. He found Isobel both extremely irritating and maddeningly appealing. She reminded him of the girls at Columbia who had turned up their noses at him, though Isobel had hardly snubbed him. In fact, she had almost seemed to be flirting with him. He banished that thought from his mind. Jayla, already fast asleep in his bedroom, was the most irrationally jealous person he had ever dated, and she could smell another woman on his mind as sure as he could smell an unopened bottle of Jack Daniel's.

He finally found the bottle tucked behind some old cookbooks his mother had given him. He set it on the kitchen counter and wiped his sweaty hands on his boxers. InterBank Switzerland was a sizeable operation. Chances were, Isobel hadn't been anywhere near the dead woman; she'd probably never set eyes on her. Still, the fact that she hadn't called him after her shift—although, he reminded himself, he hadn't asked her to—now struck him as ominous.

But was this worth falling off the wagon? He knew he

should call Bill, his AA sponsor. He also knew how much relief the Jack would give him. He shuffled back and forth between the phone and the counter, muttering to himself. Through the thin wall, he heard Jayla moan in her sleep. He began to unscrew the bottle. Then he reached for the phone, picked it up and slammed it back down.

"Shit, shit, SHIT!"

He shoved the bottle into the makeshift appliance garage behind the electric mixer and cracked his knuckles loudly. He couldn't tell if the fear he was feeling was for his job or for Isobel's safety. He tried to convince himself it was the latter, but the more he thought about it, the more he realized that what was really scaring him was the possibility, however unlikely, that Isobel had somehow, accidentally of course, plunged a pair of scissors into a secretary's chest, just like she'd dropped boiled lobsters on a nun.

He took a manila folder from his messenger bag and let the pages cascade through his fingers until he found Isobel's application. He grabbed the cordless phone off the counter and punched in her number.

Buried at the bottom of Isobel's shoulder bag, her cell phone rang and rang.

ISOBEL SMACKED HER ALARM CLOCK, rolled over and went back to sleep. She was vaguely aware that there was a reason she needed to get up, but it seemed somehow to be connected to her last dream and, therefore, not real. Fortunately, she'd hit the snooze button instead of the off switch, so the alarm blared into her consciousness again nine minutes later. As she squinted at the time, the reason burst through the fog in her head.

InterBank Switzerland. Phones, light typing—and murder.

She hunkered deeper under the thin, scratchy blanket. She did not want to return to the bank for just about every reason she could think of. After the police had released her, she had headed straight for the nearest coffee shop and wolfed down a greasy excuse for a meal. She hadn't realized how exhausted she was from the day's events until she returned to the Evangeline Residence, where she sat down on her bed to take off her shoes and promptly fell asleep.

The one thing she'd resolved before she had nodded off was to get up extra early and sign up for the second day of the auditions she had missed. With any luck, she would either be released early from the bank or be able to take a lunch break this time. She showered, dressed, and ate her breakfast, which was included in the price of her room, then headed uptown.

It was seven thirty when she turned the corner of Forty-eighth Street and Seventh Avenue. The auditions weren't set to begin until ten, so she figured she was plenty early, but her heart sank as she approached the end of a long line of people snaking down the block.

"Excuse me, are you here to audition for *Guys and Dolls*?" she asked an exotically attractive guy around her age.

He nodded and gestured to the line. "Yeah, but we're too late. They're taking names for the waiting list now."

"What?" Isobel cried in dismay. "But it's only seven thirty!"

The young woman in front of them turned and rolled her eyes at Isobel. "Let me guess—your first audition?"

Isobel took in the woman's luxurious golden curls and porcelain skin, studiously undermined by the silver stud in her nose, parade of rings up her right ear, black jeans, and tight, strategically ripped purple T-shirt.

"Obviously. Are *you* here for *Guys and Dolls*?" Isobel returned.

The blond woman snorted. "Obviously."

Isobel was irked at having been spotted so easily. But it was her own fault for not asking Nikki exactly what "first thing" meant.

"What time did the line start?" she asked.

"Who knows?" the woman said with a shrug. "I went to

one the other day and there were, like, a hundred people signed up by seven a.m. Some dinky little Bowery theater. I thought nobody would bother."

"What are you going to do?" Isobel asked.

"I'll stay and put my name on the list. Then come back at the end of the day and see what's what."

The man nodded. "Me, too."

"I guess I'll join you, then." Isobel shifted her bag on her shoulder and held out her hand. "I'm Isobel Spice."

"Sunil Kapany," he said, shaking it. "Nice to meet you." He turned to the blond woman, questioningly.

"Delphi Kramer."

They inched a few steps forward, as, groan by groan, more latecomers settled in behind Isobel.

"Delphi...that's an unusual name," remarked Isobel.

"It's short for Delphinium. My mother's family is obsessed with flower names. All the normal ones, like Rose and Lily, have been used *ad nauseum*, so my mother got creative."

"Do you have sisters?" Sunil asked.

"Ohhhh, yes. There are six of us."

"Are you going to tell us or should we guess?" Isobel asked.

Delphi gave a bored sigh. "Hyacinth is the oldest, then Pansy and Poppy—they're twins. Then me, then Aster, who believe me, can be a pain in the aster, and Zinnia. She's fourteen."

"Well, I think your name is great," Isobel said. "Very unusual and catchy."

"Thanks. I like Isobel. Anyone ever call you Izzy?"

"Let's put it this way. If you call me Izzy, I'll call you Delphinium."

"Deal."

"How long have you been in New York?" Isobel asked.

"Three weeks," said Delphi. "I spent two years singing on cruise ships, saving up money to come here. So I'm pretty much just off the boat myself. Literally."

Without realizing it, they had turtled their way down the

street, through the doorway and into a narrow hall. Behind a rickety table sat a middle-aged man in a moth-eaten argyle sweater who already looked utterly exhausted and fed up.

Delphi pulled a yellow legal pad toward her. The top page was covered with names. She jotted hers sideways in the margin next to the number fifty-nine and handed the pen to Sunil.

"Just out of curiosity," Delphi said to the monitor, "what time did the first people start lining up?"

"Six."

"This morning?" asked Isobel, taking the pen from Sunil.

The monitor raised a weary eyebrow. "Would you rather I said last night?"

"Any chance we'll be seen?" Sunil asked.

The monitor shrugged. "I've got a hundred people with appointments and," he glanced down at their names, "sixty-one on the waiting list. But hey, you never know. People sign up and then don't show. Check back around four."

"Ah, for the day we get our union cards. No more waiting in line," Delphi said as they shuffled back outside into the warm fall day.

Sunil shaded his eyes from the sun. "Equity auditions are just as bad, I hear."

"Yeah, but the pay is better if you land a job," Delphi reminded him.

"I've heard that having an agent is key," said Isobel.

Delphi paused in front of a mirrored panel on a building to crayon another layer of deep plum onto her lips. She gave them a satisfied smack and addressed Isobel's reflection. "And I've heard it doesn't make a damn bit of difference, you still wind up doing all the legwork yourself."

"That reminds me—" Isobel looked at her watch and let out a cry. "I had no idea what time it is! Sorry, I've got to run." She took off down the street, calling behind her, "The police will be furious if I'm late!"

It wasn't until she reached the subway that she realized how odd that must have sounded.

FIVE

AFTER PICKING HER WAY THROUGH YARDS of police tape and shredding half a packet of tissues sneezing from the ubiquitous fingerprint powder, Isobel arrived at her desk to find Detective Kozinski waiting for her.

"You're late," the policewoman said, pointing to the wall clock.

"I'm sorry. I didn't miss anything, did I?" Isobel asked.

"Your prints were on the stall," said Detective Kozinski curtly.

"I know. I pushed the door open."

"They were on the sink too, and the last stall."

"I threw up. Then I peed." Isobel set her Starbucks cup on the desk, then turned suddenly. "Wait a second. How do you know they're mine? You didn't take my fingerprints."

Detective Kozinski gave a little smirk. "We lifted them from the Purell bottle. We can do that, you know."

Great, thought Isobel. Now it looks like I was hiding something.

The policewoman perched on the edge of the desk and gestured for Isobel to sit down. "Why didn't you call for help immediately?"

"I was about to, when Paula came in. It took me a few minutes to pull myself together." She looked pointedly at Detective Kozinski. "As you can imagine."

"You knew your fingerprints would be in the bathroom," Detective Kozinski said. "Is that why you refused?"

"No," Isobel protested. "I just…didn't want to get ink on my pink blouse."

Detective Kozinski glared at her and walked away.

As if on cue, the phones started their symphony, but Isobel didn't bother to answer them. She wasn't entirely sure why she was back, except that the police had requested her presence. She tried Felice Edwards's extension, but there was no answer. Unsure what to do next, she took her cell phone from her bag and saw that a call had come in the night before from a number she didn't recognize. Curious to know whose it was, she dialed it back. A woman's voice answered.

"Hello?"

"Um, hi, this is Isobel Spice."

"Who?"

"Isobel Spice. You called me last night?"

"No, I didn't."

"This number came up on my cell phone."

"Well, I didn't call you."

"Are you sure?"

"Honey, I don't even know you," the woman said and hung up.

Isobel frowned at the phone and deleted the entry from the call list. Obviously a wrong number. She sat back, took a few sips of coffee, and looked around. The phone on the desk rang.

May as well start my day, she thought and picked it up.

"InterBank Switzerland, this is Isobel."

"How come you haven't called me? And what are you doing back there?"

It took her a moment to recognize James Cooke's voice.

"Oh my God, I'm so sorry! You'll never believe what happened here yesterday."

"I know all about it. It was on the news. I tried to call your cell last night, but you didn't answer."

"My cell? But I didn't—oh, wait! I did have a call, but I just called back and it was a woman—"

"What do you mean, you called back?" James said in a tight voice.

"The number wasn't familiar, so I dialed it. But the woman

said she hadn't called me."

"You called back?"

"Why, what did I do?"

"Forget it. Did you tell her your name?"

"Yes, but I thought you said to forget it?"

"Forget it."

Isobel was confused and strangely touched. "You called me? That's so sweet!"

"Why didn't you call me?" James demanded.

"I just didn't think...it was so crazy! I was going to call this morning to tell you they want me to stay on," Isobel said. Actually, she thought guiltily, she had completely forgotten about James. But she was sure she would have remembered him. Eventually.

"They want you to stay?" repeated James.

"Yes. Isn't that great? It means I did well on my first day!"

There was no answer.

"Doesn't it?" Isobel prompted.

"What if I don't want you to stay?"

"Why? You think I'm going to kill someone else?"

"Isobel!" James screamed in her ear. "This isn't a joke. If someone hears you say that, they're gonna haul your cute little ass down to the precinct!"

"Okay, okay!"

For a moment, neither of them spoke. Isobel bit her lip nervously.

"Do you want to stay? Do you feel safe?" James asked.

"I don't have much choice. The police told me I had to come back."

"What? Why? I thought you said they asked you back because they liked your work," James said.

Shit, thought Isobel. She'd blown her own cover. "They did. Doreen asked me to stay for the afternoon yesterday."

"The dead woman?"

"Yes."

"Well, I can't exactly ask her for feedback now, can I?"

"Are you telling me you think I killed her so she wouldn't tell you I'm a lousy secretary?" Isobel asked, her voice rising.

"That's not what I meant. I—"

"Then what did you mean?"

"Nobody *living* from the bank officially asked you to come back—is that right?"

"No, but," Isobel remembered Detective Kozinski's words, "they're going to need a secretary."

"It doesn't have to be you."

"Got anything else for me?"

"Not right now."

"Then I may as well stay. It's like what my mom says when a plane crashes right before you're supposed to fly. I've been pre-disastered."

James cleared his throat. "I have to talk to Felice Edwards. If they really want you to stay on, you can decide whether to take the risk. In the meantime, don't do anything—"

"Stupid? You could have a little more confidence in me," Isobel snapped. She slammed down the phone and stared at it moodily. She couldn't figure out if James was worried for her—or for the people around her.

"I'm sorry, but I don't remember your name."

Isobel looked up and saw Frank Lusardi, his BlackBerry clutched in his palm like a security blanket.

"Isobel Spice," she said, instinctively straightening her blouse.

"Right. Come with me."

As she got to her feet, he wagged a reproachful finger at her, just as Doreen had the day before.

"And no personal calls on the job."

JAMES PEERED DOWN THE HALL to make sure Ginger wasn't on the prowl. Then he shut the door to his office, slammed his right fist into his left hand, and cursed as loudly as he dared. He should have thought beforehand about what he wanted to say to Isobel, because everything had come out of his mouth completely wrong. He was supposed to be cool and professional. Instead, he'd acted like a total asshole.

What he really wanted to do was tell Felice Edwards that Isobel had another assignment and couldn't stay. He'd lose his commission, but was that really worth keeping Isobel in a potentially dangerous situation? He massaged his temples and tried to think. It was possible that a long-term placement at a company under police scrutiny wouldn't even look that good to Ginger. Then again, companies were always being investigated for one thing or another. But there was a big difference between corporate paper crime and murder. If there weren't, he wouldn't have gotten so worked up just now.

And what on earth made him say that about her cute little ass? He didn't do white girls as a rule, and Isobel was pretty lily. She was exactly the sort of overprivileged goody-goody who needed the world to knock her around some before she would be interesting. Still, there was something about the way she said his name. *James.* She sounded like a Bond girl, and he had to admit that as white as those babes generally were, they were pretty hot. Not that Isobel would ever be interested in an alcoholic, ex-quarterback Columbia dropout who was struggling to stay sober and keep his job. Even if he was attracted to her—which he wasn't.

Part of his job was to look out for his employees, he reminded himself. He'd be just as worried about anyone else. He should pull her out of there no matter what she or the police wanted.

He picked up the phone, about to dial Felice, then set it down again. Isobel wasn't any more likely to get into trouble—correction, get him into trouble—at InterBank Switzerland than anywhere else. Pre-disastered. The idea had its appeal.

If he'd learned one thing about Isobel in his few interactions with her, it was that opposing her was a recipe for aggravation. Fine. If they wanted her to stay, let her. He'd confirm it with Felice, then file Isobel as an open-ended engagement at InterBank Switzerland and forget about her. He only had to check in with the long-termers every two weeks. Once it was settled, he could pass by Ginger's office for a change and tell her he'd converted a half-day into an open-ender. She'd like that.

The phone rang. Recognizing his home number, he snatched it up.

"Hey, baby doll," he drawled.

"Who the hell is Isobel Spice?"

SIX

FRANK LUSARDI PACED BACK AND FORTH in front of Isobel as if he were a lawyer interrogating a witness.

"So you want to be an actress?"

"I *am* an actress," Isobel replied, as politely as she could. Her father, a history professor with great respect for the theater but none for the people in it, insisted on putting it the same way. Having to make the distinction always got under her skin.

"But you don't have an acting job right now?"

Isobel wasn't sure if he was trying to belittle her aspirations or simply confirm her availability. She decided, for the moment, to give him the benefit of the doubt.

"No, but I haven't been in New York very long."

"Where are you from?"

"Milwaukee."

Frank gave a dismissive harrumph. "Never been."

"Oh, it's great! The lake is gorgeous, and there's a symphony and two opera companies, and several Equity houses, and all sorts of neat experimental theaters."

"Then why aren't you there?"

Isobel's eyes widened in disbelief. "Because it's not New York! It doesn't have Broadway."

"And that's where you're heading?"

"Absolutely. I've had my Tony Award acceptance speech written since I was eleven."

Frank wandered over to the window, which looked out onto Madison Square Park. Isobel shifted on the leather sofa in his roomy corner office and checked him out. He was of medium height and build with darkly handsome Italian features, but his eyebrows projected a certain sternness, and something about the set of his mouth made her think he was not quite as smart as he wanted to be.

"The police are going to be here for a while," Frank said, almost to himself. He turned around to look at her. "I'm sure you didn't have anything to do with this."

Why, because you did? Isobel thought involuntarily.

"No, of course not," she said.

"I know the police had their reasons for asking you to come back today, but would you be willing to stay until we hire someone permanent?"

James's warning flashed through her mind, but Isobel pushed it away. A job was a job, and she'd fought hard enough for this one in the first place. Besides, she knew that if she walked away now, she might never find out what really happened to Doreen Fink.

"Sure."

"What kind of experience do you have?"

Isobel smiled stiffly. Here we go again, she thought.

"Phones, typing...." She shrugged. What the hell? "Actually, I don't have any. I've spent the last four years in college."

"You understand what this department does?"

"Nobody's really explained it," she admitted.

"We provide support to the procurement department, which supports IT purchasing and disbursements. They support the bank's overall IT function, particularly the back shop. That means we deal primarily with vendors, but only those whose businesses don't support the larger strategic functions of IT involving online banking, equities and media tie-ins." He looked expectantly at Isobel, who had lost him after the first "support."

"Seems pretty straightforward," she said.

"Plan to be here at least through next week."

"Thanks. Um, do I get a lunch break every day?"

"Of course."

"Does it have to be at lunchtime?"

"I suppose not. Why?"

"I was hoping I could leave a little early today instead of taking lunch. There's an audition I want to go to."

Frank peered at her, as if he were trying to decide whether or not she was pretty enough to be an actress.

"If it's all right with the police, it's all right with me." A sudden smile lit his face. "Hey! I know that one. 'It's the right place in the wrong time…'" he sang.

Or the right song with the wrong lyrics, thought Isobel.

She gave a pained smile. "Something like that. But you know what they say."

Frank stopped singing. "No, what do they say?"

"Don't give up your day job," quipped Isobel.

Frank's face hardened. He picked up a stack of papers from his desk and handed them to her.

"Type these," he said curtly and turned back to his computer.

Damn, damn, damn, thought Isobel, as she left his office. When will I ever learn?

NIKKI FRANCIS WAS AT HER DESK by the time Isobel returned.

"Welcome back," Nikki said.

"I appear to be the new Doreen, at least through next week." Isobel plopped down in her chair with Frank's papers in hand. "Let's hope I have a longer shelf life."

"You know what they say," Nikki said.

Isobel nodded. "I know, 'Don't give up your day job.'"

"I was going to say, 'A temp job in hand…' but it amounts to the same thing."

Isobel read down the list of names and phone extensions pinned to the corkboard above her desk: Frank Lusardi, Stan Henderson, Paula Toule-Withers, Conchita Perez, Nikki Francis, Doreen Fink, Temp. She took a pencil from the desk, crossed out Temp, and wrote her name. She briefly considered crossing out Doreen's name as well, but thought better of it.

"It'll be nice to have someone to talk to for a change," Nikki said, clacking away on her computer keyboard. "Have you met everyone yet?"

"I've met Frank and Stan. Oh, and Paula."

"Yeah, she's a piece of work. What about Conchita?"

"I saw her in the conference room when we were waiting for the police, but she wasn't here when I got in yesterday, so we never really met."

"Come on, then, I'll introduce you."

Isobel followed Nikki back to the area where the offices were. Conchita sat at a desk in the center, dissolved in tears. She hadn't been there a moment ago, when Isobel left Frank's office.

"Conchita?" prodded Nikki gently. "Are you okay?"

"It's those detectives," Conchita said, unloading her nose into a tissue. "Asking personal questions. And I don't know how to answer them. Jesus knows I can't be untruthful."

"Why would you be untruthful?" Nikki asked.

"They asked me how I felt about…about Doreen…and I couldn't…I had to tell them the truth. And then they got nasty." Conchita's fingers moved to her neck and pulled nervously on her silver and emerald cross.

"Only because everyone else is probably lying and saying that she was their best friend," Isobel said.

Conchita peered at her. "Who are you?"

"This is Isobel," said Nikki. "She was here yesterday. She's filling in for Doreen. For now."

Isobel gestured at Conchita's necklace. "That's a very pretty cross."

Conchita's hand clamped around it protectively. "I've worn this every day since my first communion. Jesus knows, I can't be untruthful," she repeated and burst into fresh tears.

"She's very religious," Nikki said unnecessarily, as they returned to their desks. "Doreen was always particularly horrible to her. Hard to know why."

Isobel leafed through the papers Frank had given her. She hoped his grammar was better than Stan Henderson's.

"I guess I'd better get going on these," she said.

"And you probably want to check the voice mails," Nikki reminded her.

Isobel copied down several messages, including two from Frank's wife. She was glad she'd missed those calls. Nikki picked up her own line when it rang and, giggling delightedly, turned away from Isobel to continue her conversation in hushed tones. Isobel passed along the phone messages, typed up Frank's memos (a few grammatical quirks, but nothing like Stan's) and stole a glance at the new issue of *Backstage*, which came out on Thursdays. After a longing glance at the Equity stage auditions, she sighed and turned to the non-Equity section. Someday she'd get her union card, but for now, she'd have to concentrate on jobs she had a shot at and build her résumé. She immediately spotted a few that looked appealing. She opened her desk drawer and felt around for the scissors that had been there the day before.

"Looking for these?" Detective Harvey appeared out of nowhere, with Detective Kozinski at his side. He was holding up a plastic evidence bag.

In the bag was a pair of maroon-handled scissors, their tips darkened with dried blood.

Isobel eyed them for a moment before she spoke, her voice even. "Anybody could have taken those scissors from my desk."

"Yes, but your fingerprints are the only ones on them," Detective Harvey said.

Isobel's heart skipped a beat. "When I got in yesterday morning first thing—I had never been here before, remember—the phones were ringing off the hook, and I was pulling things out of the drawer like crazy trying to find some paper."

"And did you find any paper?" Detective Harvey asked.

"No. Doreen gave me a memo pad."

"Did you put the scissors back or leave them out on the desk?" asked Detective Kozinski.

"I'm pretty sure I left them out."

"Did you notice at any point that they were gone?"

"I—I don't remember. Look, my fingerprints will be on everything in that drawer. And besides, where were they on the scissors? What part?"

"The handles."

Isobel silently cursed herself for always holding scissors correctly. "Okay, but not like I was actually using them. Not like I was cutting," she said.

"They were plunged into Doreen's chest," Detective Harvey said. "No cutting required."

Isobel squirmed in her chair. "I told you, yesterday was my first day here, the first day I ever laid eyes on Doreen or anybody. My first temp job ever! I just graduated from college. I'm not even really a secretary. I'm an actress!"

She caught the glance between the two detectives.

"Musicals! I do musicals!" she protested. "Everyone knows singers can't act!" She threw a pleading glance at Nikki, who had hung up the phone and was watching the exchange with a guarded expression. "Look, anybody could have taken those scissors," Isobel rushed on. "And I'll tell you this. If I were going to kill someone in an office, I wouldn't be stupid enough to use the scissors from my own desk!"

The two detectives were still staring at her.

"You're an actress?" Detective Harvey asked, finally.

Isobel took a deep breath.

"No, I'm not," she said. "I *want* to be an actress."

SEVEN

"JAMES, I'D LIKE YOU TO MEET MIKE HARDY from Dove & Flight Public Relations."

Ginger propelled forward a short, stocky man who looked like a rook on a chessboard. "Mike and I are going to have a bite of lunch and discuss how Temp Zone can support his needs," she continued, smoothing the rounded neckline of her clingy cashmere sweater.

"All right, then," James said, unsure how he was supposed to respond. Ginger slid her arm under Mike's elbow and steered him out to the elevator bank. Obviously, the man was a potential new client, but "support his needs"? He sometimes wondered just how Ginger made her business deals.

He always relaxed when Ginger was out of the office, which, he had learned, she rarely was. Anna took the opportunity to sneak out for lunch, and the other recruiters all withdrew into their offices to do whatever it was they didn't dare attempt with Ginger underfoot. James left his office door open to enjoy the cross breeze from his small window. He was just deciding how best to waste his time when the main office buzzer sounded.

His immediate, ingrained reaction when the two detectives flashed their badges was to hold his hands high above his head, but a secondary instinct thwarted his first, and he thrust them into his pockets instead.

"Can I help you?" he asked.

"Detective Harvey and Detective Kozinski. We'd like to speak to James Cooke."

"That's me," James said, careful to keep his voice as free

from the twang of the 'hood as possible. "May I ask what this is regarding?"

"We've got a few questions about Isobel Spice."

Sending up an ardent prayer thanking God for supporting *his* needs by removing Ginger from the premises, James led the two detectives to his office, where he gladly sacrificed the cross breeze and shut the door.

"Please," he said, gesturing for them to sit down. They didn't. James hovered uncertainly before deciding that he would feel more powerful behind his desk.

"You sent her to a job at InterBank Switzerland on Wednesday?" Detective Harvey asked.

"Yes."

"She said it was last minute."

"It was. I was registering her as a new employee when the call came in. It seemed like a good way to try her out. It was only supposed to be a half-day, phones and light typing."

"Have you worked with InterBank Switzerland a long time?" Detective Kozinski asked.

"I've only been at Temp Zone a week, but I believe they've been a client for a number of years."

"Who's in charge here?" Detective Harvey asked.

"Ginger Wainwright. She owns the company. But she's not here right now," James added quickly.

"Ms. Spice said you took a chance on her, that she had no office experience. Is that true?"

James cleared his throat. "Yes." He had learned long ago that lying to cops was never a good idea, even though in this case, telling the truth would mean having to explain to Ginger if she got wind of it.

"Why?"

"Ginger likes our temps to have plenty of office experience before we send them out. But Isobel seemed very bright, with a lot on the ball, and…" he paused. May as well continue with the truth. "If I'd turned her away, that would have meant not being able to fill the position. Last-minute placements always make you look good, like you've got a ready stable of skilled and available talent. Since Ginger would have been disappointed either way, I decided to give Isobel a chance."

"So you broke the rules. Do you often break the rules?" Detective Harvey asked, an unpleasant edge to his voice.

James felt the anger rise out of nowhere. He swallowed hard and counted to five before he answered. "No, I don't. But there are times when I feel it's appropriate to consider extenuating circumstances."

Detective Harvey leaned toward James, his palms on the desk. "Isobel Spice found the dead woman's body. Not only that, her fingerprints were on the murder weapon."

James's breath caught. "She didn't—um—I didn't know that."

"Do you think it was a coincidence that a last-minute call came in from the bank, just as Ms. Spice was sitting in your office ready to take the job?"

James returned Detective Harvey's gaze with a steadiness he didn't feel. "Yes, I do. How could anybody have known I would decide to take a risk and send her out? I almost didn't."

And boy, do I wish I hadn't, he thought.

He continued, "So if you're suggesting that Isobel came to me as a way to get to that bank so she could kill that woman, I think you're barking up the wrong tree."

"Did you know Doreen Fink, Mr. Cooke?" Detective Kozinski asked.

"Is that the secretary?"

"Good guess."

"You used the past tense," James said, mentally ticking off a mark in his column. "The only person I know at InterBank Switzerland is Felice Edwards, the human resources director. And I've only ever spoken to her on the phone. We've never met in person."

Detective Harvey gave a sharp nod, and Detective Kozinski followed him to the door.

"Thank you for your time, Mr. Cooke. We'll let you know

if we have any further questions."

He followed them out, willing them to complete their disappearing act before Ginger returned.

"One more thing," Detective Harvey said, holding the door open. "Do you think Isobel Spice is capable of murder?"

James shook his head vigorously. "Absolutely not. She's one of those people who is honest to a fault. A wide-open, 'what you see is what you get' kind of person. Sometimes you get more than you want, but she's real."

"Unless she's just a very good actress," Detective Harvey said, letting the door slam in James's face.

EIGHT

THE SIDEWALK IN FRONT OF THE AUDITION STUDIO was empty except for passers-by, which Isobel considered a promising sign. The hallway was another story. Bleary-eyed actors leaned against the wall or squatted on the floor. Some chatted amiably, while others were buried in loose-leaf binders silently mouthing song lyrics, their eyebrows rising as they reached for imaginary high notes. The monitor was napping, face down, on the table. Isobel nudged him.

"Excuse me?"

He jerked awake. "What?"

"My name is on the waiting list. Any chance I'll get in?"

He rubbed his neck and pushed the grubby legal pad toward her. Many of the names were crossed out.

"Did they all get seen?" Isobel asked hopefully.

"No, they gave up and went home."

"Hey!"

Isobel turned around to see Delphi emerging from the restroom. She waved as Delphi made her way down the hall.

"Did you get in?" Isobel asked.

"Nah. We're wasting our time," Delphi said, indicating the tired, waiting actors lining the walls. "You took off in such a hurry this morning, I didn't think you'd bother to come back."

"It wasn't easy to get away."

"Tough day at the office?"

"You might say that," Isobel said. Then she started to laugh. And laugh. She got so hysterical she couldn't stop. Every time she tried to say something, waves of mirth attacked her again, until tears were running down her face and her stomach cramped.

"Look at the ceiling," Delphi instructed.

"Wh-wh-at?"

"Look at the ceiling. It makes you stop laughing. It's a great trick onstage when you're afraid you're going to crack up."

Isobel looked at the ceiling and found that her body did, indeed, relax its helpless spasms.

"Oh...my...God," she panted. "Why does that work?"

"I have no idea." Delphi said, bemused. "What was so funny?"

Before Isobel could answer, a robust, stirring tenor voice invaded the dull hum of the hallway.

"Sit do-o-o-o-wn, you're rockin' the bo-o-o-at!" the voice sang.

The monitor gave an appreciative nod. "That's the best sound I've heard all day."

A few moments later, the door opened and Sunil came out.

"That was you?" Isobel cried.

"How did you get in?" asked Delphi, cutting to the real point.

Sunil smiled ruefully. "A lot fewer guys than dolls."

Delphi and Isobel whirled on the monitor, who held up his hands in self-defense. "Another guy didn't show up, so I slipped him in. It was a fair trade!"

Isobel looked around. It was true; she counted roughly one man for every five women.

"You sounded amazing," she said to Sunil, as they all headed back toward the stairwell.

He made a face. "Yeah. Fat lot of good it did me. They asked if I'd be interested in playing Ali Hakim when they do *Oklahoma* in the spring."

"But he doesn't sing," Delphi said. "How could they waste that glorious voice on a speaking role?"

Sunil stopped. "Look at me," he said.

"What? You're too good-looking?"

"I'm too Indian."

Isobel glanced at Delphi and they both looked away, unsure what to say.

"I'm not exactly as corny as Kansas in August," he went on.

"Wrong show," Delphi pointed out.

Sunil shrugged. "Same difference."

"I thought people were casting non-traditionally these days," ventured Isobel.

"Call me racist, but I think some minorities make out better than others."

"Isn't a bit too early to be bitter?" Delphi asked.

"I've been in New York for a year already," he said gloomily.

"I meant that it's only four-thirty. I try not to get jaded and cynical until after eight."

Sunil managed a chuckle, but they soon fell silent. At the corner, they stopped for the light, and Delphi turned to Isobel.

"You never told me what was so funny before. Maybe it will cheer up Sunil."

"It wasn't funny exactly," Isobel said. "More ironic."

As Isobel described the events of the last two days, she couldn't help but be satisfied at the looks of shock on her new friends' faces. Unpleasant as it all was, she knew it made her more interesting.

"That's why when you said 'tough day at the office,' I kind of lost it," Isobel finished.

Sunil nodded. "I think I saw that on the news last night. Some Swiss bank?"

"That's the one."

"I've never temped, but from what I've heard, offices are not generally breeding grounds for murder. Looks like you hit the jackpot first time out," said Delphi.

"Yeah, lucky me," Isobel said. "What do you do for money?"

"I wait tables at Vino Rosso on Restaurant Row.

Sometimes lunch, sometimes dinner. Tips are decent and," Delphi smiled slyly, "I'm picking up a little Italian from the maître d'."

As they continued walking toward the subway, Sunil asked, "You're not really going back there, are you?"

"I have to."

Delphi stopped her. "No, you don't. It's dangerous."

"I wouldn't go back if I thought there were an insane murderer on the loose," Isobel said. "On the contrary, whoever did this was very sane. Let me tell you, I wanted to kill that woman after three hours."

Delphi looked askance at Isobel. "You…didn't, right?"

For some reason, Delphi asking her point-blank bothered her less than James's confused hinting. "Of course I didn't. But I don't blame you for asking. You hardly know me."

"It sounds like whoever did it also wanted to humiliate her," Sunil mused. "I mean, think about it. Captured for all eternity on the pot!"

"Could it have been somebody from outside who came in, waylaid her in the bathroom, pulled the emergency bell and left?" Delphi asked.

Isobel shook her head. "She was such an unpleasant person that it just doesn't seem random."

"Then you definitely should not go back there, paycheck or no paycheck," Delphi said.

Sunil nodded. "Delphi's right."

"You're sweet to be so concerned, but I'll be fine." Isobel smiled. "It was really nice meeting you both. Good luck with everything."

"I think you need it more than we do," Sunil said.

As Isobel rode south on the subway, sardined between a bike messenger in need of deodorant and a young mother juggling twin toddlers, she wondered whether to take her new friends' advice. No job was worth risking her life. But what about the other people at the bank? They were all continuing to show up for work, weren't they? They had no choice. They all had jobs to do.

Well, so did she. She needed the money. James didn't have anything else for her, and even if he did, he might not send her out again. She still hadn't proven herself, not really.

And that was what she had come to New York to do. Prove herself.

NINE

DESPITE THE FACT THAT THE Evangeline Residence had the benefit of being practically around the corner from her new job, Isobel couldn't wait to get her own apartment. She knew it probably meant sharing an illegal sublet with a stranger, but that was all part of the romance of being a struggling actor in New York, and she was one hundred percent committed to that romance, hardships and all. As she reclined on a sofa in the parlor, partially hidden by a potted palm, she scoured apartment rentals on her laptop, while one of the other residents tinkered with a Chopin étude on the grand piano.

After bookmarking a few possibilities to inspect on the weekend, Isobel closed her computer. The *Guys and Dolls* audition had been a bust, but she was glad she'd gone back. Sunil really had a gorgeous voice, and he seemed like a sweet guy. Delphi was offbeat, but Isobel liked her. She was genuinely touched by their concern. Of course, she hadn't told them that her prints were on the murder weapon. That was worrying. Coupled with the fact that she'd been the one to find Doreen, it didn't look good. Perhaps if she could come up with some tidbit of information that pointed to someone else, she'd be able to convince the police she was innocent.

Then again, if going back to the bank was a bad idea, nosing around into this Doreen business was a worse one. She didn't want to wind up with her head stapled to a desk. But how much harm was there in asking a few questions?

Her cell phone rang, and she picked it up from the side of the settee.

"Hello?"

"It's James. I need to talk to you."

"Was I supposed to call you again? Everything's fine. I mean, they officially asked me to stay on, so—"

"You didn't tell me you found Doreen's body and your fingerprints were on the scissors!"

Isobel inhaled sharply. "How do you know that?"

"How do you think? I had a little visit from the cops today. Do you realize you put my ass on the line? I wasn't supposed to send you out in the first place!"

Isobel sat up. "Now, wait a minute. It's not my fault that cow got herself killed."

"If Ginger finds out that I broke the rules and you're involved in this mess, I'm history!"

"As the person working alongside a cold-blooded murderer, I'd say I'm the one with my ass on the line!" The girl playing Chopin stopped mid-phrase and gaped at her. "Sorry," Isobel whispered.

"At least you could have warned me before the cops showed up!"

"You didn't give me a chance! Besides, when I talked to you, they hadn't found the scissors."

"But you must have known your prints were on them!"

"If I stopped to think about everything I happened to touch my first day rummaging through that stupid desk drawer, I might have thought of it. But since I'm not the one who plunged the fucking scissors into her chest, it wasn't exactly top of mind!" Isobel shouted.

The Chopin girl got up from the piano bench and hurried out of the room, glancing furtively at Isobel over her shoulder.

"Did you have anything at all to do with Doreen's murder?"

Isobel was so shocked, it took her a minute to reply. Then she let him have it.

"Well, what the hell took you so long? Were you just too chickenshit to ask? Of course I didn't! I'd never met that woman before—I'd never been in an office before, as you well know—and any idiot knows that it's poor form to kill your co-workers, especially on the first day!"

Isobel was standing now, and she kicked the potted palm with her foot to punctuate her anger. The effect, of course, was lost on James. Too bad, because it hurt like hell.

There was silence on the other end of the phone. "It's just hard to know. And, I mean…"

"What? What exactly do you mean?"

"You're an actress. You could be totally bullshitting me," James said, finally.

"You don't really believe that," she said, although as she spoke, she found herself perversely wishing she were that good an actress.

"No," James said. He spoke so softly she wasn't sure she had heard him properly.

"What was that?" she pressed.

"No, I don't think you killed her. Damn cops! They get in your head and mess with you. I'm sorry."

"And here I thought you were worried about me."

"I am."

"Fine way to show it!"

Isobel caught a movement by the door of the parlor and saw the Chopin girl enter with the director of the residence.

"I have to go," she whispered.

Before James could answer, she hung up and sat down again on the settee.

"Excuse me," said the director, a prim, unsmiling woman with her hair in a tight, black bun. "I understand you were using your cell phone in a public room and screaming obscenities into it. We can't have that here, as I'm sure you understand. I'm going to have to ask you to leave."

"The room or the residence?" Isobel asked, her blood still boiling.

"The room for now, the residence if your behavior is repeated."

Isobel snatched up her things and stalked across the well-worn carpet. "That's fine with me," she called out haughtily as she left. "I don't intend to stay in this dump any longer than I have to!"

It was unfortunate, she realized later, that the person for whom she had really intended her dramatic exit hadn't seen or heard her make it.

TEN

"BABY DOLL!" James slid onto the bar stool next to Jayla's.

She was halfway through a glass of white wine, and there was already a Coke waiting for him. He leaned over and shimmied his lips up her neck to her earlobe. That usually drove her wild, but now she turned her hazel cat-eyes on him in a glare of fury.

"You gonna tell me who that was who called you?"

"Honey, she's just a new temp who started with us yesterday. Right out of school, totally green, and we sent her out to InterBank Switzerland, of all places."

Jayla folded her arms across her chest. "What's your point?"

"InterBank Switzerland? It was all over the news yesterday. Don't you read the paper or watch television?"

"I don't like your tone. You know I do, but I was tired last night."

"A secretary was killed there yesterday, and Isobel was working with her. I didn't hear about it until late when I saw it on the news, and I wanted to make sure..." He hesitated. There were several possible ways to finish that sentence. Knowing Jayla would never know the difference, he chose the one least flattering to Isobel. "I wanted to make sure she didn't do it."

"Killed a secretary? That little pipsqueaky thing who called? She could no more kill a cockroach than a person. I don't even know her, but I can tell you that much. Miss Namby-Pamby, 'Um, excuse me, but did y'all call my cell phone?'" She raised her voice to a pitch only dogs could hear.

James bounced a cardboard coaster on the bar. "You don't understand. She's kind of a walking disaster. She doesn't waitress, because she…" He paused again. Nothing wrong with stretching the truth a little. "She almost killed a nun with a lobster."

Jayla tossed her head to one side, her beautiful long dreadlocks making a slapping noise against her bare shoulder. "If she's such a disaster, why on earth did you hire her?"

Good question, thought James, but of course he couldn't say that. Or could he?

"Good question," he said.

"Well, something made you. And something made you call her last night, and it wasn't because you think she murdered someone!"

James took Jayla's hand and twined his fingers in hers. He stroked her cheek with both their hands and murmured, "Jay-Jay, baby doll, you know you're the only woman in my life!"

"Whenever a man says that, you know it ain't true!"

"Come on, Jayla, you know me better than that. What would I want some skinny little white bitch for?"

That's my story and I'm sticking to it, he thought, taking a sip of his Coke.

"So why'd you call her?"

"I told you. I wanted to make sure she isn't all mixed up in it somehow."

"Mm hmmm." Jayla pursed her lips doubtfully. "And is she?"

"Nah," he lied.

In a single, sinuous motion, Jayla slid off her barstool and rolled her palm over his thigh, landing between his legs. He reacted as she knew he would.

"Don't you get mixed up with her, you understand? I know a good thing when I've got one. And I ain't sharing."

She kissed him, slow and deep. He could taste the wine on her tongue, and for a split second, he wanted the alcohol more than he wanted her. She pulled away, satisfied.

"I'll meet you at your place later."

"I might be late," he said. "Gotta get to the gym."

"I can let myself in. Don't take too long, or I'll really get suspicious."

He watched her leave the darkened bar, her slender hips swinging gently in her tight leopard-print skirt, her endless legs disappearing somewhere into her knee-high, patent-leather boots.

"Can I get you something else?" asked the bartender.

It was so tempting. Jayla knew what she was doing when she demanded he meet her at a bar. Anything to make him feel vulnerable. He closed his eyes and counted to ten. When he opened them, the bartender had moved away to pull a beer for someone else.

"No, I'm good, thanks," James said to himself. But he wondered how true that was.

FRIDAY WAS A SLOW DAY in Procurement Support, as Isobel learned her department was called. The police were conspicuously absent, as were Stan and Conchita, although the ladies' room remained taped off. They had to use the one on the far end of the floor, which at least gave Isobel a reason to be away from her desk longer. Otherwise, she answered the phone for Frank and typed memos for Paula, whose grammar was impeccable. Nikki spent a good bit of the morning elsewhere, and Isobel kept hoping she would alight at her desk long enough for her to ask some of the questions that were piling up in her mind.

By late morning there was nothing official left to do, so Isobel pulled out her copy of *Backstage*. Without scissors, she was forced to fold and rip out the audition advertisements, which violated her sense of order, since it was impossible for the edges not to be jagged. Fortunately, although the police had dusted her Scotch tape, they hadn't seized it, so she was able to paste into her notebook the few notices that caught her eye.

"What a great idea," Nikki observed, when she finally returned. "So organized. Nothing like that would ever occur to me."

"I'm equal parts anal and scatterbrained, so it's pretty much a necessity," Isobel said, chucking the shredded remains of the newspaper into the recycling bin.

"I was just about to grab a bite. Want to join me?" Nikki asked.

Isobel brightened at the prospect. A leisurely lunch away from prying ears was even better than a hurried conversation in the office.

"Sure. I'll just tell Frank."

From Frank's doorway, Isobel thought she could hear the echo of his wife's shrills, although the receiver was pressed hard to his ear. Isobel made eating gestures and pointed down the hall. Frank looked at her for a moment like she was insane, then spun his chair around to face the window.

"There's a cafeteria on sixteen," Nikki said as they rode down in the elevator. She glanced sideways at Isobel. "But let's go out somewhere, so we can talk."

They went to a small deli café on the corner of Twenty-fourth and Park Avenue South and took their skimpy, overpriced salads to a small table in the back.

"How long have you been in the city?" Isobel asked, pushing some wilted sprouts to the side of her plastic bowl.

"Five years," Nikki said. "I taught high school drama in Albany for awhile before I moved here. One day I woke up and realized that time was running out if I had any designs on a career."

"Have you worked at InterBank the whole time?"

Nikki shook her head. "I started out temping, just like you. I wound up here about a year ago, but then I got an acting job. By the time it was over, my statute of limitations had run out."

"What statute of limitations?"

"A company can't hire you directly if you were placed there by a temp agency," Nikki explained. "But if you stop working there for three months, they can bypass the agency and hire you freelance."

"I didn't know that."

"Keep it in mind. It can really work to an actor's advantage, because we're always leaving town. And you can usually talk the company into paying you what they were paying the agency, so it's a much better deal."

Isobel was still so angry with James that the idea of cutting him out was very satisfying.

"Either way, it beats waiting tables," Nikki went on. "You can print résumés, make calls in your spare time, use the mail room, stuff like that." She gave a throaty laugh. "I like to think InterBank Switzerland supports the arts."

"And you like working there?"

Nikki nodded. "Yeah, it's good. Now that I'm completely freelance, I pretty much come and go as I please. Besides, my boyfriend works in Equities. Tom Scaletta. You took a message from him the other day."

"Ah, yes. Mr. Sexy Voice."

Nikki laughed, but Isobel could tell she was pleased.

"So, do you have any idea who killed Doreen?" Isobel asked, as she casually buttered her roll.

Nikki set down her plastic fork. "I was wondering when we were going to get around to that. Yeah, it just so happens I have a guess."

"Really? Who?" Isobel held her breath.

Nikki leaned forward. "Stan."

Isobel blinked. "Stan?" She pictured Stan Henderson's soft, sweet face and thick hair. "You mean the sad sack who never met a comma he didn't like?"

"Here's a little bit of office trivia for you. Stan and Doreen were married a long time ago. Right out of high school."

"What?!"

"Yup," Nikki smirked. "But the marriage was annulled."

"How do you know?"

"Stan got shit-faced at the holiday party last year and

cornered me by the ham station for half an hour."

"But what makes you think he killed her?"

"He had the strongest link to her. God knows what their 'marriage' was about, but obviously they still had some sort of relationship. She got him the job at the bank. Maybe he felt indebted and resented her for it. Maybe she was lording it over him and he couldn't take it anymore."

"What exactly does Stan do?"

"He's in charge of backup office equipment." Nikki sat back and raised an artfully threaded eyebrow. "In case you haven't figured it out yet, this department isn't exactly the brain trust."

Isobel chuckled. "Yeah, I gathered that. Best I can make out is that they're the support group to the support group that supports the support group that provides the support."

"In a nutshell."

"But Stan seems so self-effacing, so apologetic, like he wishes he could just disappear," Isobel said, as she turned this information over in her mind.

"Exactly," Nikki said significantly, taking a bite of grilled chicken.

Isobel gazed thoughtfully at the saltshaker, then castled it with the pepper shaker as if they were chess pieces. "Wouldn't somebody have noticed a man going into the women's bathroom?"

"During an emergency drill?" exclaimed Nikki. "You obviously haven't been in the city long. People take drills very seriously these days. It's Pavlovian. Nobody notices anything except how many stairs are left between them and safety."

Stan and Doreen. In some ways, they seemed perfectly matched: she domineering and calculating, he confused and gentle, both of them fleshy and... Isobel stopped herself. No use imagining *that*, she thought. And besides, they probably hadn't. The marriage had been annulled, after all. There was a certain logic in suspecting Doreen's ex-husband of killing her, but Isobel knew it couldn't be that simple.

"Just because they were married once and he got her a job doesn't mean he killed her. What's his motive?"

Nikki waved her fork at Isobel. "Stan will be back in on Monday. If you really want to know, chat him up. I'm sure you'll find something."

ELEVEN

Isobel was the first person to arrive outside the rehearsal studio on Eighth Avenue and Fifty-fifth Street shortly before seven on Saturday morning. Delphi was the second.

"Glad to see you're still alive," Delphi said, sitting on the stoop next to Isobel.

"So far, so good. How are you?"

"Still asleep." Delphi yawned and looked around. "Where is everyone?"

Isobel shrugged and pulled her notebook from her shoulder bag. She opened to the ad she had pasted in from *Backstage*.

"*Two by Two*," she read. "Auditions start at ten."

"Maybe we can at least go inside."

They moved into the vestibule and hit the buzzer for the studio. There was no answer.

Isobel frowned. "I don't get it. Remember how packed the other one was?"

"Who knows?" Delphi shrugged. "I'll go get us some coffee. Oh, and here." She pulled a piece of paper from her own bag and handed it to Isobel. "Start a sign-up. They don't have to honor it, but they probably will. Reduces the chances of bloodshed."

Isobel put the date and their names at the top of the page. She wondered whether the rest of the non-Equity population knew something about this showcase production they didn't. Or maybe they just liked to sleep in on weekends. By the time Delphi returned, a few more groggy actors had wandered up and added their names to the list. At nine o'clock, the super unlocked the door, and the line, still small compared to the throng the other day, filed silently upstairs. Shortly after, a gangly, effeminate man in a mustard-colored sweater appeared and took the sign-up sheet.

"We'll start at ten o'clock sharp with..." he glanced at the sheet, "Isobel, Delphi, and then Jessica. They're asking for sixteen bars of an up-tempo and sixteen bars of a ballad."

Isobel gasped. "Sixteen bars? That's it?"

"That's it."

"What can you tell in sixteen bars?"

"A lot," the man said meaningfully and started off down the hall.

Isobel called after him. "But you can't build the dramatic arc of a piece! You can't create a mood, a scene!" Delphi nudged her. "What? I'm right!"

"Rule number one," murmured Delphi, "don't piss off the monitor."

They retired to the ladies' room, where they applied makeup and changed into heels. Isobel wandered into the corner of the small anteroom and began to hum lightly. She wished she had been able to warm up more thoroughly, but she didn't dare cause another disturbance at the residence, especially at such an early hour. She tried a few scales, buzzing her lips together to trill the first few notes of Leonard Bernstein's "It's Love."

Delphi didn't seem at all concerned with warming up. She had removed the silver rings from her nose and ears and was taming her frizz into a cascade of sausage curls. Makeup in delicate pinks completed the look, and when she turned around, Isobel was shocked to see her transformed into a period heroine.

"Wow! You look totally different!"

"Thanks. I think."

"What are you going to sing?" Isobel asked.

"Not sure. The part I'm right for physically is that high soprano thing, the pagan girlfriend, but I'm an alto. And the alto character is supposed to be unattractive."

"Which you definitely are not," Isobel said.

"Well, not in this get-up." Delphi turned toward the mirror. "I guess I'll just sing my standard tune."

"What's that?"

"'It's Love,' from *Wonderful Town*," Delphi said. "Nobody does it."

That's what you think, thought Isobel, her heart sinking. Now what? They couldn't go in one after another singing the same song. What if Delphi sang it better?

"What key do you sing it in?" Isobel asked casually.

"A. I had it transposed down, just because I like the song so much."

Isobel sang it higher, in the score key. It would have a distinctly different sound, but it was still the same song. The same mood, the same scene—even in sixteen bars. She suddenly understood what the monitor meant. But Isobel had only grabbed two songs from her music book that morning, "It's Love" and a comic number by Irving Berlin that wasn't as appropriate.

Before she could figure out an alternate plan, the monitor called her name. She threw a helpless look at Delphi, who gave her a thumbs-up, and followed the mustard sweater into the audition room.

Isobel slapped on a smile and approached the two middle-aged men behind the desk. "Good morning. I'm Isobel Spice!" she chirped.

She handed her headshot and résumé to them and walked over to the pianist.

"Can you play "I'll Know" without the music?" she whispered. "I was going to sing something else, but I've changed my mind."

The accompanist, an acne-scarred, nerdy-looking boy, scowled at her. "No, I can't. Don't you know you should always bring your whole book with you?"

Isobel sighed and set the sheet music for "It's Love" on the piano.

The accompanist's face broke into a smarmy grin. "This is a much better choice anyway. Nobody does it."

The joke's on you, buddy, thought Isobel.

He started playing before she'd even reached the center of the room. She had no choice but to go with it, strolling along as if she were just discovering how she felt. Her bright, silvery soprano filled the room, and she was relieved to find that her voice was in fine shape. Suddenly, the bottom dropped out and she caught herself short.

"Hey!"

"That's sixteen," announced the pianist.

"What else do you have?" asked the older of the two men behind the desk. He had a beard but no moustache, which made him look as if a small hamster was glued to his chin.

"Can I finish 'It's Love'?" she asked.

"We'd rather hear something else for contrast," the second man said.

"The monitor should have told you. One ballad, one up-tempo," Hamster-chin added.

"Well, what do you consider 'It's Love?'" Isobel asked. "Yes, it's a love song, but it's not a ballad in the traditional sense. The tempo is too bright." She was aware of a second Isobel looking on from outside her body, urging, "Shut up. Stop talking now. Shut UP!" But she didn't. Instead, she turned to the piano player.

"Don't you agree? I mean, what would you call it?"

He frowned at her and shook his head ever so slightly. But Isobel pressed on, turning back to the two men.

"I've never understood why people insist on categorizing songs that way, ballad and up-tempo. It's meaningless. Take Cole Porter's 'Miss Otis Regrets.' That's a comic song, but it's definitely a ballad." She paused, considering. "I think what you really mean is sixteen bars comic and sixteen bars serious. I've got 'The Secret Service' by Irving Berlin. I can do that."

The auditioners gaped at her. Hamster-chin finally spoke.

"I'm afraid we need to move on. But thank you for the

musical theater pedagogy lesson. It was most enlightening."

Mortified, she returned to the pianist to collect her music. He was waiting for her, the music already in his hands, an evil grin on his pimply face.

"It's a ballad, you idiot," he sneered.

Isobel left the room, still reeling from her mouth's betrayal of her common sense. She walked past Delphi, who shot her a furious look before following the monitor into the studio. Isobel plopped down on the chair her friend had vacated.

In her confusion about what to sing, she had forgotten to savor her first New York audition. Now that it was over, she only wanted to forget it. Would she ever learn to keep her stupid mouth shut?

Through the door, she heard the brief piano introduction to "It's Love." She stood up again and put her ear against the door.

The melody was only barely recognizable as the same one that Isobel had just sung. Could transposition to a different key make a song so unrecognizable?

Isobel closed her eyes and focused on the words.

No, it was definitely the same song. It was Delphi. She was terrible.

The door opened a few seconds later and Delphi emerged. She and Isobel stared at each other for a moment, then Isobel croaked, "That was great."

"It sucked," Delphi said, pushing past her.

"Wait!"

Delphi whirled on her, and Isobel could see her struggling to sort her emotions. "Why didn't you tell me you were singing the same song?"

"I...I don't know...I'm sorry!"

"You could have warned me!"

"I was trying to think of something else to sing!"

"You had the advantage, going first."

That isn't why I had the advantage, Isobel thought, then mentally smacked herself for the disloyal thought.

"I didn't have any other music with me. I asked the pianist if he could play 'I'll Know' and he said he couldn't. I think he was lying. He was a total jerk."

"They didn't even ask me for anything else," Delphi said.

"Maybe they heard everything they needed?" I certainly did, Isobel thought, and mentally smacked herself again, harder.

Delphi shook her head angrily. "No, it's because they'd already heard you, and you were better."

Her words hung in the air between them. It was true, and they both knew it.

"You're, like, a real singer. You could do opera," Delphi went on, hurt. "How come you didn't tell me?"

"I don't know, I—what do you want me to say? That's my voice."

"Goddamn sopranos," muttered Delphi.

"Well, at least your audition wasn't a complete disaster." Isobel proceeded to tell Delphi how she had behaved in front of the auditioners. "So, you see? I'm not getting a callback, either."

"What makes you think I'm not getting a callback?" Delphi's eyes flashed.

Isobel flapped her arms helplessly. "I didn't mean—"

"Hey!"

Sunil was striding toward them, his leather shoulder bag bulging with sheet music. Clearly, he knew to bring his whole book.

"What? Did they start a waiting list already?" he said, stopping at their grim looks. "I've heard crappy things about this company, so I figured it wouldn't be too crowded."

"If it's not a good gig, why are you here?" Delphi asked.

"Practice. Besides, probably only a lousy outfit like this would consider hiring an Indian to play Noah, even if I am Jewish."

"Very funny," Delphi said.

"No, I'm serious," he said. "I'm Jewish."

"*I'm* Jewish," snapped Delphi. "I know one when I see one. And you're not."

"You're cranky, that's what you are," Sunil said. "But I really am. There aren't a whole lot of us."

"I didn't know there were Indian Jews," Isobel said.

"We eat really well," Sunil said with a wink.

Delphi looked closer at Sunil, and it seemed to Isobel that she was suddenly considering him in a slightly different light.

"Sorry, I didn't mean to be insulting," Delphi said, after a moment.

"Believe me, that barely registered on the insult scale." He looked down the hall. "It doesn't look that crowded. Is it really full?"

"No," said Isobel. "You'll get in."

"What's up with you two, anyway?"

"Nothing," Isobel and Delphi said together.

Sunil raised an eyebrow. "You guys need some acting lessons." He walked over to the monitor.

"He's cute," Isobel said, trying to rescue them from the awkwardness they had created.

"Thanks, Yente," said Delphi. "I noticed."

"I should have sung that other song from *Wonderful Town.*"

"Which one?"

Isobel smiled ruefully. "'One Hundred Easy Ways to Lose a Man.' Only I could have sung 'One Hundred Easy Ways to Lose a Job.'"

Delphi couldn't help but laugh. Isobel held up her hand. "Okay, to enumerate: rule number one, don't piss off the monitor. Rule number two, don't lecture the director."

"Rule number three, tell your friend if you're singing the same song," Delphi added.

"And rule number four, bring all your music," Isobel finished.

Sunil came back. "I just put my name on the list. Shouldn't be too long." He looked from Delphi to Isobel. "You look a little happier. If you wait for me, we can hang out afterwards. There's a flea market downtown I want to check out."

"Really?" Delphi asked.

"Yeah, I love to shop," said Sunil.

"Don't tell me you're gay!" Isobel blurted. Delphi poked her in the ribs, but Sunil just laughed.

"Nope. Two minorities is my limit."

"Well, thanks for the invite, but I'm apartment hunting today," Isobel said.

"You don't have a place?" Delphi asked.

Isobel shook her head. "I'm staying at the Evangeline Residence on Gramercy Park South. You get breakfast and dinner, and there's a rooftop garden and a parlor with a piano. But it's run by Mrs. Danvers, so I have to get out of there."

"Wow, I didn't even know such a thing existed," Delphi said.

"It's not bad. But you have to say good night to your date in the parlor, which I imagine could become a problem after a while. At least I hope so. I pulled a few online listings to check out."

Delphi twirled a stray curl around her finger. "Listen, I know we only just met and we don't really know each other, but I've been staying on my friend Jason's couch, and it's time I moved on, either to another couch or my own place. We could try to find something together."

Isobel thought back to their little disagreement a few moments before. Living with another actor was probably a terrible idea. How could she be an encouraging friend when they were in competition, especially when Delphi's singing left so much to be desired? But Isobel liked her, even if she was a little prickly. And despite any potential conflicts, it had to be better than sharing with a stranger.

"Forget it," Delphi said, when Isobel didn't respond. "I'm sure you have a better—"

"That would be great!"

"Are you sure?" asked Delphi, looking pleased. "I mean,

for all you know, I could be an axe murderer."

"No, for all *you* know, I could be a scissors murderer," returned Isobel. Delphi gave her a look, and she held up her hands in self-defense. "Kidding!"

"I sure as hell hope so," muttered Delphi.

TWELVE

JAMES DISENGAGED HIS BULK from Jayla's endless, dark chocolate legs and stood up.

"Where are you going in such a hurry? It's Sunday morning," Jayla purred from the mass of brown silk sheets that cascaded around her like the train on a wedding dress.

"Shower."

"Mmmm. C'mon and lie here with me a bit. Where's the fire?"

"You're the fire, baby," James said reflexively. He knew a cue when he heard one. "That's why I need the shower."

"I thought I put your fire out already," she murmured.

Here we go, James thought. Do I have to turn on the sweet talk right now? I just want a goddamn shower.

What he really wanted, of course, was a drink, but a shower would have to suffice. He needed to clear his head. Something strange had happened while he and Jayla were having sex. Right at the critical moment, an image of Isobel had flashed through his mind, completely unbidden and definitely unwanted. She looked pissed off as hell, which he knew she had been the last time they spoke, but the weirdest part was that the fury he'd imagined on her face had turned him on.

He stepped into the shower and ran the water as hot as he could stand it. He did not want to be thinking of Isobel that way. He knew he was the envy of his friends, dating the gorgeous and talented Jayla Cummings, who had two business degrees from NYU and was on the fast track at a hot new consulting firm, but who could still turn on the neighborhood when she wanted. In every sense.

But as much as he was into Jayla, she was starting to smother him. She'd been the one to get him into AA, and while he knew he should be grateful, he couldn't escape the feeling that she was tracking his every move. Worse, she had Plans, with a capital P. At twenty-seven, newly and barely sober, James was nowhere near ready for marriage, but it was hard to take Jayla's comments about single black mothers as anything other than big-ass hints.

He soaped himself vigorously and found himself thinking again about Isobel. Of course she hadn't killed anyone. What had he been thinking? He was a patsy for buying into the detectives' suspicions. Isobel was right, he was chickenshit. When was he going to start thinking for himself?

He needed to sort her out in his mind, like his mother used to do when she separated eggs. The yolk (Isobel's infuriating perkiness) in one bowl and the white (her safety) in another. He had a sudden picture of her swimming in a life-sized bowl of egg whites, slipping under the surface and calling to him to save her, in her best Bond-girl voice.

He shut off the water and wrapped himself in a towel. There was one more thing he could do to set his mind at ease. He had finally confirmed Isobel's extended employment, but why not ask Felice Edwards to lunch? He could find out what kind of people Isobel was in with. Felice might even have a sense of what direction the investigation was taking and how seriously the cops suspected Isobel. Ginger Wainwright was always urging her staff to take clients out to lunch to solidify their relationships. Other recruiting firms didn't bother, but that was what made Temp Zone different, she always said. Relationships.

Yes, he thought, jumping onto the scale, where the needle bounced and landed just above where he wanted it. First thing Monday, he'd call Felice. Isobel would never have to know he was checking up on her.

Neither, he reminded himself, would Jayla.

THIRTEEN

BY THE TIME MONDAY MORNING rolled around, Isobel was exhausted. After rejecting one apartment the size of a walk-in closet, another with room for only one bed (although Isobel was pleased at the thought of rooming with Delphi, she didn't exactly want to sleep with her), and a third whose eat-in kitchen was undermined by suspiciously chewed-up baseboard moldings, she and Delphi had finally taken a sublet in Hell's Kitchen. It cost more than either of them had budgeted, but it was too good to pass up: an L-shaped studio with a galley kitchen on the fourth floor of a brownstone. It had two large windows overlooking a weedy courtyard and somebody's rusting Hibachi, but more importantly, it was in midtown, convenient to all the audition studios.

After his callback for *Two by Two*, Sunil had taken them first to the flea market and then to the giant Salvation Army store on Forty-sixth Street, where he proved to be an expert haggler. With his help, they came away with a barely-used futon and frame, an almost-new air mattress, a small table with two chairs, two bookshelves, a filing cabinet, and assorted pots, pans and dishes, all for three hundred and fifty dollars. It had taken Isobel and Delphi all of Sunday to move, and with Sunil's help, they'd unpacked, organized, and rearranged the furniture until late.

Isobel had trouble falling asleep in her new surroundings. When she finally nodded off around two, she dreamed that they were still apartment hunting, but Doreen kept turning up dead in every bathroom. After a few hours of fitful slumber, Isobel was awakened at six by what sounded like a nuclear apocalypse but turned out to be garbage trucks, and that was the end of her night.

Now, armed with the largest coffee money could buy, Isobel settled at her desk at InterBank Switzerland and, since nobody was looking, put her head down. Her thoughts drifted back to the conversation the night before that had precipitated her bad dreams.

"Do you think the murder was premeditated or spontaneous?" Sunil had asked, wiping down their new kitchen cabinets.

Delphi had looked up from arranging her scripts alphabetically on one of the bookshelves. "Does it matter?"

"If it was a cold-blooded, calculated murder, Isobel is marginally safer than if it's somebody with a hair-trigger temper who might flip out if she misplaces a comma."

"I'm the one most likely to do that, given the grammatical skills of this bunch," Isobel pointed out.

But it was a good question. Had somebody followed Doreen into the bathroom in a rage and just let fly? Or was it planned ahead of time? If it was the latter, then the person who killed her knew there was going to be an emergency drill—and that Doreen would be in the bathroom at that particular moment. But who could possibly know a thing like that? Even Doreen couldn't have predicted exactly when she'd have to pee.

Something else struck Isobel, and she stopped inflating her new air mattress to pose a question to Delphi.

"When you go into a bathroom stall, do you lock the door?"

"If I'm the only one in there, I don't always bother," Delphi answered. "Then if I hear someone come in, I lean over and lock it. Why?"

"When I went into the bathroom, the stall door was ajar," Isobel said. "I was rushing and didn't look, and I just pushed it in without thinking anyone would be there."

"What does this have to do with anything?" Delphi asked.

"I might not lock the stall if I knew there was going to be a fire drill and nobody would be coming in. And if Doreen knew about the drill in advance, maybe somebody else did too. So the murder could have been premeditated."

Sunil nodded thoughtfully as he wrung out a dirty dishtowel. "Makes sense," he said. "What better time to slip into a bathroom unnoticed than when everyone is running around in a panic saving their own asses?"

Delphi shook her head. "I don't know. It still seems a little dicey. I think the person was just waiting for an opportunity and grabbed one when it came along."

"Like they grabbed my scissors," Isobel said. "Maybe the emergency drill just happened to coincide with his or her last straw."

"Or maybe the person planned to strangle her and changed his mind when he saw the scissors lying out. And maybe the lock on the bathroom stall was broken. None of this matters," Delphi had said. "Premeditated or not, it's still risky for you to be there, and I really don't want to have to find another roommate."

And that was the end of the conversation. Isobel opened her eyes and looked at the scuffed laminate of her desk, wondering anew who might have known in advance about the emergency drill.

"Napping, are we?"

Isobel jolted upright to see Paula Toule-Withers, her arms sagging under the weight of a banker's box spilling over with papers. She dropped the box onto Isobel's desk.

"Doreen handled all the filing for the department." Paula wiped her hands together dismissively. "And you're the new Doreen."

Isobel looked at the overflowing box and a fresh wave of fatigue washed over her. "Where do they go?"

Paula pulled back her brightly-sticked lips into what, for her, passed as a smile. "You're smart. I'm sure you'll figure it out."

Isobel opened the top folder, which held a jumble of invoices, order forms, memos and receipts. It was impossible to know where to begin. She fortified herself with a big gulp of coffee and dragged the box over to a wall of filing cabinets. She pulled open the bottom drawer and fingered the tabs on the hanging folders. There were designations for receipts, vendor invoices, memos, and just about every other kind of document she had spotted in the box. Pay dirt on the first drawer. She pulled up a small stepstool and began filing. She spent close to two hours sorting documents, taking frequent breaks for coffee and hoping Nikki would show up and provide her with a distraction. When she didn't, Isobel decided to orchestrate one of her own.

She stretched her tired arms, rounded the bend to the office area, and peered into Stan Henderson's office.

"He's not in today." Conchita Perez was sitting primly at her desk. "He called this morning to say he's ill, Lord help him."

Isobel hoped Conchita's imprecation was a measure of her devoutness and not an indication of the seriousness of Stan's malady.

"Oh, that's too bad. I wanted to talk to him about something," Isobel said.

"Maybe I can help?"

"No, that's okay, I—" Isobel paused. If Stan had confided in Nikki, perhaps he'd confided in Conchita, too. She was his secretary, after all.

"Actually, there are a few things," Isobel said, circling around the older woman's desk. "I'm still not entirely clear on what everybody does in the department."

Conchita plumped herself in her chair like an inflatable pillow. "Well, Frank is in charge, but you knew that."

"What's his title, exactly?"

"Senior Vice President of Procurement Support," Conchita said. "And Paula is Assistant VP, but you probably knew that too."

"Actually, I didn't," said Isobel. Conchita beamed with satisfaction. "And you're Paula's assistant?"

"Yes, and Stan's. Doreen worked for Frank."

Isobel noticed there was no "God rest her soul" after Doreen's name.

"I gather Doreen didn't get along all that well with everyone," Isobel said. Conchita looked at her, as if sizing up whether or not she could be trusted. Isobel continued quickly. "I mean, I only spent one morning with her, but I found her completely intolerable."

Conchita couldn't resist. "Well, I don't like to speak ill of the dead..."

"Oh, go for it," said Isobel with a confidential wink.

"She was a first-class bitch," Conchita said and immediately crossed herself.

"I'm guessing she was the kind of woman who doesn't get along well with other women."

Conchita nodded. "Paula hated her, too." She glanced around and then whispered, "But she's no prize either, that one."

"You're telling me!" Isobel whispered back. "What about Stan? Did Doreen get along with him?"

Conchita set her mouth in a line and shook her head. "That's not for me to say."

"Nikki told me they were married once. Is that true?"

Conchita's mouth dropped open. "Lord help us!" she gasped.

Isobel was taken aback. "You didn't know?"

Tears squeezed out from the corners of Conchita's eyes. "I—I have to get back to work. So much to do..." She shook her head and fumbled with a stack of pencils.

Isobel watched the rise and fall of the little knobs of wool on the back of Conchita's hand-knit sweater. Obviously she'd just dropped some sort of personal bombshell. But what? Was there something going on between Conchita and Stan?

"Isobel!"

She looked up to see Frank gesturing to her from the doorway of his office.

With a guilty backward glance at Conchita, she followed Frank, who closed his office door behind them.

He rolled his eyes. "Conchita's like Niagara Falls. She cries when the copy machine breaks. How are you managing?"

"Fine so far."

"Good. Because I may wait a while before hiring somebody permanent."

"Really?"

Frank looked squarely at her. "I know people didn't like Doreen. I didn't always like her. But she was devoted to me. Really devoted. I knew I could trust her with anything. And I did. She knew...well, she knew a lot about me, both professionally and personally. You can't buy that kind of loyalty. I don't want to rush into finding a new assistant. I need to take some time."

"I have to admit, working in an office where somebody was killed makes me a little nervous," Isobel said.

"We're all on edge."

"Do you think it was somebody who came in from outside?" she asked.

"I don't know." Frank tapped a pen on his desk blotter. "I'm trying not to think."

Isobel attempted what she knew was a clumsy segue. "Well, at least there are emergency drills to help keep us safe. How often do those happen?"

"Every six to eight weeks. But they're not really designed to prevent random murders."

Isobel laughed self-consciously. "Right. But still, it's good to have them. Who schedules them?"

"The building management."

Isobel nodded. "Sure. I figured. Although I suppose any of the firms in the building could request one if they wanted?"

Frank gave her an odd look. "Why would anyone want to do that? They're a pain in the ass. They disrupt the day."

But they provide lovely cover if you want to kill someone, thought Isobel.

"No, of course, you're right," she said. "But do they at least let you know in advance when there's going to be one?"

"They're pretty good about that."

Ah, thought Isobel. Now we're getting somewhere.

"So everyone knows beforehand?" she asked.

"Not everyone, just the fire marshals. Each floor has two marshals, one male and one female. It's their job to make sure everyone is out safely."

"Who are ours?"

"Paula and Stan."

"So they were the only people who knew about the drill the other day?" she asked.

"And Doreen. She was the one who coordinated with the management." He shook his head in confusion. "Why are you so worried about emergency drills?"

"I'm just trying to figure out what's part of my job and what isn't," she said, trying to look earnest. Not entirely false, she thought—although not entirely true, either.

"Well, if you get a call alerting you to an emergency drill, now you know who to tell," Frank said.

Whom, Isobel thought involuntarily, invoking her one-second delay. "I should probably get back to my filing," she said instead. Also not entirely false, but mostly she wanted to digest this information elsewhere and with elsewhom.

"I still have some administrative things to go over with you, and I want to make sure you're clear on your duties as my assistant. Let's talk later, around two."

Isobel walked out past Conchita, who had stopped crying and was murmuring into the phone in Spanish. She didn't look up when Isobel passed.

So, three people had known in advance about the emergency drill: Paula, Stan, and Doreen. That was one person too many to be conclusive, but not a bad place to start. Doreen had said she was on her way to lunch. Had she forgotten about the drill? Maybe she was trying to avoid participating. As Frank pointed out, emergency drills were a pain. Why not be absent if you could?

Isobel rounded the bend and tripped over the stepstool she had left in front of the open filing cabinet.

"Damn!" She rubbed her shin.

"That's precisely what I said," said Paula. She was standing next to the stool, her eyes stormy and her arms folded across her chest.

"Sorry," muttered Isobel. "I was talking to Frank."

"Well, next time close the drawer, please. And move the stepstool aside." Paula pushed past Isobel and headed back toward her office. Then she paused and looked over her shoulder.

"What were you doing in that drawer, anyway?" she asked, a strange glint in her eye.

"Filing the stuff you gave me," Isobel said, resisting the temptation to add "duh."

"But the documents I gave you are all from this year. That drawer has last year's files."

She grinned maliciously at Isobel and disappeared.

FOURTEEN

FELICE EDWARDS, IT TURNED OUT, was just his type. Smart and sexy like Jayla, but not as intense, and nothing perky about her. She was the kind of grounded, earthy woman who knew how to have fun, but relished her independence. And, apparently, her alcohol.

"I really shouldn't," Felice said with a flirty grin, when the waiter came around again. "And I hate to drink alone," she hinted.

James cleared his throat and counted to ten, double-time. "No, thanks."

"Well, what the hell! It's been a wacky week at the office." She turned to the waiter. "Another glass of Merlot, please."

"And I'll have another Coke," added James.

Felice leaned toward him, her blouse slipping alluringly to one side, exposing the top of a juicy-looking breast. "I never drink at lunch, you know. I don't want you to get the wrong idea. But I really need to unwind. I'm telling you—a murder in the office? Not in the job description, you know what I'm sayin'?"

She took a bite of her grilled chicken sandwich, tearing off the extra meat with a fervor that James could have put down to hunger, anger, relief, or a nicely brewing buzz.

"I'm sure it's been a zoo over there," he said.

Felice wasn't in need of much prompting. She had jumped at his invitation to lunch so quickly that he wondered if she'd been expecting his call. He hadn't necessarily intended to meet her today, but she had made that assumption, and he had gone with it. When he stood up to introduce himself in the restaurant, he noticed, with some satisfaction, the telltale shift of light in her eyes that women always thought they were hiding, but never were. Felice found him attractive, and there was no ring on her left hand. That was the real reason she was having a second drink, he thought. She was trying to turn a business lunch into a date.

"The police need to know everything they can about all the employees, so naturally they came to me," she said proudly.

"So, where are they are heading with this?"

Felice shook her head. "They don't give up much, that's for sure. They interviewed me for a long time, then they took my files and that was that."

"I'd like to know everything I can about all the employees, too. I guess that makes me no better than the police."

"Better looking," Felice said sweetly.

James gave a self-deprecating laugh. "Well, thank you. But seriously, I want to know more about the people Isobel is in with. I'm worried about her. And, uh, all the other Temp Zone employees you have."

Felice eyed James. "Isobel's the only one on the books right now."

He cleared his throat. "Well, I'm trying to get a handle on how safe it is for her to be there. As her employer. Given the murder."

Felice sipped her wine. "How safe is it for any of us? Isobel's only temporary."

"But do you think it was somebody in her department? Or somebody who came in from outside? Or maybe from another company in the building?"

"Slow down, buddy!"

James made a mental note to start counting to five between questions.

Felice bit off another chunk of her sandwich and chewed thoughtfully. "The police asked me the same things. I wish I thought it was somebody from outside, but to know Doreen Fink was to want to kill her. So I think whoever did it probably works for us."

"If she was so awful, why didn't you just fire her?" James asked.

Felice shrugged. "Her boss liked her. We got tons of complaints about her, but he wouldn't let her go."

"Couldn't you overrule him?"

"The complaints were never actionable. It's not like she was helping herself to people's wallets or making mistakes that cost the company millions. You can't fire a person just because she's a pain in the ass. If you could, we'd none of us have jobs!" Felice tossed her twisted coiffure and laughed heartily.

"Maybe one of the people who complained about her finally snapped and killed her."

"Maybe. Maybe, James." She leaned forward again as she said his name. She was more than a little buzzed now. He closed his hand over hers, and she gave a little shiver of delight.

"Come on, Felice. I know something's cooking in that sweet noggin of yours!"

"Oh, I have an idea. I've got a few. Trouble is, I don't know which one is right."

"Okay, then tell me about these people. What are they like?"

She dipped her head coyly. "It wouldn't be ethical to talk about my employees that way," she said. As the waiter came up behind her, James caught his eye and gave the nod. In a moment, he had refilled Felice's empty glass. James didn't care how much this little lunch was going to run Ginger Wainwright. He was close to getting some real information, and he was counting on Felice's loose lips to start letting in the water.

She took another long sip of wine. "Ooooh, that's divine!" She set down her glass. "Okay, I'm telling you this because," she paused for a dainty hiccup, "because Temp Zone has always given us good help. And because you're a brother. But this goes no further, understand?"

"Got it," said James.

"Paula Toule-Withers. Uppity British bitch. Divorced. Wants Frank's job."

"Who's Frank?"

"He's the Senior VP. Doreen was Frank's secretary. Oops, administrative assistant. We're not supposed to say secretary. Like you can't say stewardess anymore, either."

"Right. Go on."

"Frank is up for promotion from Senior VP of Procurement Support to Senior VP of Procurement. Doesn't sound like much of a promotion, but actually it is. Paula is angling for Frank's job, but she knows we'll bring in someone else."

"Why would you do that?"

"Because there aren't any women Senior VPs, and she's a bitch. Can't fire someone for that, but you can decide not to promote them. Doreen used to rag on her. Said she'd never go anywhere, and she'd better get used to it."

"Okay, who else?"

"Let's see, Stan Henderson. Kind of a wet dishrag. Doreen brought his résumé to us. Knew him from high school. High school, can you imagine? He's pretty harmless, so I don't think he could have done it. Besides, she got him the job. Then there's Conchita Perez. Puerto Rican. Very Catholic. Wants off for every damn saint's day. Oh, I'm not supposed to say damn and saint together, am I? Sorry about that."

"I'm not religious," James said with a smile.

Felice gave a delighted giggle. "Me neither! Well, Conchita thought Doreen was evil. Said she made good people do bad things. Whatever that means. There's also Nikki Francis. Came in sideways through a temp agency about a year ago, right before I started. I think it was Temp Zone, actually. She does the billing for the department, but she's freelance. She's an actress. Dating a guy in Equities and thinks nobody knows."

"An actress, huh?" They're everywhere in this town,

thought James. "What's she been in?"

"Not much of anything, so far as I can tell. Can't be very good, can she? She complained the most about Doreen," Felice said, massaging her brow. "Man, I'm getting a headache. Doesn't usually happen to me on two glasses of wine."

"Nikki complained the most?"

"Yeah. Funny that somebody who isn't even full-time would push so hard to get Doreen fired."

"Did she give a reason?"

"Nothing actable. Actionatable. Actionatingable."

"Actionable."

"She got real snarky with me too, when I said we couldn't do anything. Said something kind of weird, now that I think about it. Said Doreen was poking around too much in people's personal business and it was going to bite her fat ass. I asked her what she meant by that 'xactly, and she said one day Doreen would open her big mouth so wide, someone else would have to shut it for her."

Felice sat back on the banquette and undid the next button on her blouse. "I'm not feeling so good. Do you think you could take me home now?"

FIFTEEN

ISOBEL COULDN'T BEAR THE THOUGHT of undoing two hours' worth of filing, so she dumped the remaining contents of the box into the bottom of last year's drawer and kicked it shut. She wasn't even supposed to work for Paula anyway, and she didn't believe for a minute that Doreen had happily done anyone else's work but her own. Paula had a secretary, and when Conchita had used up both sleevesful of tissues, she could finish the damn filing.

Isobel surreptitiously plugged her flash drive into her computer, then transferred her résumé into a folder she had created and innocuously named "Background." Her printer was cheap and unreliable, so she had decided to take Nikki's advice and avail herself of the office equipment. She recalled Nikki's comment about InterBank Switzerland supporting the arts and smiled to herself as she sent ten copies of her résumé to print.

Nikki appeared a moment later. Isobel was about to call out a greeting, when she noticed the slump of Nikki's shoulders and her swollen, red eyes. Nikki sat down heavily at her desk with her coat still on. Isobel walked quietly past her to the printer and collected her résumés, but she couldn't ignore Nikki's obvious distress.

"You okay?" she asked.

Nikki nodded. "Acting class. I'll be fine in a minute."

Isobel sat down and began stapling the résumés to her headshots.

"Nice picture," Nikki said, glancing over.

"Thanks. Is your acting class always so traumatic?"

Nikki gave an insulted sniff. "It's not traumatic. It's exhilarating."

"Well, you look pretty miserable," Isobel said.

"I'm not. I feel cleansed."

"Oh."

"It's an emotional reality class," Nikki explained. "We do a different emotion each week. You bring up a past experience that triggers that emotion, and then you filter your monologue through it."

"What if your monologue doesn't have anything to do with that emotion?"

"Half the time it doesn't. But half the time your words don't reflect what's going on underneath emotionally. Life is subtext."

"Well, yes, I know, but it seems kind of manipulative to work it that way."

"What do you know about it?" Nikki snapped. "You said it yourself, singers can't act."

Isobel had only said that to the police to keep them from suspecting her. True, that was the stereotype, but she prided herself on her acting ability, particularly her comic timing. She gave Nikki a dirty look and turned back to her computer.

"I'm sorry," said Nikki a few moments later. "We did sadness today. I guess I didn't get rid of it all."

"I happen to be a very good actress," Isobel said stiffly.

"I'm sure you are."

"How often do you take this class?" Isobel asked.

"Once a week. I also do scene study on Thursday nights."

"What's the next emotion?"

"Joy."

"Well, that's a relief," said Isobel.

"Can I see your résumé?" Isobel handed it over. "Not bad," Nikki commented. "You don't list any acting teachers except your college ones. You should take class."

"Who's your teacher?"

"Terence Hoff."

"Thanks. I'll keep it in mind." Isobel retrieved her résumé and made a mental note to steer clear of Terence Hoff.

Nikki was not providing the sort of distraction she'd hoped for, and Stan Henderson was still MIA, so Isobel resigned herself to typing and emailing memos, taking phone calls and sneaking peeks at online casting notices. She ate lunch by herself, grabbing two hot dogs and soaking up the fall warmth in Madison Square Park. At two o'clock, she poked her head into Frank Lusardi's office.

He was on the phone, but he signaled for her to wait. She glanced around his office, and her eyes lit on a framed photo of a glamorous woman in a floral print dress. Expensive-looking sunglasses sat on her forehead, pushing back long, wavy red hair.

Frank hung up the phone and nodded at the picture. "My wife."

"She's stunning," said Isobel, wondering how someone that beautiful could sound so shrewish.

"That's why I married her."

"And so stylish."

"If shopping were an Olympic sport, Audrey would be a medalist," he said.

"Do you have kids?"

"Bit of a sore subject." Frank grabbed a small box of flash drives. "Let's go."

Nikki was gone when they returned. Frank set the box on Isobel's desk.

"These are Doreen's files. I need you to load them up onto your computer so you have access to everything for the department." He indicated Doreen's desk, which was still taped off. The police had emptied its contents and taken her computer the first day. "I understand why they took everything, but we still have work to do." He tapped the box. "Fortunately, she'd just done a backup. Inventory lists, vendor contact information, and miscellaneous forms. For correspondence, take a look at the format Doreen used and be sure to copy it going forward."

Minus the bad grammar, thought Isobel.

"You'll have to check in with Procurement every other day to see what needs to be ordered and for which department. Your contact person is Candy O'Hara. Her number is on the wall there." He pointed to the sheet of phone extensions.

"Okay."

Frank put a hand on her shoulder. "Oh, and this is very important. If Edmund Jeffards calls, put him through immediately. He's the Head of IBS North America. Jeffards. J-E-F-F-A-R-D-S. Got it?"

"Yes," Isobel said. She wrote down the name and circled it twice.

"If you have any questions, please ask me. Only me. Not Paula. All right?"

Isobel didn't need to be told twice to avoid Paula. As soon as Frank was gone, she sat down and picked up the first drive, labeled "Correspondence." She was about to insert it into the computer, when a familiar deep voice startled her.

"Isobel."

James was towering in the space between her desk and Nikki's.

"James! What are you doing here?"

"I wanted to apologize for the way I acted on the phone the other day."

Points for you, thought Isobel. A man who apologizes.

"I'm impressed that you came by just to say you're sorry," she said.

"Well, I was having lunch with Felice Edwards, so I thought I'd poke my head in."

So much for that. Still, he had made the effort.

James leaned down and lowered his voice. "You don't have to stay here."

"We've been through this. Unless you have something else—"

"That's not a reason to stay."

"For me it is," Isobel said firmly.

"Felice told me about some of the folks you're working with. And, well...just be careful."

Isobel craned her neck to look up at his face and noticed for the first time what a lovely liquid brown his eyes were. They were looking at her with real concern.

"I suppose I should be flattered that you're so worried about me," she said.

James shifted away from her slightly. "I would be about any employee."

Isobel turned over the flash drive in her hand. "Is there anything...specific...you think I should know?"

James cleared his throat and leaned in toward her again. She felt a slight charge of excitement, although she wasn't sure if it was due to the physical proximity of such a large man or the certainty that he was about to impart something significant.

"There's a woman here who's freelance."

"Nikki Francis?"

"Yeah, she tried to get Doreen fired."

"Maybe, but—"

"Listen to me. She also said something a little freaky."

Isobel caught her breath. "James—"

"Will you listen? This Nikki apparently told Felice that if Doreen didn't shut up, someone would shut her up for good, because Doreen was poking around in her personal business."

"James—"

"And she's an actress too, so I figured you'd probably make friends with her. Just be on your guard, okay?"

"James, please—" Isobel shook her head at him.

"Watch out for all of them, but be especially careful of Nikki Francis."

Isobel closed her eyes and put her hands over her face.

"Why should she be careful of me?"

He staggered around to face Nikki, who had come up behind him.

"I tried to tell you," Isobel whispered.

"And who the hell are you, anyway?" Nikki's face was red, though her eyes no longer were.

"I'm Isobel's—um, she's my...we're..."

"This is James," Isobel broke in. "He's my rep at Temp Zone."

Nikki looked furiously from Isobel to James. "Oh, really? Well, maybe you should be careful of *him*!"

SIXTEEN

JAMES KICKED THE LATTICED METAL trash can on the corner of Twenty-fourth and Madison, scattering nervous passersby. Then he whipped out his cell phone and dialed furiously.

"Bill? I've counted to ten twice, now tell me why I shouldn't have a drink."

The calm voice on the other end answered, "Because it's been almost a whole month, and that's a major milestone. You're so close, don't give up now."

"You gotta do better than that, man, because the way I'm feeling right now, I don't give a shit about milestones—I just want a drink."

"Count to ten again."

"Goddammit, Bill, I told you—"

"Do it! Out loud."

Through gritted teeth, James counted to ten.

"All right," Bill said steadily. "Let's think about what's important here. You've got this far, don't let it slip away. Whatever happened, I'm sure it can't be as bad as you think. You wanna tell me about it?"

James kicked a small pile of leaves, which rose and fell in a crunchy swirl. "Nah, it's too stupid."

"Well, if it's so stupid, then it's definitely not worth falling off the wagon."

Bill had a point. Why should he care if that Nikki woman knew he thought she might be dangerous? As far as he was concerned, they all were. Dangerous until proven innocent. No, what was eating him was the helpless look on Isobel's face. He'd painted her into a corner, and then he'd hightailed it out of there. He'd run away like a freaking coward, leaving her to explain.

"Let's focus on the positive." Bill's voice broke into his consciousness. "Anything positive happen today?"

"Lunch with a sexy babe," James admitted. Lunch had been good in that Felice was easy on the eyes and he'd gotten some information out of her. But that thought led him right back to the mess he'd made.

"Well, that's good, isn't it?"

"Mixed, actually. Like a nice scotch and soda."

"James," warned Bill.

"She had too much to drink. She asked me to take her home, but it was a business lunch, and I had no intention of taking her home for just about every reason you can think of. I managed to get her back to her office, and right now she's passed out on her sofa."

"Okay."

"And then I went by to check on this girl—this woman— this girl I've got working for me, and I was telling her something about a co-worker of hers. But I didn't know that this co-worker had come up behind me and heard every goddamn thing I said."

"Ahhhh."

"Don't fuckin' say 'ahhhh!' Just listen. You got me talking, now let me finish. I left my girl hanging. And I went by in the first place to apologize for something I shouldn't have had to apologize for at all, and now both of them think I'm an asshole. And when the sexy babe wakes up on her office couch with a hangover the size of Staten Island, she'll think I'm an asshole, too."

"So three women think you're an asshole."

"That about sums it up."

"You're feeling vulnerable, your self-esteem has been wounded, and the natural thing to do is drink, right?"

"Right."

"Wrong! This is when you need to just stop in your tracks

and repeat the Serenity Prayer."

"You don't understand! I might have put my girl in danger!"

"Is this Jayla we're talking about?"

"No, it's not Jayla. I told you, it's a girl who works for me. One of our temps. She's at an office where—" He suddenly found himself too tired to rehash Doreen's murder. "Never mind. You're right. Three women think I'm an asshole. So fuckin' what?"

"Got any gum?"

"Yeah."

"Take out two pieces. Put one in your mouth, and as soon as the flavor runs out, add the second. Then walk from wherever you are now to wherever you're going and don't stop. Call me again when you get there. Okay?"

"Okay."

"Call me!"

James shoved his phone in his jacket pocket and pulled out a packet of wintergreen Orbit. He popped a piece in his mouth and chewed mightily. He would call Bill when he got back to his office like he promised, but he was already a bit calmer. Two things he'd told Bill had triggered pictures in his mind. The first was Felice, her plump face slack, the curves of her body gyrating gently against his as he steered her back to her office past her wide-eyed colleagues. It had been a long time since he had been sober looking at someone who'd had too much to drink. It was amazing how unattractive she had immediately become. He was beginning to understand what he must be like drunk, all 250 pounds of him. No wonder Columbia had given him the boot, not to mention the other recruiting firms he had worked at. Who could work, study, play football, or even carry on a conversation like that?

But it was the second thing he'd said that had brought him up short. It was possible, even likely, that his clumsiness had put Isobel in even more danger. If that was the case, he owed it to her to try to keep her safe.

And he wasn't fool enough to think he could do that drunk.

NIKKI AND ISOBEL STARED at each other for a long time after James stumbled out. Isobel finally broke the silence.

"I don't believe him," she said.

"Maybe you should," Nikki said in a thin voice. "Maybe he was telling the truth."

"Well, was he?" Isobel asked.

Nikki shook her head, defusing the tension slightly. "I did try to get Doreen fired—he's right about that. And I did say that if she wasn't careful, someone would shut her big fat mouth for her. But I'm certainly not the one who did it. I'm not dangerous. A little overdramatic, maybe."

"I see," said Isobel.

But her mind was racing. James the giant jerk had completely jeopardized her one decent relationship on the job. She had spotted Nikki approaching and had seen her about to tap James on the shoulder to ask him to move. The worst part was that Isobel hadn't had time to process any of it before being left to face Nikki.

"What made you say a thing like that, anyway?" she asked.

"I'd had my emotional reality class that morning. We'd done anger that day, and my monologue was from *The Duchess of Malfi*, so you can imagine where my head was. I would never be dumb enough to say something like that if I intended to follow through on it," Nikki said.

"Was Doreen poking around in your personal business?"

Nikki gave a shallow laugh. "Doreen was poking around in everybody's business. I guarantee you that in the few hours you were here, she found out more about you than you think. She was a nasty, nosy person, and one day I got particularly fed up."

"When was this?" Isobel asked.

"About a month ago." Nikki rubbed her neck with her

long, graceful hands. "The class is great, but it can sort of screw with your head. You saw how I was with you this morning. It was the same thing that day. I don't want you to get the wrong idea."

"So I don't have to be careful of you?"

"No, you don't." Nikki's expression softened. "In fact, I hope we'll be friends."

Isobel nodded. "Thanks. Me, too."

"And if you ever want to try my acting class, just let me know," Nikki said, returning to her desk.

Isobel plugged Doreen's correspondence drive into her computer and squinted at the screen, pretending to work. As furious as she was with James, she knew it would be foolish not to proceed with at least some caution where Nikki was concerned. She recognized the temptation to fall into a friendship with a fellow thespian adrift in the business world, but this was a good reminder not to trust anybody at InterBank Switzerland. She looked over at Nikki, who was reapplying her lipstick, and wondered what Doreen had found out that had set her off. Was an emotional hangover from an acting class the real reason behind Nikki's outburst, or was she using that as an excuse for behavior that was, given recent events, potentially incriminating? Isobel had never heard of an emotional reality acting class. Was it even for real? She picked up her résumé and glanced at the Training section.

There was only one way to find out.

SEVENTEEN

As Delphi passed by the bar at Vino Rosso with a tray of appetizers on her shoulder, Isobel tried to catch her eye.

"Talk," she mouthed.

Delphi frowned and continued on her path. In a moment, she was back, empty tray in hand.

"You have to order something if you're going to sit here," Delphi said.

"I'll get a glass of wine. Have you ever heard of Terence Hoff?" Isobel asked.

"No. Who's he?"

"An acting teacher."

"Look in *Backstage*. All the acting teachers advertise in the back," Delphi said.

"I did. He's not there."

"I can't talk now, I'm working—"

"*Bellissima!*" A tall, handsome Italian man drew up to them. "Table four wants you." He put his face close to Delphi's. "They are not the only ones." Delphi raised a weary eyebrow at Isobel and walked off toward the tables.

"What can I get for you to drink, eh?" the man asked Isobel.

"What red wine do you have by the glass? Nothing too expensive."

"Complimentary! It will be my pleasure. Any friend of *la bellissima* is a friend of mine," he said with a wink.

He circled around behind the bar and poured her wine. This was obviously the maître d' Delphi had mentioned. He was definitely attractive, with wavy black hair and dark shining eyes, but Isobel had little patience for Latin machismo. She liked men with a little humility. She couldn't imagine this guy ever apologizing for anything.

"I must apologize," he said, setting a glass in front of her. "I wanted you to try our house specialty, a lovely Nero d'Avola, but we have run out."

Well, not for anything serious, anyway, she thought.

"This is perfect, thanks," she said, tasting the wine.

"It is our best Barbera," he said proudly.

"It's excellent." Isobel found it even smoother on the second sip. It was far superior to the wine she usually drank.

He moved in closer. "You know the secrets of *la bellissima*, maybe?"

So there was a price to pay for the free wine. "Perhaps I do," she said. "But I'm certainly not going to reveal them to anybody whose name I don't know."

"I am Carlo. Carlo Alessandrini, maître d' of Vino Rosso. Although I think to persuade the owner to change the name to La Bellissima, after your friend, the exquisite Delphinium."

Isobel laughed. "You won't get anywhere if you call her that."

"I do not understand. It is so beautiful and unusual. Like her."

"Yeah, well, she hates it."

"There is one thing I would like to know, and perhaps you can tell me, eh?"

"Depends," said Isobel.

"Does she have a *ragazzo?*" he said in a stage whisper. "A boyfriend?"

Before Isobel could answer, Sunil burst into the restaurant and spotted her at the bar.

"Sorry I'm late. That showcase company just called—I got the part in *Two by Two!*"

"That's fantastic!" She jumped off the stool and threw her arms around him.

Sunil looked around excitedly. "Where's Delphi? I can't

wait to tell her!"

"I'm sure she'll be back in a moment." She turned to Carlo. "Oh, and in answer to your question? Yes." She cocked her head in Sunil's direction. Carlo's handsome Roman features flushed.

"I see," he said.

"Well?" She gazed expectantly at Carlo.

"Well…what?"

"Another glass of Barbera on the house? I believe you said that any friend of Delphi's was a friend of yours?"

Carlo glowered at her and returned a moment later with a second glass, barely half full.

"Hey, thanks!" Sunil said.

Carlo ignored him and strode away to the front door where he greeted a party of six with loud air kisses.

"Clearly you have the touch and I don't," Sunil said wryly.

"But you have it where it counts. You got the job. That's great!"

"Well, that remains to be seen. This company has a reputation. And it's a showcase, so there's no pay."

"I'll help you send out flyers to agents and casting directors if you want," said Isobel. "I can use the equipment at my office."

"That would be great!"

"My office," she mused. "That sounds so strange. But I suppose, for now, it's true."

"You'll get an acting job. Don't forget, I've been here for a year already."

"And this is your first gig?"

"Not exactly. I had a summer stock job last year." He smiled sheepishly. "Playing Ali Hakim in *Oklahoma*."

"Well, here's to the first of many fabulous singing roles," Isobel said, raising her glass.

"And here's hoping you survive your office job long enough to get one yourself!"

They clinked glasses and drank. Delphi joined them a

moment later.

"Sunil has news," Isobel said, elbowing him.

"I got Noah in *Two by Two*."

"That's fantastic!" Delphi crowed.

"Thanks," he smiled, slightly embarrassed. "I'm sure you'll get something soon."

"I've been thinking about Shakespeare." Delphi turned to Isobel. "Something you said the other day about my having a good period look."

Isobel nodded enthusiastically. "You do! I'm hopelessly contemporary. But your curls, your features. When you lose the heavy silver and the nose ring, you have this amazing china doll look."

"Why do you think I got the nose ring?" said Delphi drily.

"I can totally see you doing Shakespeare," Isobel continued. "Helena, Olivia, Beatrice…"

"Lady Macbeth, Goneril…" added Sunil.

"Very funny." Delphi punched him playfully on the arm. "Anyway, I thought I might try a class. Just to see if it suits me."

"That reminds me." Isobel told them about Nikki, leaving out James's intrusion. She would fill Delphi in on that later. "So I want to find out if this emotional reality class is for real. Who wants to join me?"

"Sounds ridiculous," scoffed Sunil.

"I'm game," Delphi volunteered. "Besides, I don't want you going anywhere alone with anyone from that office. Even—no, especially—with that actress."

"It's Monday morning," Isobel said. "I guess I'll have to ask for time off."

"What if an audition comes along later in the week?" Sunil asked.

"I'll take my chances," Isobel said. "I need to find a good acting class, anyway."

"Doesn't sound like this is it," Delphi said doubtfully.

"No, it doesn't. But it will be an object lesson in what I

don't want." Isobel raised her glass and downed the rest of her wine in a satisfied gulp.

ISOBEL WAS UNPACKING THE LAST of her things into the apartment's one small closet when Delphi returned home after her shift later that night.

"I'm beat," Delphi said, flopping onto the futon. A puff of dust rose up. "I have to do something about that," she said, coughing.

Isobel lay down on her air mattress, which was tucked into the opposite corner. It was hard to reconcile the slumber party atmosphere of two faux beds in one room with her first adult living space, but as far as she could tell, this was the standard of habitation for recent college graduates who insisted on living in Manhattan.

She watched Delphi unload her wrists, piling up her silver bracelets neatly on the edge of her futon. "What do you think of Sunil?" Isobel asked.

"Hold it right there!" Delphi held up a link of silver skulls. "No matchmaking!"

"Don't tell me you're interested in that sleazy maître d'?"

"Carlo isn't sleazy, he's Italian. They're all romantics, and they all love blondes. Why?"

"Because I told him Sunil was your boyfriend."

"What?!"

"I didn't like the way Carlo was talking about you," Isobel said. "Very possessive and intrusive."

Delphi gave an exasperated sigh. "Italians are notoriously jealous! It's part of their charm."

"I know," Isobel said. "But if he's interested in you for something more than a quick hookup, now he has to fight for you. And if he isn't, he'll leave you alone."

"What if I want a quick hookup? What if I don't want to be left alone?"

"Do you?"

"Maybe! And if I were looking for some fun, I'd take it with Carlo. If you like Sunil so much, why don't you go after him yourself?" Delphi heaved herself up from the futon and stabbed a bright pink comb into her topknot. "Don't poke your nose too far into other people's business. If you pull that kind of stuff at your job, you're liable to get yourself killed!" She flounced off to the bathroom, her pink comb bobbing in disapproval.

Isobel's phone rang. She swallowed down a lump in her throat and answered it.

"Hello?"

"Iz? It's Percival. You okay?"

"Yeah."

"Liar."

She smiled ruefully. Percival, younger by seven years, had a level of emotional maturity that far surpassed hers. She could date her first awareness of it to one night when he was a tiny, bespectacled three year-old and they were both sick. She'd brought him some water in the middle of the night and made herself comfortable on the edge of his bed. Percival had stroked her hand and said, "You go back to sleep. You're sick, too." Not long after that, the indications of his uniqueness multiplied too quickly to count.

"Why do I always mess everything up?" Isobel said.

"What did you mess up?"

She was grateful to him for not adding "this time." Percival had a way of neutralizing her upsets, and just hearing his supportive, gently curious voice made Isobel realize how much she missed her little confidant and confessor.

"Why have I never learned to stop the big cup that is my mouth from running over?"

Percival laughed. "It's part of your charm, Iz."

He was the only one allowed to call her Iz. And she was the only one who didn't call him Percy.

She picked at a seam on the air mattress. "Maybe it's time to cultivate a new kind of charm."

"Don't be so hard on yourself. You're in a new situation, meeting new people. Your insecurities are bound to come out. Take that vulnerability and channel it into your acting. You can do it, I've seen you," Percival said.

"Thanks. I knew you'd make me feel better."

"Then you shouldn't have waited for me to call you," he chided.

"Right as always. How are you? How's school?" she asked.

"That's why I'm calling. I'm coming to New York next week for my Columbia interview."

"Wait a sec," Isobel sat up. "You're applying this year? I thought you'd decided not to graduate early."

"I changed my mind. There's nothing more for me here. I'm taking all my classes at the junior college, except Latin. My guidance counselor agrees."

"What do Mom and Dad think?"

"They think it's the right thing for me. So can I stay with you?"

Isobel looked around at the apartment, which felt a lot smaller now that it was crammed with furniture. "I have to ask my roommate, and I don't know what she'll say, especially since I just pissed her off. It's only one room."

"I could stay with Uncle Jake, but the cigar smoke might kill me."

"I'll ask her," Isobel said, as the bathroom door opened. "I'll call you tomorrow, okay?"

"Okay. Love you, Iz. Hang in there."

"Love you, too," Isobel said.

"Who was that?" Delphi asked, rubbing her wet hair with a towel.

"Percival."

"Who the hell is Percival?"

"My brother."

"I didn't know you had a brother." Delphi shook out her curls. "What's 'I'll ask her'?"

"Maybe *you* shouldn't poke your nose into other people's

business," Isobel said.

"Am I 'her'?" Delphi asked. Isobel nodded. "Then it is my business."

"He's coming to look at Columbia for next year, and he asked if he could stay here."

Delphi pulled a Nine Inch Nails T-shirt over her head. "Depends. Is he cute?"

"He's fifteen."

"And he's applying to Columbia?!"

"He's a genius. Math, physics, computers. And people," she added.

"Do you have a picture?"

Isobel pulled a photo from her wallet. She and Percival were standing by the shore of Lake Michigan, their arms draped around each other, grinning at the camera.

"Oh my God, it's Harry Potter!" Delphi exclaimed.

"With the wisdom of Albus Dumbledore."

Delphi handed the photo back. "I don't know, though, it's pretty tight in here. Where would he sleep?"

"I could go back to the residence for a few nights," Isobel said.

"And leave me alone with Harry?"

"Or you could spend the night with Carlo," Isobel suggested.

"Or Sunil," Delphi said.

Isobel took that as an olive branch. "Sorry. I was just looking out for you. No more meddling, I promise."

"It's okay. I overreacted. But just so you know, I'm perfectly capable of handling the menfolk all by myself."

Isobel nodded gratefully. "Got it. So what about Percival? Can he stay here?"

"Is he anything like you?"

"Nothing at all."

Delphi smiled and patted her damp hair. "In that case, he's more than welcome."

EIGHTEEN

THERE WAS SOMETHING COMFORTING about being part of the big city masses reporting to work every morning, Isobel decided. Her first rootless week in New York had demonstrated how easy it was to feel inconsequential without some sort of routine and a place, no matter how small and shared, to call home. Even if the routine involved going to an office every morning instead of to an audition or, better yet, a rehearsal, it gave her a sense of usefulness. She was a real New Yorker, she was paying her dues, and she was finding her place.

So it was a bit of a shock when she arrived at work a few days later to be reminded that her place was still the focus of a police investigation. The police, in the form of Detective Kozinski, served as an unassailable reminder.

"Can you tell me who this is?" Detective Kozinski asked without preamble. She held out a grainy black and white photo of a tallish woman in a flowered skirt with a scarf over her head and a long jacket.

"It's hard to say," Isobel said.

"Quick impression. Familiar or not? Ring any bells at all?"

"The skirt looks like one Paula Toule-Withers has, but it's impossible to be sure, and it doesn't really look like Paula. I mean, it doesn't give the impression of Paula. Why? What is this?"

"A still from the security camera. This woman exited the building just after the fire drill started, and we haven't been able to identify her."

"When did she enter the building?"

"I can't answer that."

"You won't tell?"

"We don't know," Detective Kozinski admitted. "For whatever reason, she seems to have dodged the cameras coming in."

"Maybe she was dressed differently?" suggested Isobel.

Detective Kozinski nodded. "We're reviewing the tapes with that in mind."

As Isobel set down her coffee, she noticed that the drawers of the small credenza adjacent to Doreen's desk were open. She looked questioningly at Detective Kozinski, who held up a key in response.

"Found this in Doreen's desk. It goes to that cabinet. There's something in particular I'm looking for."

"Can I help?"

"Doubt it," Detective Kozinski said with a smirk.

Isobel sipped her coffee and watched the detective remove stacks of papers without even looking at them. She slowed down when she reached the bottom shelf on the right. From this she withdrew a small, quilted toiletry bag and gingerly began to remove its contents. When she extracted a square tan plastic case, she gave a satisfied nod and dropped it into an evidence bag.

Isobel knew immediately what it was. Unable to help herself, she jumped up from her chair and darted across the room.

"What on earth do you need that for?" she asked, unable to contain her surprise.

"Evidence."

Isobel stared at her. "Doreen's diaphragm is evidence?"

Detective Kozinski shook her head. "Just the case. We already have the diaphragm." She considered Isobel for a moment, then said quietly, "She was putting it in when she was killed."

Isobel gasped. "Seriously?"

"Any idea who she was going to meet?"

Isobel shook her head. "I told you, I only knew her for three hours."

"If you happen to pick up any details about Doreen's love life, let me know." Detective Kozinski handed Isobel her card.

"Why would the person she was going to meet want to kill her?" Isobel asked.

Detective Kozinski gave her a curious look. "Why would you think that's who killed her?"

"I don't know," Isobel faltered. "Isn't that what you were getting at?"

"Not necessarily. We just want to know who it was. Maybe the person who killed her was jealous that she was meeting someone else."

Isobel laughed. "I'm sorry, but Doreen was not the sort of woman that men fight over."

Detective Kozinski gave Isobel an appraising look, as if determining whether or not *she* was that sort. "You got that in three hours?"

"I got that in three minutes."

Detective Kozinski picked up the evidence bag and the toiletry kit. "If you get wind of anything, my numbers are on the card. Call my cell if it's urgent."

Isobel looked into the policewoman's clear blue eyes. "Does this mean I'm not a suspect anymore?"

Detective Kozinski held her gaze. "Everyone's a suspect. Just some more than others."

Isobel watched her go, then knelt by the credenza. Detective Kozinski hadn't bothered to put back any of the papers and office supplies, so she began stuffing them back onto the shelves. Then, changing her mind, she rifled through them, searching for a date book, address book or appointment book of any kind.

Nothing. If there was such a thing, the police must have grabbed it on round one. She heaved the last of Doreen's property back into the credenza, which she left unlocked, since Detective Kozinski had taken the key. Then she returned to her desk and her latte.

So, Doreen was on the make. This was shocking partly because she was such an unattractive person—although Isobel supposed it took all kinds—but more so because she'd been heading for a tryst in the middle of a workday. It settled one thing, however: Doreen never had any intention of participating in the emergency drill. But why was she putting in her diaphragm in the office bathroom? Why didn't she wait until she got to her love nest? And furthermore, thought Isobel, if I were putting in my diaphragm, I'd definitely close the stall door, even if I didn't think anyone else would be coming in.

In her peripheral vision, she spotted Stan Henderson scurrying around the corner to his desk. Finally. Maybe now she'd be able to get a read on how he really felt about his ex-wife. Isobel looked at her watch. It was only nine forty-five. She would give him a little time to get caught up from his absence.

Then she'd find a reason to pass by.

"JAMES! I WAS JUST PASSING BY."

Ginger Wainwright appeared in his doorway, waving an invoice in her hand. "I see that you expensed a lunch with Felice Edwards of InterBank Switzerland. I'm glad to see you're taking that kind of initiative."

But…? James thought.

"But next time, no booze. It runs up the tab. I'm not a bottomless pit, you know."

"Understood."

"And just so you know, we're phasing out InterBank Switzerland. Let's see, who else are you working with?"

"Gilbert Brothers Publishing, Dove & Flight Public Relations since the other day, and—"

"Stay on top of Dove & Flight. You met Mike Hardy. You can take him out to lunch next month. He's a sports nut. You two should get along well."

"Sounds great," James said with more enthusiasm than he felt. "Hey, Ginger, I was wondering...do you remember a temp named Nikki Francis?"

Ginger frowned and shook her head. "Doesn't ring a bell. But that doesn't mean anything. They come and go so quickly, you can't expect me to remember all their names. That's why God invented computers." She flounced out the door and continued her morning rounds.

"Anna? I was just passing by..."

James returned to his computer and continued searching the employment records for Nikki Francis. His instinct told him Felice's memory was more accurate than she gave herself credit for. Alcohol, as he knew only too well, tended to uproot the truth, while sobriety only buried it deeper. He plugged in Nicole, Nicolette, Nicola and every other name for which Nikki was a plausible nickname. He tried every conceivable spelling of Francis. Nothing came up.

He stood up and paced the length of his tiny office. One of the reasons he liked Temp Zone was that Ginger had divided her modest space into actual offices instead of cubicles. This was becoming more and more rare, but Ginger was old school. It was why she stubbornly refused to hire over the internet. Her holdout technique appealed to a certain kind of client, allowing Temp Zone to enjoy a reputation for selectivity. He had no doubt that Doreen Fink's murder was behind her decision to phase out InterBank Switzerland.

He walked down the narrow hallway to the makeshift kitchen and grabbed a Coke from the fridge. Anna came in a few moments later.

"Hey," he said. "Enjoy your morning chat with Ginger?"

"Oh, please. I'm so used to it by now, I respond on autopilot."

"How long have you been here?" James asked.

"Too long," Anna said with a groan. "One of these days I'm going to place myself in a nice, long-term gig and get the hell out of the recruiting business."

"Do you remember an employee named Nikki Francis? Actress probably in her late twenties, early thirties. She worked at InterBank Switzerland, at least for a while."

"What does she look like?"

"Tall, slender, attractive, but a little hard-looking. Short reddish-brown hair. Kind of androgynous."

Anna shook her head. "I don't think so. And I've done most of their placements. Why?"

"Not a big deal. She's just someone I met over there the other day. Well, I'd better get back to it."

He had just reached the door to his office, when Anna called his name. He walked back to her.

"There was an actress in her late twenties a few years ago who was tall and sort of coltish. Her hair was different and so was her name. Annika Franklin. Could that be her?"

"Could be," he said, his pulse quickening. "What happened to her?"

"She was terminated."

"Why? Did she go permanent?"

"No. We fired her, but I can't remember why."

NINETEEN

"CAN I GO WITH YOU TO YOUR emotional reality class next week?" Isobel asked Nikki, who had come in just before noon and was wearing a sensational pair of lemon yellow leather pants that showed off her long, slender legs.

Nikki raised an eyebrow at Isobel. "Really? You didn't seem so into it when I invited you."

"I've been thinking about it, and, like you said, singers aren't always so truthful in their acting. I really should get back in class."

Nikki considered this a moment, then nodded. "All right, then. But you'll have to ask Frank for the time off. It's from ten to twelve on Monday."

"I can skip lunch on Tuesday and Wednesday. Is it okay if I bring a friend?"

"Terence usually allows only one auditor per class, but I'll ask. Is your friend a singer too?"

Isobel shook her head vigorously. "Not at all."

They worked in silence for a while. Isobel had almost finished uploading and organizing the contents of Doreen's flash drives. There were only a few files left to transfer, but the urge to procrastinate was strong. She considered trying again to see Stan. She had happened by twice already, but both times he was behind closed doors with Frank.

She looked over at Nikki, who was manipulating an incomprehensible spreadsheet on her computer.

"Nikki?"

"Mmmmm."

"Did Doreen have a boyfriend?"

Nikki snorted. "That cow?"

"Somebody might have found her attractive," Isobel said.

"Who? And believe me, from the way that woman talked about sex, it was obvious she wasn't getting any."

"What do you mean?"

"Didn't you notice how obsessed she was? Doreen could find sexual innuendo in the most banal sentence. She was always making lewd, insinuating comments about other people's sex lives. And whenever anyone did something she didn't like, she'd threaten to spank them. Believe me, that didn't go down well with Paula."

"We know Stan found her attractive," Isobel reminded her.

"We know Stan married her." Nikki rolled her chair away from her desk to look at Isobel. "Not the same thing. And don't forget, the marriage was annulled. I'm guessing one look at Doreen naked sent Stan running back to City Hall."

"Maybe," Isobel said, "but I still think Doreen must have had somebody."

"What on earth makes you think that?"

Isobel was about to share the diaphragm tidbit with Nikki, but James's warning flashed through her mind. She couldn't quite convince herself that Nikki was dangerous. Still, it was probably best not to confide.

"It just—I don't know—boyfriends and murders seem to go together so often."

"I never heard her on the phone with anyone who could have been a boyfriend," Nikki said. "And her conversations weren't exactly discreet."

Isobel remembered overhearing Doreen massacring metaphors on her first day. Nikki was right; if she'd had a boyfriend, it would hardly have been a secret. But how did that explain the diaphragm?

"You're right. I don't know what I was thinking," Isobel said. She stood up and stretched her legs. "I'm going to take a little break."

Now that she'd exhausted every possible distraction except

trying Stan again, she headed back his way. Maybe he and Doreen had had some kind of latter-day reconciliation and were finally consummating their non-marriage. In any case, there was a reasonable chance that he held the key to the diaphragm, whether Doreen was putting it in for him or for someone he was jealous of.

Conchita Perez was seated at her desk, her eyes closed, her head tilted toward the ceiling, and her lips moving in a silent appeal. She opened one eye when she heard Isobel approach.

"Hola," Isobel said cheerily.

"Hello."

"Is Stan…?" Isobel noticed that Frank's office door was open now and Stan's was closed.

"He's in his office and doesn't want to be disturbed."

"I just wanted to see if there's anything he needs," Isobel said.

Conchita bristled. "*I'm* his assistant."

"I know," Isobel said quickly, "but on the first day, I did a few memos for him, and I thought maybe—"

"That was only because I was out. He doesn't need anything from you," Conchita said, with surprising force.

For the first time, Isobel caught a steely determination in Conchita's eyes, and she decided not to press her luck. She pointed at Frank's door instead and lifted her eyebrows at Conchita, as if to ask permission to enter. Conchita shrugged and looked away.

"Frank?" Isobel said, glancing in through the door.

He looked up from his computer. "Yes?"

"Would it be all right if I came in late on Monday morning? I could be here by twelve thirty, and I won't take lunch on Tuesday or Wednesday."

"Is this some acting thing?" he asked, with a disdainful emphasis on the word "acting."

"More or less." But rather less than more, she thought.

"Nikki's out on Monday mornings, so Conchita will have to take all the phones. If it's okay with her, it's okay with me."

Great, thought Isobel. When she returned to Conchita's desk area, she caught sight of Stan retreating into his office. He shut the door firmly behind him once more. Conchita was gazing after him with a wistful expression that easily took five years off her. Isobel cleared her throat.

"Could you cover for me on Monday morning? I'd be happy to return the favor sometime."

Conchita scrunched her eyes and dipped her head to keep the tears from falling.

"I'll take that as a yes," said Isobel.

WITHOUT A PHOTO, James couldn't be certain that Annika Franklin and Nikki Francis were the same person. One thing was clear, however; Anna's recollection was correct. According to Temp Zone's records, Annika Franklin, whoever she was, had been fired, first from her position at Credit Exchange Bank, and subsequently from Temp Zone. There were no details about the reason for her dismissal, but there was a note that read, "Do not rehire." Prior to her position at Credit Exchange Bank, she had indeed worked at InterBank Switzerland, although there was no indication that she'd been fired from there. James stepped out into the hall. He could hear the other reps talking among themselves or on the phone, and above them all, Ginger loudly trying to convince someone to take advantage of her services. James returned to his office and closed the door. Then he used his cell phone to dial the number for the director of human resources at Credit Exchange Bank.

"May I speak with Gretchen Bryars?"

"This is she."

"Gretchen, this is James Cooke with," he hesitated ever so slightly, "Temps in Time. We've had an application from someone who worked for you once. Name is Annika Franklin."

"Don't hire her," Gretchen said, firmly and immediately.

"Ah, I thought there might be a problem," James said. "What can you tell me about her?"

"We hired her from an outfit called Temp Zone. They have an excellent reputation, but this woman was bad news. She was an actress, or said she was."

"What exactly did she do? Was there something specific?"

"Absolutely. She stole money."

"Really?" James didn't know what he'd expected to hear, but it wasn't this.

"Yes. Unfortunately, we were never able to prove anything, which is why no charges were pressed. But we're reasonably certain that she was siphoning off cash under cover of the accounting department. She was supposed to be handling receivables, but she was helping herself to the payables, if you know what I mean."

"Why weren't you able to prove anything?" he asked.

"She had created a spurious vendor and cut checks to them. But she set it up very cleverly, with a post office box in another state and checks endorsed with a company stamp."

"What makes you sure it was Nikki—I mean, Annika—if you weren't able to prove it?"

"The rest of the personnel in that department were long-term, full-time employees, and they all claimed they'd never heard of…Computer Accessories, that was the name of it. Plus, the invoicing was all done from her terminal. I suppose we didn't know for sure until we fired her, but it stopped as soon as she left, so you can draw your own conclusions."

"What did she look like?"

"Tall, with long, very straight auburn hair. Sharp dresser. I remember admiring one pair of trousers of hers in particular—leather pants in a buttercup yellow." Gretchen laughed. "Of course, I don't have the figure to pull those off!"

"Do you know what happened to her after she left?" James asked.

"I know Temp Zone let her go. I had a long conversation afterwards with Ginger Wainwright, the owner. She reassured me at great length that her company's reputation came first, and she would never keep on a dishonest employee."

"Do you still use Temp Zone?" he asked. He knew they didn't, but he was curious to hear the reason.

"I don't. Their fees went up, and I get a better deal from Temporama, although honestly, the help isn't as good. Tell me about your outfit. What did you say it was called?"

"Um, Temp..." James scrambled to remember the name he'd made up on the spur of the moment. "Temps..." James quickly hit a button on his keypad. "I'm sorry, Gretchen, but I think I'm getting another call. I appreciate your help. I'm sure we won't be hiring her."

"Oh, one other thing," James heard Gretchen say, as he was about to hang up. He brought the phone back to his ear.

"You referred to her as Nikki," she continued. "That's what she was called here, as well. Nobody ever called her Annika."

James smiled triumphantly and fist-pumped the air. "Thank you, Gretchen. Thank you very much."

TWENTY

IT SEEMED LIKE CONCHITA was never going to take a lunch break, and there were only so many excuses Isobel could invent to pass by Stan's office. She planned to give it one last shot for the day, but Paula stopped her.

"You're spending an awful lot of time wandering about. If you don't have enough work to do, I'd be happy to fill out your dance card."

Isobel didn't feel like defending herself. Instead, noticing the return of Paula's flowered skirt, she said, somewhat slyly, "Nice skirt."

That brought Paula up short, as she'd hoped it would.

"What's that supposed to mean?" she asked sharply.

Isobel shrugged. "Oh, nothing. It's just that Detective Kozinski showed me a security photo of a woman leaving the building in a hurry right around the time Doreen was killed, and she was wearing a skirt that looked an awful lot like yours."

Paula narrowed her small, brown eyes. "Yes, she showed me that photo too. But as you well know, it wasn't me. The physique was all wrong."

"It wasn't *that* wrong," said Isobel, an inner devil taking hold of her. "Besides, the perspective is always funny in those security photos."

"Nonsense. I was busy executing my duties as fire marshal."

"Which are...what, exactly?" asked Isobel, feigning politeness.

"Making sure everyone on the floor is proceeding

downstairs accordingly. I am not permitted to exit until I have confirmed that everyone else has evacuated the premises."

"How selfless. But, of course, it explains why you came into the bathroom when you did."

"Exactly. I was looking for Doreen. I'd forgotten about *you*," she said with a sneer.

"Then again," Isobel said, unable to stop herself, "as one of the few people who knew in advance that there was going to be an emergency drill, perhaps you popped in there a bit earlier to stab her and were just coming back to make sure she was dead."

Paula's eyes flashed fire, and for a moment, she looked positively dangerous. She leaned closer to Isobel, who instinctively took a step backward.

"I would be very, *very* careful about making accusations, Sarah Bernhardt," Paula hissed. "Doreen took her lunch every day at one p.m. sharp, preceded always by a trip to the ladies' room. Emergency drill or not, everybody on this floor knew precisely where they could find her at that particular moment."

"Everybody except me," Isobel said.

"Then what were you doing in the bathroom?"

"Using it," Isobel retorted.

"You ignored an emergency drill to use the loo?" Paula gave a thin, witchy laugh. "The police must believe you're an absolute moron to do such a thing. Then again, that isn't much of a stretch."

Isobel shook her head in disbelief. "Why do you dislike me so much?"

"Let's see…where to start? Perhaps with the fact that you just baldly accused me of murder?"

"Bullshit!" The word exploded from Isobel with surprising force. "You've been horrible to me since my very first day."

"I find all women in your position distasteful," Paula said.

"Temps?"

"Temps, secretaries." Paula clenched her fingers into fists.

"I've fought hard to get where I am, and I'm not nearly where I want to be. Why? Because as long as there are women willing to be underlings, men will think that's where we belong."

"So who do you think should have these jobs? Children? Midgets?"

"Men. And women too, as soon as there are enough of us balancing out management."

"So you've taken it upon yourself to be nasty and unhelpful to every secretary or temp who comes along until they...what? Vie for your job?" Isobel laughed at the absurdity of Paula's reasoning. "You'd better give that a little more thought."

Isobel stalked back to her desk, confused and angry. Was Paula deliberately egging her on? Didn't she realize that admitting her dislike for secretaries only corroborated Isobel's suspicions? At what point did distaste morph into hate?

And at what point did hate turn murderous?

Isobel knew she had gone too far in actually accusing Paula. But by provoking her, she had gleaned one interesting bit of information. It was common knowledge that Doreen took lunch every day at one o'clock with a stop in the bathroom first. The emergency drill may have provided a lucky stroke of cover, but the killer didn't need to have known about it in advance. It was enough that Doreen was a creature of habit.

That widened the field considerably.

TWENTY-ONE

"OKAY, BUT HERE'S WHAT I DON'T UNDERSTAND," Delphi said, attacking her toes with nail polish in her signature delphinium blue. "If you're putting in your diaphragm in the office bathroom—which, I agree, is weird to begin with—why would you take it out of its case at your desk? Why not bring the case with you into the bathroom?"

"Maybe she was doing the tampon trick?" Isobel suggested. "You know, where you slide a tampon up your sleeve so nobody sees it."

"I know, but a diaphragm? And what about the jelly? Did she put the tube up her sleeve too?"

"Not everybody uses the jelly. I had a roommate in college who refused. Her boyfriend used a condom too, and she felt it was overkill."

"Aren't you overlooking the obvious?" Delphi asked, admiring her left foot and turning her attention to her right.

"What's that?"

"Maybe she was taking it out."

"But Detective Kozinski said—"

"Why would she be straight with you?" asked Delphi shrewdly.

"Maybe she thinks I can help."

"Okay, but think about it. Taking the diaphragm out makes more sense on every level."

"Well," Isobel said thoughtfully, "it would explain the missing jelly tube, and it seems right that she could have had sex the night before with…whomever, it doesn't matter…and just forgot to take her diaphragm out until that moment."

"Exactly," Delphi said. "She suddenly remembered, and she didn't want to leave it in any longer because that can be dangerous. So she took it out and was probably going to wrap it in toilet paper and stash it up her sleeve until she got back to her desk to put it back in its case."

"I honestly can't imagine who in a million years would have wanted to sleep with her. And Nikki seemed pretty certain that Doreen wasn't getting any."

"You believe Nikki?"

"On that? Yes. Although Nikki is moody, no question." Isobel paced into the galley kitchen and poured out what was left of the Diet Coke. "Paula is a dragon, Conchita is a religious nut, Frank is preoccupied, and Stan is a hologram." She leaned on the counter. "What do you think?"

"Look to the religious nut. They'll do anything in the name of God."

"I just can't see Conchita driving a pair of scissors through somebody's chest. She's like a little Hispanic grandmother. If you saw her, you'd know what I mean."

Delphi capped her nail polish and waved it at Isobel. "Don't be fooled. Those little Hispanic grandmothers are tough!"

Isobel looked at her watch. "I wouldn't mind some fresh air. And more Diet Coke. Wanna take a walk?"

"Can't, I'm still drying," Delphi said, wiggling her toes.

Isobel grabbed her coat and walked down the three flights to the newsstand on the corner. The newsman was just cutting open the plastic binders around a stack of copies of *Backstage* and was happy to unload one on Isobel. She stopped at the deli for another bottle of Diet Coke and a bag of pretzels and headed home, waving cheerfully to two male prostitutes in drag, who were camped out on the stoop a few doors down. They waved back and continued to chug from bottles ineptly concealed in brown bags. Isobel liked the "local color," as she called it. Familiarity had eased any fears she may have had, as the unknown became known and thereby less menacing.

Delphi was talking agitatedly into her cell phone when Isobel got back.

"Just tell her to stop! Aster, look…I know, but Pansy has always had her issues with Mom, and I think if she's going to…fine, don't listen to me, you never do. No! Poppy's got her own shit to deal with right now. That guy dumped her… Well, I don't know why she didn't tell you. I have to go. Right. All right. Look out for Zinn, okay? Bye."

Delphi skipped her phone across the floor like a stone on a lake.

"You are so lucky you have a brother," she said to Isobel. "What did you get?"

"Provisions," said Isobel, holding up the pretzels and the soda. "And a copy of *Backstage*. Let's see if there's anything good."

They settled down on the floor and began to leaf through the listings.

"Look," Isobel pointed, "here are some auditions for *Othello*."

Delphi shook her head. "I've got to get into the groove first. My Shakespeare class doesn't start for another couple of weeks." She flipped the page. "Here's a production of *High Society*. That could be fun! It's on Friday. Wanna go? I can sign us both up in the morning."

It was tempting. Isobel loved Cole Porter, but she wasn't keen on going to another musical audition with Delphi. On the other hand, without Delphi signing her up, there was no way she could make it, as it would require both being late to work and ducking out during the day. Until and unless Delphi decided to give up musicals altogether, there was no avoiding going to auditions with her.

"Sure, let's go for it."

"Are you interested in straight theater at all?" Delphi asked.

"Not as much. I'm always waiting for the song cues. What about you? Have you, uh, always done musicals?"

"Yeah. I got to play a lot of great roles in high school. I really love to sing." Delphi twirled the silver stud in her nose and glanced self-consciously at Isobel. "But I don't have the kind of training you and Sunil have. That's why the Shakespeare idea interests me."

"It does seem to me," Isobel said carefully, "that with so many people trying to break into show business, the more specific your goals are, the better chance you have of getting work."

Delphi shrugged. "I always heard you should just try out for everything, and the work will find you."

"It's such an unpredictable business. Hard to know what's best," said Isobel lightly, aware that they were skirting dangerous waters.

"You might like doing Shakespeare," Delphi said. "The language is so musical."

"I don't know. Why don't you try your class first and tell me how you like it?"

"Why don't you try that emotional reality class first and tell me how *you* like it?"

Isobel laughed. "Oh, no, you're coming with me. As my bodyguard. And I promise, if it's truly horrible, I'll try Shakespeare with you."

"Deal," said Delphi. They spread the paper on the floor, settled in with the pretzels, and continued to scout the audition listings until well past midnight.

JAMES EMERGED FROM THE SHOWER to find Jayla dressed and sitting on the edge of his bed, her arms and legs crossed in full defensive girlfriend position.

"Are you drinking again?" she asked.

"Do you smell it on me?"

"No."

"Then what makes you think I'm drinking again?"

He pulled a pair of jeans from his closet. He had promised

her they'd run out for a bite to eat, although he wasn't particularly hungry. He would rather have just gone to sleep.

"You're acting funny."

"Funny weird or funny ha-ha?"

Jayla uncrossed her legs in order to stamp her foot on the floor. "Don't mess with me, James. It's that girl, isn't it?"

"What girl?" James asked, taking a moment to straighten the hangers. He knew damn well what girl, but he couldn't begin to explain why he felt guilty about Isobel.

"That white bitch," Jayla said.

He sighed. It was time to level with her. Partly. "I admit, I'm a little preoccupied, because I found out something about one of the people she's working with."

"So pull her out of there and be done with it," Jayla said. "I want her out of this bedroom!"

"She is not in this bedroom!"

"Mm hmmm," said Jayla knowingly. "Your head was somewhere else just now. Your bigger head, that is."

James shrugged on a T-shirt. "You're creating a problem where there isn't one."

"I'm not a fool, James. I know when somebody isn't telling me the truth."

James whirled on her. "Maybe I'm just not into you anymore, Jayla. And that has nothing to do with Isobel!"

As soon as the words were out of his mouth, he regretted them. It wasn't a new thought, but it hadn't crystallized as truth until that moment. Now there was no going back.

Clearly, that possibility hadn't occurred to Jayla. James could tell from her shocked expression that she couldn't fathom how he could give her up unless there was somebody else.

She softened a bit. "James...James," she purred. "I thought we wanted the same thing."

"Which is what?"

"Marriage. Children. A strong black family."

He sat on the edge of the bed and took Jayla's hand.

"Listen, it's not that I don't want that, and it's not that I don't want that with you." He allowed himself that white lie. "But I'm not ready. I haven't even been sober for a month. This is new ground. It's like a new me. I need to feel what the world is really like."

Jayla pulled her hand away. "You mean you need to see who else is out there," she said in a brittle voice. "And after I stood by you and everything. Who got you into AA, huh?"

He stared at his hands. "I know, and I'm grateful. But I need to spread my wings a little. I need," he paused, realizing he hadn't quite admitted this to himself, "I need some time alone to figure out who I am without the booze."

Jayla stood up and looked down at him, which made him feel like a child about to be scolded.

"You expect me to believe that you, who are afraid to be alone—and don't tell me otherwise, you know it's true—are leaving me...for *nobody*?"

He sighed. He was telling the truth, but it was so far removed from Jayla's image of him that he knew no amount of protesting would convince her. There was only one way to make this stick.

"All right. There is somebody else."

"I knew it!" Jayla's eyes blazed triumphantly, but her voice settled lower as she realized what this meant. "Who is it?"

James paused. "Her name is Felice Edwards. She works in HR at InterBank Switzerland."

Jayla looked for a moment like she didn't believe him. Then she slapped him hard across the face and walked out.

TWENTY-TWO

ISOBEL HAD HOPED TO GET TO Stan before Conchita set up her guard post, but the Diet Coke had kept her awake, and, as a result, she didn't arrive at her desk until nine thirty. She'd have to wait until Conchita's lunch break and hope that she could snare Stan then. She set aside Doreen's flash drives to return to Frank, took phone messages, placed a few equipment orders, and researched non-Equity performing opportunities.

"InterBank Switzerland, this is Isobel," she said, picking up the phone absent-mindedly as she clicked on the Blue Hill Troupe, the oldest Gilbert and Sullivan company in the city.

"It's James. I have to talk to you."

Isobel turned her back on Nikki's desk, even though Nikki wasn't in yet. "More suspicions to fling around? Shall I put you on speaker phone?"

"It's important," he said. "Meet me for lunch."

"I'm not taking lunch today. There's an audition tomorrow—"

"There's a diner at Twenty-third and Park Avenue South, northeast corner. Twelve thirty." Before she could argue, he hung up.

She stared at the phone, vaguely irritated. He hadn't given her much choice. On the other hand, maybe he planned to apologize for putting her on the spot with Nikki. She hoped he'd gotten more from Felice Edwards or knew where the police investigation was heading. She had certainly picked up a few interesting tidbits since they'd last spoken, although she hadn't yet decided if she wanted to share them.

The morning dragged on, leaving her plenty of time to

speculate about the urgency of James's phone call. At twelve
twenty, Isobel walked around the bend to Frank's office to let
him know she was taking a quick lunch. He nodded his assent,
but when she turned to leave, she saw that Conchita was
nowhere in sight and Stan's door was open.

Damn, she thought, glancing at her watch. I don't have
time for this now.

But she knew this might be her only chance to avoid the
self-appointed Cerberus. She banished James from her mind
and darted into Stan's office.

"Hello!" she said, rather too energetically.

Stan squinted at her through his doughy cheeks.

"Who are you?" he asked, his speech high and adenoidal,
probably a result of his cold.

"Isobel Spice. We met last week? I'm temping. I mean, I
was temping, but now I'm filling in for Doreen. Not filling in
exactly…replacing her. But not permanently! Remember, I
took a message for you last week?"

Thank God this isn't an audition, thought Isobel.

"Oh, right. Is there something you need from me?"

"Actually, I wanted to see if you needed anything from me.
Any, um, filing or anything?"

"No, I'm okay. Thank you."

"I'm sorry about Doreen. I know you and she were—"

"What?" His features altered, for the first time, into a
slightly less squishy demeanor. She noticed for the first time
that he had remarkably long eyelashes.

"You were…" she paused. How much should she know?
"You knew her outside of work."

Stan regarded her warily. "We went way back," he said.
"I'm sorry, I have work to do." He picked up a yellow legal pad
and flipped through the pages.

"I mean," Isobel stuttered on, "I'm sure it was a great loss.
And, um, I just wanted to say that I'm sorry."

She wasn't exactly sure what had led her to say that,
considering that Stan was still fairly high on her list of

suspects. A pained expression crossed his face, and he ran his fingers through his thick hair.

"Thank you. It was a loss. Nobody else here gets that. Even Conchita doesn't appreciate—" he stopped. "Doreen was not an easy person. But nobody will ever understand the things she did for me. The sacrifices she made. I'm not sure why she made them." He shook his head sadly. "And now I'm on my own."

"So you didn't kill her?" Isobel blurted out, startled by this odd confession.

"Jesus wept! Of course he didn't kill her!" Conchita cried from behind her. "I told you to leave the poor man in peace. I can take care of everything he needs."

"Not everything," Stan said, locking eyes with Conchita over Isobel's shoulder.

Conchita set her mouth in a thin line and nodded her head sharply, like a genie granting a wish.

"Everything," she said firmly.

ISOBEL WAS PANTING WHEN she slid into the booth across from James at the Moonstone Diner.

"Sorry I'm late! I finally got to talk to Stan Henderson, and it wasn't what I expected. I thought since he was married briefly to Doreen years ago, he might have killed her. But he seems genuinely distraught. I can't understand why—I mean, I can't imagine anyone really liking that woman, but he said something intriguing about her making all kinds of sacrifices for his sake, stuff nobody else would do. Anyway, now I'm thinking he probably didn't do it, unless he's a really good liar, but he doesn't strike me as that bright. Now Conchita, his secretary, she's another case altogether, and I'm pretty sure she has a thing for Stan. She doesn't seem the type—she must be pushing sixty—but even though she's kind of grandmotherly and all, there's real metal underneath her. You know what I mean?"

James blinked. "I'm fine, Isobel, thanks. And you?"

She blushed and sat back against the banquette. "I was blathering, wasn't I?"

"No problem. I like a good monologue with my lunch."

"I'm sorry." She seemed genuinely dismayed, which James found inexplicably endearing.

The waitress appeared, pen and pad in hand. "What can I get you?"

"I'll have a grilled cheese sandwich," Isobel said, without glancing at the menu.

"Turkey on rye, mustard, lettuce, tomato," James said. "And a Coke."

"Oh! Me, too," said Isobel.

James couldn't resist. "All that caffeine. Do you think it's wise?"

"It's okay, I'm not driving," Isobel said.

James found himself resisting the urge to say, "Not funny. I'm an alcoholic." Instead, he said, "You look very nice today," and immediately wished he hadn't.

Isobel's hand flew to her hair, smoothing it behind her ears. "Thank you. What's so urgent?"

James shook his head. He wasn't quite ready to burst her bubble yet. "No, you go on about Stan Henderson." He cast his mind back to his lunch with Felice. "Didn't Doreen get him the job?"

Isobel looked surprised. "How did you know?"

"Felice told me at lunch the other day."

"Ah, yes. You seem to be making a habit of this sort of thing," said Isobel, indicating their surroundings. "Tell me, was that lunch with Felice purely business?"

"I have a girlfriend." Although as soon as he said it, he realized it wasn't true anymore.

Isobel's lip curled in amusement. "That wasn't what I asked."

Damn, he thought. What is wrong with me?

"Yes, it was business," he said. "Mainly to find out what

kind of people you're in with."

"I wonder why Stan and Doreen's marriage was annulled," Isobel went on. "Annulment—the 'oops, I made a mistake' divorce."

James shrugged. "Probably one of them discovered something about the other they didn't know before. Like inability to perform in bed. Isn't that the big reason marriages are annulled? Failure to consummate?"

"But they were high school sweethearts. Wouldn't they have known that?"

"Maybe they chose to abstain."

Isobel feigned shock. "I didn't know you could do that!"

"Seriously, though, nothing you've said makes a good case for him killing her. Prior failed marriage? Not enough." He sucked a cold mouthful of Coke through his straw.

"I guess not. But the way Nikki presented it to me, it sounded logical. I thought maybe Stan resented Doreen for helping him."

"Nikki?"

"She's the one who pointed me toward Stan."

I'll bet she did, thought James. He knew he should tell Isobel what he'd learned about Nikki, but he wasn't quite ready.

"Tell me about Conchita," he said instead, when their sandwiches arrived. "According to Felice, she's very religious."

"Maybe. I'm not so sure."

"What do you mean?"

"It's a great cover, isn't it?" Isobel said. "Crying and praying all the time. No one would ever think she was capable of killing someone. This is a woman who claims she's worn the same silver and emerald cross since her first communion! But she's fiercely protective of Stan. She's going out of her way to make sure I don't talk to him."

"Felice said Conchita thought Doreen made good people do bad things," he said.

Isobel's eyes grew appealingly wide. "What do you think

that means?"

James shrugged. "Something. But who knows what? What about the boss, Lusardi?"

Isobel frowned and shook her head. "Can't quite get a handle on him. He liked Doreen." She paused. "No, liked isn't the right word. Appreciated her. But even so, he doesn't seem all that broken up. He and Paula Toule-Withers don't get along at all. Then again, she's a bitch. I hope she gets offed next."

"Isobel!"

"But she did tell me something interesting." Isobel waved her pickle for emphasis. "Apparently, Doreen was in the habit of leaving for lunch every day at one p.m., and she always stopped in the ladies' room first. I was the only person who didn't know where to find her. And, of course, I'm the one who found her."

There was a pause, and James knew the time had come.

"I know you're not going to like this, but you have to listen. The thing I have to tell you—it's about Nikki."

Isobel set her Coke glass down on the table with a thud. "Are you going to tell me to be careful of her again?"

"No, I'm going to tell you why."

He proceeded to tell her everything he'd learned from Gretchen Bryars at Credit Exchange Bank and what he had read in the Temp Zone files.

"Your monologue wasn't as good as mine," Isobel said when he finished.

"This isn't a competition."

"Well, you're wrong," Isobel said haughtily. "I happen to know that the reason Nikki is freelance now at InterBank is that she left for three months for an acting job, and her statute of limitations was up."

"How do you know it was an acting job? How do you know she didn't switch over to Credit Exchange, get caught, get fired, then contact Felice's predecessor about freelancing directly?"

Isobel gave an exasperated sigh. "Because she's an actor! Actors don't leave temp jobs for other temp jobs, they leave for *acting* jobs. Why don't you people take us seriously?"

"What do you mean 'you people'?" James asked, feeling his neck grow hot.

"All you buttoned-up corporate types. You, Frank Lusardi. My father's just as bad. You all think it's a big joke. 'Oh, look! Isobel and Nikki are going to be actresses. I mean they're going to *try* to be actresses. They won't succeed, of course. There are too many people out there who are *really* talented, but isn't it cute that they're giving it a shot?'"

He'd obviously struck a nerve, but she wasn't assimilating the facts. He reached across to touch her hand, but she snatched it away from him.

"I'm sure you're a good actress," he said. "And believe me, I'm sure Nikki is, too. I imagine she can fool people very well. I think she's got you fooled."

"Well, you're wrong about her," Isobel snapped. "And haven't you overlooked one tiny detail?"

"What's that?"

"They have different names!"

"I know, but look how similar they are! Isobel, don't be stupid—you're the college graduate, I'm the dropout. Gretchen even said Annika went by Nikki."

Isobel stood up. "You're just trying to cover your ass for making a fool of yourself the other day."

"Okay, I admit it—I started snooping because I wanted to prove to you that I wasn't overreacting. But where there's smoke, there's fire." Isobel turned away, but he pressed on. "Do you trust Nikki?"

"Yes."

"You don't think there's anything a little off about her?"

"No."

"I'm sorry, but I don't like what I've heard about her, and I didn't get a good vibe from her the other day—"

"Of course you didn't! You were casting aspersions about

her behind her back in front of her face!"

"And what I learned this morning confirmed them! Come on, Isobel, can you honestly say you like this woman?"

"Better than I like you!"

They stared at each other for a moment. Then Isobel said coldly, "And besides, Nikki's leather pants are lemon yellow, not buttercup." She turned and marched out of the diner.

James watched her leave, stunned. Isobel's words had hurt just as much as Jayla's slap.

No, not just as much. More.

He was too angry to go back to his office. Angry at Isobel for being childish and stubborn, and angry at Jayla for being right about Isobel. He should have either made the executive decision to pull Isobel off the job or left her to fend for herself. Trying to arm her with information was obviously a mistake.

We are never angrier than when we're angry at ourselves.

James heard Bill's voice in his mind and mentally punched him in the face. He was angry at Bill too, for keeping him away from the booze.

You're into your second month, he could hear Bill saying. Don't blow it now.

"Fuck you!" James exploded, and an elderly woman in front of him on the sidewalk turned around and shrieked. He growled at her, and she hurried away as fast as she could. He sulked all the way home on the subway, but instead of making the turn toward his apartment, he went in the opposite direction and paused outside City Liquors on 125th Street. He pulled out his cell phone and started to dial Bill, when an image of Isobel's face flickered through his mind. He saw her delighted expression when he told her how nice she looked.

He powered off his phone, pushed open the door to City Liquors, and went inside.

TWENTY-THREE

ISOBEL SAT ON A BENCH in Madison Square Park, thoroughly disgusted with herself. She knew she'd been awful to James. Even worse, she knew deep down he was probably right. While she was grateful for Nikki's presence at InterBank Switzerland, there was something about her that didn't quite add up. Given that, she wasn't sure why she had felt the need to defend Nikki so ferociously. James was going to a lot of trouble to look out for her, and what had she done? Insulted him. And stuck him with the check.

She kicked a crumpled soda can, but her conscience got the better of her, and she tossed it in the garbage, wishing the city would commit to public recycling bins. Her imagination had been so fired up by her conversation with Stan Henderson that by the time she'd arrived at the diner, bursting with theories, she'd forgotten she was mad at James. Maybe if she'd shown up angry, she wouldn't have left angry.

Why did they always argue? Their first encounter at Temp Zone was far and away the most collegial, and even that had been a skirmish. They obviously brought out the worst in each other. It was too bad, because there was something about him she found intriguing. A college dropout? His comment came back to her now. Why hadn't he graduated? And why had he felt compelled to tell her he had a girlfriend? Did he think she was interested in him in that way?

Isobel knew she was being irrational, but she felt as if she were flailing about on a patch of ice and couldn't stop herself from falling. She would just have to wait until she landed, and hope she didn't get too bruised. Then she would look at the facts with detachment and make her own decisions about who could and could not be trusted. Maybe she'd decide that Nikki was right and James was the one who should be approached with caution.

She trudged back to the office, wondering what she could do to take her mind off him. Reformatting her résumé seemed like a good place to start. When she got back, she saw that Nikki had returned and was busy with a stack of invoices.

"Hey, I spoke to Terence and he said it's okay for your friend to come on Monday. Here's his card."

"Thanks."

Isobel glanced at the address and wondered whether going to the class was still necessary. Probably more so now, given James's suspicions. She needed to confirm whether the class really messed with one's emotions that much, or whether Nikki was faking hysteria to excuse her behavior. She was glad Delphi would be with her, although she couldn't quite believe that Nikki would invent a class in order to lure her to some parking lot, beat her senseless, and leave her for dead.

"I've been meaning to ask you," Isobel said, as casually as she could. "When you left here for that acting job, before you came on freelance, what was the show?"

"It was a whole season of summer stock," Nikki said, without hesitation. "The Oldyard Theatre in Ludlow, Vermont."

"What did you do?"

"Two original plays that weren't very good. And *Summer and Smoke* by Tennessee Williams." She gave Isobel a wry smile. "I was miscast."

Isobel felt her anger toward James rise again. It was one thing to lie about a play you'd done, but why say you'd been miscast? James just didn't understand how an actor's mind worked. Yes, their names were similar, and yes, they both had yellow leather pants, but why would she start out at InterBank Switzerland using one name, and then come back after the summer with another? The evidence that Annika Franklin and

Nikki Francis were the same person was still basically circumstantial.

She reached for her flash drive, but it was gone, along with Doreen's.

"Have you seen the box of flash drives?" she asked Nikki.

"Yeah, Frank came by earlier to take them back."

"There was another one that was unlabeled. Did you see where that went?"

"I think he scooped it up with the others. Why?"

"That had all my personal stuff!" She jumped up and sprinted around the corner.

Isobel was so intent on getting her drive back that she was halfway into Frank's office before she realized there was a woman speaking to him from his visitor's chair.

"It's all done in a petri dish. You won't even have to—" The woman whirled around, a furious look on her face. "Don't you knock?"

"I'm so sorry," Isobel said.

"What is it?" Frank barked.

"I—um, my flash drive is in there."

Frank thrust the box at her, clearly annoyed.

Isobel fished out her drive and turned to the woman. "You must be Mrs. Lusardi. It's nice to, um, put a face to the voice." Audrey Lusardi was as glamorous in person as she was in her photo, and even though she was seated, Isobel could tell she was statuesque. She wore a sweater with faux fur trim at the cuffs and boot-cut velvet jeans. In fact, she looked more like a naturally occurring actress than Isobel.

"You must be that temp." Audrey wrinkled her pert nose in distaste.

"Isobel's staying on until I hire someone permanent," Frank said.

"Frank, I only have a few more minutes," Audrey said, giving her husband a meaningful nod.

Isobel turned to leave, but Frank's voice stopped her. "Hang on. Since you're here, I need you to pull an invoice for me." He scribbled something down on a piece of paper and handed it to her.

"Where will I find—?" Isobel began, but a sharp shake of Frank's head told her she'd have to figure that out herself.

She closed his office door quietly behind her. She had no idea where to find the vendor invoice Frank had asked for. It was for a computer consultant named Lou Volpe, dated from March of that year. Lou Volpe—the man who had called for Stan on her first day.

"Conchita? Do you know where I would find this?" She held out the paper for Conchita to see.

"*Nunca te ayudería, querida*," said Conchita. The phone rang. Conchita grabbed it and switched immediately to English.

Thwarted, Isobel returned to her desk. She was so distracted that she cut the corner too sharply and kicked over a stack of folders on the floor by Doreen's desk. Papers cascaded out.

It was all the junk that Detective Kozinski had removed from the credenza. Isobel was sure she'd stuffed it all back, but apparently someone had taken it out again, and arranged it in haphazard piles on the floor. With a sigh, Isobel knelt on the floor and started shoving the papers back into the credenza. All the annoyances of the last two hours suddenly overwhelmed her, and she began pitching the piles into the cabinet with increasing force. A pale pink envelope slid into her lap from one of the manila folders. It was a fine weave, not office paper, and it was unsealed. She withdrew a matching piece of pink stationery from the envelope.

It was an invoice of sorts, but it was not from or intended for InterBank Switzerland, that much was clear. The paper was covered in Doreen's handwriting, and Isobel recognized several of the names written on the page.

She also immediately and with certainty recognized the significance of the recurring dollar amounts next to each one.

TWENTY-FOUR

EVERY TIME JAMES TRIED TO SPEAK, the words came out all wrong. He knew Jayla couldn't understand him, because he kept trying to tell her that he wanted her to leave, but she kept saying, "Shhhh, don't worry, I'm not going anywhere." After a while, he could barely understand himself. It sounded to him like he was speaking with a pillow over his mouth. Then he realized that he was in bed and his face really was crushed into a pillow.

"Don' want you to stay," he muttered again.

"Shut up and drink this." Jayla heaved him over, propped his head up, and tipped a glass of ice water into his mouth. The sudden rush of cold made his teeth hurt, and for a moment he thought he was going to be sick. He wanted to brush away her hand as she caressed his forehead, but his arms felt as if they were tied to the bed.

"And take these. It's Advil for your headache," she said, prying his mouth open and dropping in two pills. Again, she held the glass to his lips, and he managed to wash down the pills.

"Nothing to do but sleep it off," she said.

He watched helplessly while Jayla rummaged through his bag for his cell phone. She turned it on and scrolled through for the number.

"Is this Bill? This is Jayla, James's girlfriend."

He tried to object from the bed—not to her calling Bill, but to her calling herself his girlfriend—but his tongue felt like an out of control garden hose.

"James has had a little relapse... Honey, he's in no shape to talk! I guess you could come over, but..." She met James's eyes. "He's about to conk out. Maybe tomorrow? I just wanted to make sure you knew, in case he tries to hide it from you."

Jayla sat down heavily on the end of the bed, which sagged under the weight of her disappointment.

"I know. I'm trying real hard and you are too," she said. "We'll all keep on trying. He needs us."

I don't need either of you, James thought. He tried to form the words, but they came out like "Donneedya." Jayla waved a hand to shush him.

"Thank you for being there for him, Bill."

Jayla hung up and set the phone on James's bedside table. She leaned over and rested her finger tenderly against his lips.

"We're just going to forget all about that little chat we had the other day. It's a good thing I came back to get my appointment book, or Lord knows what kind of shape you'd have drunk yourself into. You are not fit to be alone, James, even if that's what you think you want."

The long lashes fringing her cat-like eyes arched up so gracefully that he wished he could make himself small enough to recline in one. He wouldn't mind simply floating through life, curled up on an eyelash with a Jayla's-eye view of the world, enjoying the prettiest part of her, without having to deal with the rest.

"I'll spend the night tonight, and then tomorrow we'll see." She disappeared into the bathroom. He lay silent as the room spun and imagined himself settling down for the night on a bed of eyelashes.

When the phone rang, he couldn't tell whether it was his cell phone or his land line. They were right next to each other on his nightstand, and he threw out an arm to try to answer them both at the same time.

"Hlo!" The receiver from the land line hit the floor with a crash, dragging the rest of the phone with it.

"James!" Jayla scolded. "You're going to fall out of bed!" With surprising strength, she pushed him back onto the pillows with both hands and placed a cool, wet washcloth on his forehead.

"Who is this?" Jayla said into his cell. "Oh, Miss Isobel Spice! I know all about you. Now you listen to me!"

The cold of the washcloth sharpened his hearing and the name cut through the fog in his brain. His mind was suddenly clear, although his body was still beyond his control. He tried to reach for the phone, but Jayla pulled away from him.

"He doesn't want anything more to do with you. No, he does not want to talk to you right now. Don't call him again, you hear me? He's through with you!"

She threw the phone in the drawer of the nightstand. "You'll thank me for that," she said. "It's for the best."

Maybe it is, James thought, as he slammed into a hard, black sleep.

ISOBEL STARED AT THE PHONE in her hand.

"Well?" Delphi asked.

Isobel shook her head. "I don't know what just happened."

"What did he say?"

"He didn't. It was his girlfriend. She says he doesn't want to talk to me anymore and never to call him again."

Delphi gave a dismissive snort. "That's ridiculous. You work for him."

"I knew I should have waited until tomorrow."

Actually, Isobel thought, I should have called him this afternoon instead of waffling about it so long.

When she realized what Doreen's little invoice meant, her first instinct was to tell James. She had come so close to completing the call, standing on the corner of Twenty-third and Broadway, safely out of range of InterBank Switzerland. She had dialed his number five times, stopping just short of the last digit each time. But she couldn't bring herself to apologize for the way she'd behaved at lunch, and she knew there was nothing else to be said until she did. She still wasn't convinced that she was in the wrong, but her hesitation had ensured that the damage was done. Now she was on her own.

"You have to go to the police," Delphi said.

"I know, but I wanted to show it to James to make sure I wasn't reading too much into it."

"Reading too much into it? Give me that!" Delphi snatched the paper out of her hand. "Conchita Perez: $475, $475, $475, $475. Nikki Francis: $2,300, $2,300, $2,300, $2,300. Stan Henderson: $5,000, $5,000, $5,000, $5,000. Okay, I don't know any of these people, but from what you've told me about all of them, especially Doreen, I'm willing to bet it's a blackmail log."

"Eight hours ago, that's what it looked like to me too, but now I'm not so sure. It could be anything."

"Trust your gut. On stage and in life. It always knows more than your brain. If you don't call the police, you're withholding evidence."

"I know. It's just—"

"What?"

"His girlfriend sounded like she was personally mad at me."

"Who gives a shit what your temp agent's girlfriend thinks of you? You just found something that could shed some light on the killer's motive."

"Or that could be absolutely meaningless."

"That's why you should leave it to the professionals to decide. And that does not include James." Delphi padded over to the light switch and flipped it off. "I have to go to sleep if you still want me to get up at six and sign us up for that Cole Porter audition."

"I do."

"Then good night."

Within moments, Isobel heard Delphi's faint snoring, but she lay awake, thinking first about how rude she had been to James, and then about the paper. Finally, she switched on her lamp and pulled it out again. She ran down all the names, figures, and dates. First was a name she didn't recognize, with the repeating figure of $200, then Conchita, then two other names she didn't recognize for $750 and $1,275, then Nikki, and finally, a bit farther down the page, Stan. Poor Stan. Doreen had hit him up for more than anyone else.

Isobel still had Detective Kozinski's card. Delphi was right. She would call first thing in the morning. She switched off the light again and lay awake, pondering the list. If James was right about Nikki's past, it was pretty clear what Doreen was holding over her, and given her strange history with Stan, chances were good she knew something about him, too. But what could she possibly have on Conchita? And why weren't Frank and Paula on the list? Had Doreen tried and failed to find any dirt on them?

This led her to the disconcerting thought that had Doreen lived, she might have tried to blackmail her, too. Although, as Isobel drifted off to sleep at last, she couldn't imagine what Doreen would have found to taunt her with.

TWENTY-FIVE

GINGER WAINWRIGHT WAS NOT PLEASED.

"Will you be back on Monday?" she asked, without a grain of sympathy in her voice.

James glanced at Jayla, as if she could advise him how best to answer, although of course, she couldn't hear Ginger's question through the phone.

"I'm sure I'll be feeling better by then," he said.

"Glad to hear it. Anna's taking a personal day, so I really need you here."

James hung up the phone and lay back on the bed. His head was throbbing, and he felt worse than he had in a long time. Come hell or high water, he would be back at work on Monday. If he weren't, he'd have to hate himself even more than he already did, and he didn't have the energy for that.

"You hungry?" Jayla asked.

"I'm fine. You should go to work."

"I told them I'd be late."

"Stop hovering."

Jayla knelt by the bed and took his hand. "James, if you're alone, the demons will come again."

He snatched his hand away. "You don't know shit about the demons." His eyes bored into hers until she turned away and stood up.

"I'm not leaving you alone."

"What are you planning to do—take me to work with you?"

He divined the answer from her silence. She hadn't told them she'd be late, she'd told them she wasn't coming in. If only Jayla hadn't come back for her stupid appointment book. He hated being rescued. He hated feeling grateful. And she twisted everything he said to make it seem like she knew what he wanted more than he did. What he wanted was for her to go away. But he supposed this was his punishment for being a coward. He probably deserved it.

"You're right," he said. "I'll call Bill."

Jayla eyed him doubtfully. "You will?"

"I'll go to a meeting with him today. Then you can go to work. Although I really appreciate your offering to take the day off," he added quickly.

"I didn't offer." She handed him the phone and folded her arms across her chest.

"I'll do it."

"Now."

He knew she had him, so he dialed Bill's number. After a few moments, Bill's voice mail picked up. James cleared his throat and spoke over Bill's outgoing message.

"Bill? It's James. I, uh, kind of lost it last night... Is there a meeting we could go to together? I'll come to you...Thanks. I'm sorry."

When the voice mail prompted him to please leave a message, he hung up. He looked at Jayla and lied with the easy skill of a practiced alcoholic.

"There's a meeting near his office at noon. I'm meeting him there. So you can go."

"It's only ten thirty."

"I'll just shower and leave. You don't have to stay."

"We can walk out together."

James sat up on the bed and, with considerable effort, got to his feet. He pressed a hand onto the nightstand to steady himself.

"Look. I'm glad you found me last night, and I appreciate your staying over. But I can get to Bill's office by myself. I don't need you babysitting me."

"Are you really going?"

"Call Bill and ask him." James held out his cell phone, betting that she wouldn't take it. But he was wrong. She grabbed it and glanced down at the call log. Then she handed the phone back.

"I'm coming back later to make sure you went. And I'm spending the night."

James held his tongue, with difficulty. He needed to sort himself out. He wanted another plan in place to deal with Jayla by the next time he saw her. Maybe he really would call Bill. But if he did, it would be because he wanted to, not because she made him.

Jayla threw on her coat and grabbed her bag. "I'll cook something nice for us tonight. Full of protein." She trailed her fingers across his cheek, but while her touch was tender, her voice was not.

"I'm going to make sure this doesn't happen again."

She was gone before James could ask her how exactly she planned to do that. Which was fine, because he didn't really want to hear the answer.

ISOBEL ALMOST DIDN'T MAKE IT to the audition in time. First, she had to wait for Detective Kozinski to show up and collect Doreen's blackmail log, which, to Isobel's annoyance, she did without so much as a thank you. Then she had to wait for Frank to get off the phone so she could ask permission to leave, and then she missed a train and had to wait ten minutes for the next one. She was completely out of breath when she arrived at the studio. The hallway was clogged with the usual crush of optimistic actors, but Delphi was standing just outside the audition room, her ear to the door.

"I was starting to think you weren't going to show," she whispered. "There are only two people ahead of me and then we're on."

"What's the drill?" Isobel hurriedly threw off her flats and slipped on a pair of spiky heels.

"They said they would type us when we came in, and they might ask us to sing, but they might not. If we do sing, they might cut us off after a few bars, and no matter what, the most they want is sixteen."

"That's even more ridiculous than the last one!"

Delphi indicated a mousy young woman with a clipboard perched on the end of a bench. "You'd better check in."

"Isobel Spice," she said, pointing to her name. The monitor dutifully put a check next to it.

"They're typing when you go in, so you may or may not get to sing," the woman droned.

"So I've heard," Isobel said.

A man came out of the audition room, grumbling, and an older woman in front of Delphi went in.

"Typing—what exactly does that mean, anyway?" Isobel asked.

"They give you a quick once-over to see if you look right for any of the parts, and I guess they run down your résumé—Oh, this is me!"

The older woman was in and out, without singing a note. Delphi went in, leaving the door slightly ajar, and Isobel strained to listen. This time they had compared audition material beforehand, and she knew Delphi was planning to sing "Good-bye, Little Dream" from *Anything Goes*, transposed to a more suitable key. Isobel was armed with "De-Lovely" from the same show. She smiled to herself when she heard the piano intro begin. It seemed Delphi had made it past the typing test.

"Good-by-y-y-y-y-e-e-e-e-e—" Delphi began.

"Thank you!"

A moment later, a stunned Delphi appeared in the doorway.

"Son of a bitch," she gasped.

Isobel gave her arm a sympathetic squeeze, took a deep breath and walked past her into the room.

"Hi! I'm Isobel Spice and I would like to sing "De-Lovely.""

She bit her lip to keep from adding anything else that could be used against her.

She knew her singing was tentative, because she expected to be cut off at any moment. When neither of the men behind the table stopped her, she relaxed and began to enjoy herself, only to find herself suddenly singing without accompaniment.

"That was sixteen," the pianist called out.

"Thank you," said one of the men behind the table. "Please send in the next person."

Isobel joined Delphi in the hall. Before she could say anything, Delphi held up her hand. "Don't say a word. At least you got to sing more than one bar."

Isobel shook her head in silent commiseration.

"Did I really sound so awful?" Delphi asked.

"It was fine," said Isobel. "Honestly." It was true. The two notes Delphi had sung hadn't been enough to offend. "Maybe they were still deciding about your type."

"That's it. I'm going Shakespearean," Delphi grumbled.

"If it makes you feel any better, I didn't get much more from Detective Kozinski when I gave her Doreen's paper."

They walked to the subway in silence.

"I was thinking," Isobel said, pausing at the entrance. "It might be worth tracking down the names on Doreen's list that I didn't recognize."

"I'm sure the police will do that."

"That doesn't mean I can't also."

"Don't get involved," Delphi warned.

"I'm already involved," Isobel said. "And I want to find out whether that paper is a blackmail log or not. It's a good guess, but it might not be. It might be something else."

"Why don't you just ask Nikki?"

Isobel shook her head firmly. "If Nikki and Annika Franklin really are the same person, then she's a thief. What if Nikki killed Doreen because she found out? If she knows I know, then I could be next. I'm better off getting the information from somebody who doesn't know who I am or where to find me."

"You're better off not getting the information at all," Delphi said.

"I'll be careful, I promise. But I have to figure out what is really going on in that office. That's the only way I'll know who might be dangerous."

Delphi threw up her arms. "That's easy—all of them!"

"I have to sit there all day with them. I'm not in a vacuum."

"Isobel, I know you're a...how can I put this nicely...a naturally curious person, but let's not forget what happened to that curious cat."

"Yes, but cats have nine lives."

Isobel gave Delphi a quick peck on the cheek and trotted down the subway steps.

"You're not a cat!" Delphi called after her.

Isobel waved over her shoulder and continued on her way back to InterBank Switzerland. And she knew exactly what she was going to do once she got there.

TWENTY-SIX

IT TURNED OUT THAT THERE WAS an Alcoholics Anonymous meeting at noon near Bill's office, and James found himself there—not because he eventually brought himself around to calling Bill, but because Bill showed up at James's apartment only moments after Jayla had gone.

"She called me last night," Bill reminded James.

James had a vague recollection of Jayla talking to Bill the night before, but it was so fuzzy, he thought he'd dreamed it.

"You didn't have to drag yourself all the way up here," James said.

"Were you going to call me?" Bill asked.

"I did."

"But you didn't leave a message…"

"Okay, maybe. I don't know, I feel so, so…" James struggled to find the right word, but Bill was ready with it.

"Ashamed. We've all been there. Falling off the first time is, in some ways, the worst. But now you know better what you're in for."

Yeah, a lifetime of folding chairs, James thought, taking a seat in the meeting room of Park Avenue Presbyterian Church on Twenty-second and Park Avenue South.

"Are you going to speak?" Bill whispered to James, while a young NYU student with curly black hair and glasses shared her struggle to stay sober in the face of campus temptation.

James shook his head.

"You might find it helpful. This group always leaves time for additional speakers."

James stole a glance at Bill. He was in his mid-thirties, a

divorced insurance broker with two small children he rarely saw. His sandy blond hair was thinning, and there was a permanent sadness in his eyes, which morphed into pain when he talked about his kids. He was a good sponsor for James. Steady, but careful not to push too hard. He had been sober himself for three years. Obviously, he'd had a good role model.

"Do you still have a sponsor?" James whispered back.

"Of course. She's great. Sweet, but tough." Bill scanned the small gathering. "I don't see her here today, or I'd introduce you. She hasn't been to our home group for a while, but she works nearby and comes to these lunchtime meetings when she can get away."

James turned his attention back to the black-haired girl. James wondered if he should talk to her after the meeting. Although he'd started drinking in high school, the real problems had kicked in at Columbia. He probably knew better than anyone else there what she was going through.

She finished speaking and returned to her seat, wiping her eyes.

"Thank you, Jill." The leader smiled warmly.

"Thank you, Jill," the room repeated.

Jill nodded and continued to cry quietly in her chair.

"Does anyone else want to speak? We have a few extra minutes," the leader said.

The room fell silent, and although nobody was looking at him, James felt an acute desire to confess. But he didn't want to do it here. He wanted to save it for his home group, which met at a community center near the Columbia campus.

"Then let's recite The Serenity Prayer," said the leader.

James closed his eyes and mouthed along. He kept them closed a few moments longer, adding his own private prayer. "Lord, help me lick this thing. And help me do what's right."

By the time he opened his eyes, the group had begun to disperse. He caught sight of Jill, the NYU student, standing alone by a rack of folding chairs. He hesitated, unsure whether or not she would appreciate his empathy. Then, remembering how much kind gestures always meant to him, he took a step toward her.

"Hang on." Bill stopped him and waved to a woman who had just come in.

She walked toward them, shaking her head in frustration. "Is it over already? The temp took lunch early, and I couldn't get away."

"I'm glad you came. There's someone I want you to meet," said Bill. "Hey, James!"

James pulled his eyes away from Jill and met those of the short, round woman standing next to Bill.

"This is James," Bill said. "I'm teaching him everything you taught me."

She waved off Bill's compliment with a shy laugh, but nodded her head just the same.

"James, this is Conchita, my sponsor."

As she held out her hand, James's eyes lit on the silver and emerald cross around her neck.

"Pleased to meet you," she said with a smile.

EVEN THOUGH ISOBEL HAD MADE a photocopy of Doreen's personal invoice before turning it over to Detective Kozinski, she had committed the unfamiliar names and amounts to memory. Kim Wong, Susan Hart and Lenny DeCarlo, whoever they were, were linked to the $200, $750 and $1275 sums respectively. If Doreen was blackmailing them, she must have stored their contact information somewhere. Friday afternoon was relatively quiet, so Isobel set about searching her copies of Doreen's computer files for an address book or contact list.

After a fruitless hour, she sat back in her chair, massaging her temples.

"What are you working so hard on, anyway?" Nikki asked, glancing over at her.

"Oh, just organizing information so I know where

everything is. What about you?"

"Billing. That's all I ever do."

Nikki was wearing her yellow leather pants again, and Isobel tried to decide whether she would ever describe them as buttercup. She tried to envision the sixty-four-count box of Crayolas. Lemon she remembered, but not buttercup.

"I love those pants," she said. "They're really great on you. In my next life, I want long legs."

"Thanks," said Nikki. "I want big boobs."

"What color would you say those are exactly? Lemon? Buttercup?"

Nikki rubbed her hands thoughtfully over her leather-clad thighs. "Dunno." Nikki looked up, and her face brightened. "Tom! What color would you say these pants are?"

"Yellow," intoned a deep, throaty voice that Isobel recognized instantly. But when she saw where it was coming from, it was all she could do to keep from laughing.

Tom Scaletta, Nikki's boyfriend, may have had the best bedroom voice around, but he was short and squat, with graying hair that stuck up in tufts around a balding pate. His voice was so at odds with his appearance that Isobel had to assume his prowess in the sack was more in line with the former than the latter.

Nikki gave a flirty laugh. "We know they're yellow, but what kind? Buttercup? Lemon? Sunshine?"

"Sexy," said Tom.

Nikki turned to Isobel. "There you have it. Isobel, this is Tom. Tom, Isobel."

Tom took Isobel's hand and shook it heartily. "I've heard a lot about you."

Isobel hesitated, unsure how to respond. The usual answer to such a statement was "And I've heard a lot about you." Except that she hadn't.

"It's nice to finally meet you," she said. She was tempted to add "and put a face to the voice," but she didn't trust herself not to crack up.

Tom turned back to Nikki. "I made a reservation for bottle service at Xavier's. Are we still on for tonight?"

"You bet!"

"Excellent," said Tom. The way he taffy-pulled the word out of his mouth, it sounded to Isobel more like 'egggggggg-salad.'

"I'll meet you downstairs in ten, okay?"

"Sure." Tom gave Nikki a peck on the cheek. "Nice to meet you, Izzy."

She instinctively recoiled from the nickname she loathed, although she had to admit that, generated by those vocal cords, it sounded rather appealing.

"What's bottle service?" she asked Nikki when Tom was gone.

"It's the only way to get a table somewhere like Xavier's. You know about Xavier's, right?" Isobel shook her head, and Nikki continued as she gathered her things. "Xavier Barques, the movie director, owns it. It's *the* nightclub right now. Although in a few months it'll probably fade. They do. Anyway, with bottle service, you order a bottle of whatever you want to drink, and you pay anywhere from $500 up."

"Five hundred dollars—are you kidding? Is it a special bottle?"

"No. But it buys you a table and you can sit there all night and host your friends. It's fabulous."

It didn't sound so fabulous to Isobel, but maybe there was more to it. "Do you get food, too?"

"That's extra," Nikki said, pulling on her jacket.

"Couldn't you get the same bottle at the bar for a lot less?"

"Sure, but that's not the point."

"It sounds pretty extravagant," Isobel said.

"Tom does very well." Nikki gave Isobel a significant wink.

In more ways than one, thought Isobel. "Do lots of places do this?" she asked.

"Oh, sure. But Xavier's is hot. It draws a completely wild and diverse clientele. Hipsters, money, celebrities. Big gay and transgender crowd too."

"Sounds neat," said Isobel, unconvinced.

"You should try it sometime."

Isobel laughed. "I'll have to get myself a boyfriend in Equities first."

"Better than a boyfriend in Equity. That'll get you nowhere." Nikki laughed at her own joke and threw her bag over her shoulder. "See you Monday!"

"Wait! I almost forgot. Should we just meet you at Terence Hoff's studio?"

"Yes. Ten o'clock. What's your friend's name?"

"Delphi."

"That's cool. Is it short for something?" Nikki asked.

"Delphinium. But she hates it."

"Yeah, I hate my full name too."

Isobel's heart began to beat the tiniest bit faster.

"What's your full name?" she asked.

"Annika," said Nikki. "But only my mother calls me that. Have a good weekend!"

TWENTY-SEVEN

"YOUR IMAGE ISN'T STRONG ENOUGH! I want to see joy! JOY!"

Isobel and Delphi exchanged dubious glances as Terence Hoff, a slim, effeminate, beaky man, shouted at the quivering young woman at the front of the small, dark room.

"I—I'm trying," she stammered. "It's just that I'm not…well…I'm not by nature a very happy person."

"That's why it's called ACTING!" screamed Terence.

"If it's acting, then why is she working so hard to remember something that actually happened to her?" Isobel whispered to Delphi. Nikki, seated next to them, shushed her. Isobel sat back and watched the young woman repeat the exercise.

"Think of an image that brings you great joy," Terence insisted. "It doesn't have to be an event from your own life. It could be a scene from a movie or some music that sets your heart a-twitter."

"But I told you—"

"No excuses! Think, April. Think!"

April stood in front of the class and thought. A flicker of emotion crossed her face, and one side of her mouth pulled up in an involuntary smile.

"That's it! Go with that! Whatever it was you were just thinking!" shouted Terence.

"It's not joyful, it's funny," April protested.

"Just GO WITH IT!"

April began to leap around the room, letting out ahs and whoops that, to Isobel, sounded completely phony and forced.

"Physicalize it more!"

April swung her arms wide and twirled around.

"Use your whole body!"

She flung herself every which way, until Terence shouted, "Now, start your monologue!"

Accusations and invective streamed forth from April in a high-pitched, singsong voice that was completely at odds with what she was saying.

After a minute, Terence cut her off. "Perfect! Brilliant!"

"Ridiculous," Isobel muttered.

Terence rose from his chair and took the panting, shaking girl by the arm. "Now, how did that feel?"

April hesitated. "Good?"

"Excellent work. A big breakthrough, I think."

"I don't get it," Isobel whispered. "That monologue has nothing to do with joy. There's nothing joyful about it."

"What do you expect?" Delphi stifled a giggle. "It's from *Look Back in Anger*."

"That's not the point," Nikki hissed. "I told you, it's all about subtext. It's about being able to call up any emotion at will and use it to color the words."

"But that's not acting, that's, that's..." Isobel paused.

"Masturbation?" Delphi let out a snort of laughter.

"Excuse me," Terence broke in. "Is there a question?"

"Yes," said Isobel. "Why didn't April use material that fit the emotion better?"

"Because that isn't the point of the exercise. Wednesday evening's class is for monologue and scene study. The point here is to experience the integration of genuine emotion with any available text."

"But when would you ever need to do such a thing?" Isobel asked.

Terence walked over to her chair and looked down at her, his baggy reptilian eyes glinting.

"If my methods are not clear, I'd be happy to discuss them with you after the session. I'd prefer not to waste the time of my students who are paying good money to be here."

Isobel looked around the room. A blue-jeaned Adonis in the back row caught her eye and smiled. Emboldened, she addressed the room. "Isn't the whole point of acting to make believe? And to let the audience experience the emotion?"

"That is what I refer to as the 'nobody cares how you feel' school of acting, and I do not subscribe to it. Genuine emotion inspires genuine emotion," Terence said grandly.

"But this isn't genuine emotion," Isobel said, exasperated. "It's completely manufactured, and it has no connection to the play!"

"If you're on a movie set and you have to make an entrance sobbing because your mother has just been shot, you're going to have to film that scene ten times from three different angles, so you'd better have a solid technique in place to get yourself there emotionally," Terence said, through gritted teeth.

"What about simply imagining yourself in the character's situation?" Isobel argued.

"It's not as immediate."

"Maybe if you have no imagination, but if that's the case, you shouldn't be an actor to begin with."

"Young lady, are you here to audit the class or teach it?" Terence snarled.

"Sorry." Isobel retreated back into her chair.

"Now," Terence continued, struggling to compose himself, "if we're not too rattled by that little…digression…let's continue to bring up joyful images in our chairs. When you feel you have yours, come on up."

Nikki glared at Isobel, then placed her hands over her face to shut her out while she conjured a joyful image. Isobel stole a glance at the hot guy in the back row. He was sitting thoughtfully in his seat, and when Isobel caught his eye, he winked at her.

"That's it, concentrate. Concentrate." Terence stalked among the students like a panther on the prowl. "Remember, joy is difficult. Joy is elusive. I know you're all relieved when I schedule joy, but it rarely produces your best work. We're not as accessible to joy as we are to anger or frustration." He glowered at Isobel as he passed her seat. "We don't have to dig very deep for those emotions, do we?"

There was a movement behind Isobel, and the hot guy leaped from his seat and practically pirouetted to the front of the class.

"That's it! Yes, Justin, yes!"

Justin soared around the room like an airplane, spinning his arms wildly, escalating into peals of wild laughter.

"Your monologue! START YOUR MONOLOGUE!"

"Now is the winter of our discontent! Made glorious summer by this sun of York! And all the clouds that lour'd upon our house in the deep bosom of the ocean buried!" Justin wailed ecstatically.

"Fabulous! Class, did you see how free he was? How joyful?" Terence preened triumphantly and began to applaud. The rest of the class dutifully followed suit.

"Now, Justin, you must have had a very strong image. Will you help the rest of the class understand why it has to be that strong in order to attain that level of emotional release? Tell us your image, Justin. What were you thinking about?"

Justin caught Isobel's eye and winked again. Then he threw his arms wide and turned to Terence.

"Nothing," said Justin. "Not a goddamn thing!"

"HALF THE CLASS IS FAKING IT," Justin said. He leaned against the railing of the brownstone next to Terence Hoff's studio and took a long drag on his cigarette, blowing the smoke away from Isobel and Delphi. "But if you admit it's all bullshit, that means you've been suckered into spending a ton of money on nothing."

"What about you?" Delphi asked.

"I was going to quit anyway." He stubbed out his cigarette on the bottom of his boot and flicked it into the street. Littering offended Isobel greatly, but she bit her tongue and focused instead on the way his jeans hugged his butt and thighs.

"How did you find this class, anyway?" she asked.

"Terence is an old friend of my mom's. I promised I'd give it a try. But he's a complete crock."

"Obviously some people in the class get something out of it," Delphi said.

Isobel wondered if Nikki was one of them. She still wasn't sure. Apparently, anger and frustration had interfered with Nikki's access to joy, keeping her in her seat for the entire class. So in the end, Isobel hadn't been able to assess her acting. But from her silent, furious looks, Isobel was willing to bet that Nikki was a true believer. It wasn't hard to imagine her blind with rage, threatening to go after Doreen.

"You certainly fooled Terence," Isobel said.

"Nah. He just wants to fuck me." Justin smoothed a brown curl off his forehead.

That makes two of us, thought Isobel. Beside her, Delphi gave a quiet sigh. Make that three.

"Is Nikki any good?" Isobel asked.

"Is that the tall babe who was sitting next to you?"

"Yeah."

"She seems to really get into it. When we did sadness last week, she was a mess. Anger...she was good at that one too. I get the feeling that if you really let yourself go there, it's kind of hard to shake it off afterwards."

Isobel nodded. That settled that.

"Do his students get a lot of work?" Delphi asked.

Justin shook his head. "Terence won't let you audition for anything until you've completed his course," he said scornfully.

"That's crazy," Isobel said. "It's all well and good to take class, but you only really learn by doing it."

Justin turned to her. "Listen, half of New York City is made up of people who call themselves actors, but haven't done a play since college. Acting teachers play into that. It's a

Svengali thing."

"Don't you think it's important to study?"

"Oh, sure. But you gotta be careful. Terence isn't the only phony out there. And he's by no means the worst of them."

"Sounds like you speak from experience," said Delphi.

"Nah, my friends' experiences. I'm not that interested in acting, anyway."

"What do you do, then?"

"I'm an underwear model." He reached into his leather satchel, pulled out a catalogue and handed it to Isobel, who coughed self-consciously.

"Um, that's not much underwear," she said.

He smiled. "Keep it. As a souvenir of our time together." He snapped open a baseball cap and swiped it onto his head. "I gotta run. See you around."

Delphi watched him go, a lascivious smile on her face. "Well, I wouldn't call this morning a total loss." She pointed to the catalogue in Isobel's hand. "He didn't happen to scribble his phone number down, did he?"

Isobel shook her head sadly.

"No," Delphi said with a sigh. "They never do."

TWENTY-EIGHT

DAY THREE WAS PASSING TOO SLOWLY for James's taste. Contrary to Bill's assurances, his second attempt at sobriety was proving more difficult than the first. He blamed Jayla entirely. She was back, not with a vengeance, but with a purpose, which was much worse. James was no longer a boyfriend—he had become a cause.

As he waded through the day's placements, James thought back to his two most recent AA meetings. Sunday night, he had shared his lapse with his home group and been overwhelmed by the outpouring of unconditional support he had received, which was making it both harder and easier to stick to his goal. He felt more than ever like the group had a stake in his sobriety, and he didn't want to prove himself unworthy of their confidence. He made a mental note to ask Bill if he'd ever felt this way and how he handled it.

Then there was the Friday lunch meeting and the shock of meeting Conchita. It wasn't that common a name, she was wearing a silver and emerald cross like the one Isobel had described, and InterBank Switzerland was right around the corner from Park Avenue Presbyterian.

Twice he had picked up the phone to share this latest tidbit with Isobel, but he couldn't bring himself to complete the call either time. His only memory from the night of his binge was Jayla on the phone telling Isobel that he never wanted to speak to her again. Somehow, that conversation had penetrated his stupor and branded itself on his brain. He didn't want to have to explain Jayla or answer any questions about why he wasn't answering his own phone. And he knew Isobel well enough by now to know she would ask.

James took a long swig of Coke from the open can on his desk. He felt paralyzed, unable to do anything else until he had a drink or called Isobel, and he didn't want to do either. He picked up his nameplate from his desk and ran his sleeve over it, his customary tension reliever. In a sudden swift motion, he set down the nameplate, picked up the phone and, before he realized what he was doing, dialed InterBank Switzerland.

"Hello, this is Felice Edwards."

"Hi, Felice, James Cooke here."

"Oh. I'm, um, glad you called."

She didn't sound it. "You okay?"

"Yeah, sure. I'm just…"

"I can call back another time," James said quickly.

"No, it's just… Oh, hell! I'm completely embarrassed about the way I acted at lunch the other day. I'm afraid I made a complete fool of myself. I don't know what you must think of me, getting ripped like that in the middle of the day."

Alcohol makes fools of us all, he thought.

"No need to apologize. You were charming company. You can prove yourself over another lunch sometime."

Felice paused. "Or we could have dinner, where behavior like that is more acceptable."

James wasn't sure whether to laugh, say yes, hang up the phone, or invite her to his next AA meeting. He settled on a combination of the first two.

"Well, yeah, we could do that sometime. I was really just calling to make sure you were all right."

"When?"

"Now."

"No, I mean, when do you want to have dinner?"

"Oh, I…" James paused. Man, she was slick. He wasn't even sure if he meant it. On the other hand, maybe Jayla would finally get the message if he actually did take Felice out. "Friday night?" he asked.

"Sounds great."

He could hear the smile in her voice, but he was eager to regain control of the conversation.

"I was wondering…how much do you know about the personal lives of the people you employ?"

"No more than I can reasonably ask as an HR director."

"You must pick up gossip, though. Like when you told me that Nikki Francis is dating a guy in Equities and thinks nobody knows."

"Well, there's always talk."

Suddenly, James realized he'd run aground. He couldn't ask her pointblank if she knew about Conchita—that would be violating the anonymity promise of AA. He also realized that while he was pretty sure Nikki Francis was Annika Franklin, he could be on shaky legal ground if he contributed to her being fired without proof.

"Is there…anything else you can tell me?"

"I've told you everything I know."

"Well, if you think of anything else—"

"I can tell you on Friday."

"Sure. Okay, see you then."

James hung up, strangely relieved. Even though he hadn't gotten any more information from Felice, the conversation seemed to have moved him past his paralysis. The pull to call Isobel had waned, and so had the desire for a drink. He took another sip of Coke and realized with sudden clarity that, on some level, he knew the prospect of forgetting Isobel had been what prompted him to call Felice in the first place.

Unfortunately, Conchita remained a mystery.

ISOBEL WASN'T SURPRISED WHEN NIKKI didn't return to the office after Terence Hoff's class, but she didn't come in the next morning, either. While Isobel was relieved to further prolong the inevitable blow-up over her behavior, she was finding Nikki's extended absence worrisome. Although Nikki claimed to come and go as she pleased, her presence was surprisingly dependable, with the exception of Monday mornings.

At eleven o'clock, Paula buzzed through to ask Isobel to bring in Nikki's vendor invoices to sign for payment. Isobel grabbed the forms, which were stacked neatly to the side of Nikki's computer, and waited in the chilly silence while Paula fixed her stiffly legible signature to each one. Finally, Isobel cleared her throat and asked, "Um, do you know if Nikki's coming in today?"

"No idea. Why? These look all in order."

"I don't know, I was just—"

But Isobel stopped. Her eye had fallen on the name of the vendor whose invoice for $1,280 Paula was now approving. Computer Accessories. That was the name of the false vendor Annika Franklin used to siphon off money from Credit Exchange Bank. Despite her foul temper during her lunch at the diner with James, Isobel had managed to absorb the details he'd relayed regarding Annika Franklin's prior schemes.

Isobel could no longer deny they were the same person. Somehow Annika/Nikki Franklin/Francis had managed to spend her summer at the Oldyard Theatre and Credit Exchange Bank simultaneously. Paula was holding the proof Isobel needed that Nikki was still up to no good—and that Doreen had tangible evidence to prove it.

"Computer Accessories," she said aloud. "Why is that name familiar?"

Paula paused and ran her pen down the side of the form. There were line items for various computer hardware extras, backup drives, storage media, and a big sum for miscellaneous. She frowned. "That's odd. We generally purchase this sort of thing from Staples or PC Connection."

Either Paula did not see the value in reading what she signed, or this was the first time a Computer Accessories invoice had crossed her desk.

"Maybe their prices are better?" Isobel suggested.

"If you're dying to know, you can ask—" Paula gave a

surprised laugh. "I almost said ask Doreen, but of course, you can't. Ask Candy O'Hara in Procurement. She'll know."

"Would Doreen have known anything about them?"

Paula nodded. "Doreen knew all the vendors, where we held which accounts, and what we generally purchased from whom. For better or worse, she made it her business to know more than her job. That's the key to advancement, you know," Paula added, more to herself than to Isobel.

Isobel couldn't help but ask, "But Doreen didn't advance, did she?"

"She didn't want to," Paula said, with obvious disgust.

Isobel scooped up the forms and returned to her desk. She'd take them to the mailroom later. First things first.

She glanced down the corridor to make sure that Nikki was nowhere in sight, then she quickly switched on Nikki's computer. While it was starting up, she pulled open Nikki's file drawer and began thumbing through the hanging folders, looking for other invoices for Computer Accessories. There were neatly organized, clearly marked folders for myriad vendors, including overstuffed ones for Staples and PC Connection, but nothing for Computer Accessories. She looked up Candy O'Hara's extension on the sheet on the wall and dialed.

"Hey, Nikki," chimed a voice as sweet as her name.

"Oh, sorry. It's Isobel. I must have used her extension by mistake."

"Hey, Isobel. What's up?"

"Paula wanted to know why we use Computer Accessories for our hardware extras instead of Staples or PC Connection."

"Who?"

"Computer Accessories."

"We don't. We have accounts at Staples and PC Connection," Candy said.

"And we don't ever get stuff from Computer Accessories?"

"I've never heard of them. We sometimes have to get specialty items direct from the manufacturer, but maintenance items, new equipment, all that stuff comes from one of the other two."

Isobel began to giggle. "You know what? Now I see, it's an invoice *for* computer accessories from PC Connection. I think Paula needs reading glasses!"

"You want to be the one to tell her?" Candy asked.

Isobel laughed. "Not me! Sorry to bother you."

"No problem."

Isobel hung up and tapped her foot nervously as Nikki's computer came to life, displaying the welcome screen.

And a password window.

Damn, thought Isobel.

If her brother Percival were here, he could hack into it before she could say embezzlement. Thinking of Percival gave her another idea, and a few moments later, she was back on the phone, this time to Richie in the IT department. She got his voice mail.

"Um, hey, Richie, it's Isobel in Procurement Support. Do you happen to know the password to Nikki's computer? She's not in today, and I need to print out some invoices that are due. Thanks."

Every few minutes, she jumped up to peer down the hall to make sure Nikki wasn't on her way in. She saw the bearded man gesticulating angrily at a cowering delivery boy.

He's right, thought Isobel. They should move his desk. And put a nice person in his place.

When the phone finally rang, she grabbed it.

"Richie?"

There was a pause, and then a man's voice with a thick Brooklyn accent said, "I thought you screwed me in the back last time, but this time, you really done it!"

Isobel inhaled sharply as she recognized the hilarious malapropism from Doreen's phone conversation on her first day. Clearly, this guy didn't read the papers. But before she could say anything, he went on.

"Ya know who came to the house whiles I was out? The

fuckin' cops! I just wanna know one goddamn thing. No, two goddamn things! Why the fuck was I payin' you out all that dough to keep your big, flappin' trap shut, and how much do I get back 'cuz you didn't fuckin' do it?"

Isobel glanced at the console and saw she'd answered Doreen's extension. It took her a minute to find her voice, but when she did, she spoke as softly and steadily as she could.

"Lenny DeCarlo. I know who you are."

"Doreen?"

"No, it isn't Doreen. But I know all about you," Isobel said.

"Fuckin' bitch, what did she do, broadcast it on the news?"

"I have some information that will make you feel a whole lot better about your situation, but first you have to tell me two things."

"Who the hell are you?"

"That doesn't matter," she said, maintaining her even tone. "But I can help you. First of all, I don't care what it was about, but was Doreen Fink blackmailing you?" There was silence on the line. Isobel tried again. "Were you paying her $1,275 a month to keep your secret, whatever it is—and I don't want to know?"

There was a pause. "Yeah," Lenny said huskily.

"Do you know anything about anybody else she was blackmailing? Because I've got news for you, Lenny, you weren't the only one."

Lenny gave a harrumph. "Figures. I don't know nothin'. Now what do you got to tell me?"

"Doreen is dead."

Lenny gasped. "Are you shittin' me?"

"That's why the police came by. They know she was blackmailing you and several other people, but listen—she was killed here, so if you can prove you were somewhere else at one o'clock last Wednesday, you're golden."

"Do you know if she told anyone else about my...my secret?"

"Not that I know of. I think you're done paying out."

"Shit. Thanks. It was cuttin' into little Joey's piano lessons."

"There's one more thing I should tell you," Isobel said.

"What?"

"You can't screw someone in the back, even metaphorically speaking. You can stab them in the back or you can screw them over, but you have to pick one."

"Shit," Lenny said, and hung up.

Isobel stared at the receiver in her hand, which was trembling. Now there was no doubt that Doreen's paper was a blackmail log. Nikki/Annika was playing the old Computer Accessories game at the bank, and Doreen had found out. Pretty careless of Nikki to use the same fake company name on the invoices. On the other hand, she'd never officially been caught or prosecuted the first time, so why not?

The phone rang again.

"Hey, Isobel, it's Richie. You wanted Nikki's password?"

"Please. I need to pull an invoice for Frank."

"Password is Alma."

Isobel thanked him and hung up the phone. She should have guessed. Whether Nikki was miscast or not, Alma Winemiller was a great part.

She clicked open Nikki's hard drive, but there wasn't a whole lot there. Certainly nothing to justify the hours Nikki spent glued to her computer. She spotted Nikki's theater résumé and couldn't resist sneaking a peek. There were the three plays she'd done at the Oldyard Theatre, listed right at the top. Isobel frowned. That was the one thing that still didn't add up. How could Nikki have been in two places that summer? Isobel opened up the web browser and pulled up the theater's website. There was Nikki's name next to *The Great Kazoo* by Claude Heck, *Soup and Sandwich* by Helena Bauer, and Tennessee Williams's *Summer and Smoke*. She wasn't lying about that, at least. Isobel absently clicked on the lineup for next year's season.

They were doing *Lend Me a Tenor*, one of the few straight

plays that interested her. She clicked for more information. Oooh, no, Isobel thought. *I would not want to do a complicated farce in one-week stock.*

Of course.

Isobel navigated back and quickly scanned the dates of Nikki's plays. They were all one-week runs. That meant each show rehearsed for one week and then performed for one week, and they were consecutive. So Nikki was only at Oldyard for a total of four weeks: one to rehearse *Summer and Smoke*, one to perform that and rehearse *Kazoo*, one to perform *Kazoo* and rehearse *Soup and Sandwich*, and then one more to perform *Soup and Sandwich*. One month. Nikki had spent a month at Oldyard, worked at Credit Exchange for two, then come back to InterBank and gotten them to employ her directly using her stage name to avoid any chance of connection to the Credit Exchange scheme.

With renewed enthusiasm, Isobel whipped down the list of files in the folder marked "Vendors." She opened the one for PC Connection, which revealed a long list of invoices. There was nothing for Computer Accessories, but two files near the bottom of the long list caught her eye.

She held her breath and clicked on the first, which was named "Untitled."

It was, as she had hoped, an invoice for Computer Accessories with multiple iterations piggy-backed into the same document. The amounts varied, but the bimonthly invoices seemed to date back only as far as Nikki's current employment. Isobel grabbed a flash drive and quickly copied the file onto it. Then she clicked on the second one, which was marked "Untitled2."

It took her a moment to figure out what she was looking at, but when she did, everything about Nikki Francis suddenly fell into place.

TWENTY-NINE

"SHE'S MAKING A BLOODY FORTUNE!" cried Delphi, staring the contents of Untitled2 on Isobel's laptop.

"I know. That's why she could afford to pay out so much to Doreen every month, even though the invoices for Computer Accessories aren't for that much."

"I'd like her boyfriend to be my investment advisor."

"Tom Scaletta's a crook," Isobel pointed out.

"We don't know for a fact that he's doing any insider trading," Delphi said.

"We don't have to. She's embezzling company money, and he's investing it."

"That's quite a scam." Delphi sat back on Isobel's air mattress. "And quite a profit."

Isobel paced the small apartment, detouring around the furniture. "Doreen must have asked Nikki about Computer Accessories and not been satisfied with the answer. So she went snooping around on Nikki's computer and found what I found. Richie's pretty free with the passwords."

"It explains how Nikki and Tom can afford bottle service," Delphi said.

"It also explains what she sees in him. The appeal isn't in the bedroom, it's in the portfolio."

"Well, it beats the hell out of waiting tables," Delphi said, massaging her feet.

"Unless you count the jail time," Isobel said. "I guess I'd better call Detective Kozinski."

"You're turning Nikki in?"

Isobel paused, cell phone in hand. "You sound surprised."

Delphi hesitated. "Maybe you should cut her a break? I mean, she is a fellow actress."

"Actress? I've got two words for you," Isobel said tartly. "Terence Hoff."

"Point taken. But once you call the police, it's done."

"You were the one who told me to give them the blackmail log!"

"But this is going to result in an arrest."

Isobel sat down next to Delphi. "All right, what are my options?"

"You could warn Nikki and let her get out of there."

"Is that what you would do?"

Delphi sighed and traced a seam on the wooden floor with her finger. "I don't know. No." She looked up at Isobel. "Do you really think she killed Doreen?"

"You know, I don't," Isobel said thoughtfully. "With that profit margin, it wasn't costing Nikki that much to keep Doreen quiet."

"Unless Doreen was threatening to raise her fee."

Isobel snapped her fingers. "There's something else. Nikki and I were together when Doreen left. And she went down the stairs ahead of me during the emergency drill."

"Couldn't she have made a beeline back up to the bathroom?"

"Swimming against the tide on the stairs? I only barely made it back up. And even if she had, there's no way I wouldn't have seen her." Isobel shook her head firmly. "Nikki didn't kill Doreen. I'm her alibi."

"If you call, you should tell the police that."

"What do you mean 'if'?"

Delphi wound a wayward curl around her finger. "It's just…weird. I've never been involved in the arrest of someone I know."

"You're not. I am," Isobel said grimly. "But if I don't call the police, I'm withholding evidence."

"You're right," Delphi conceded. "Go for it."

Isobel dialed Detective Kozinski's number and left a detailed message. "There," she said, setting down her phone. "It's done."

They sat in silence for a while. "I guess we won't be invited along for bottle service," Delphi said finally.

"No. If we're ever deluded enough to think we want it, we'll have to pay for it ourselves," said Isobel. She closed her laptop and stood up. "If Nikki didn't kill Doreen, we'd better look to Conchita and Stan. She was blackmailing them, too."

"Stan especially, don't you think?"

"Yes, all things considered."

Feeling distinctly unsettled, Isobel wandered into the kitchen and opened the refrigerator. There wasn't much: a loaf of bread, some cheese, and a peach. As she washed the peach, she found herself thinking of James. She wanted to call and tell him what she'd found and what she'd done. But something was holding her back, and it wasn't just the nasty girlfriend.

"WHAT EXACTLY IS THAT GOING TO BE?" James asked, gazing at the array of ingredients lined up on the counter.

Jayla set her hands defiantly on her hips. "Chicken Marengo. Any fool could see that!"

James attempted a laugh. "You know me...I'm not just any fool."

Jayla had cooked for him every night since his binge, and he wasn't sure how much more his stomach could take. She refused to follow a recipe, insisting that her instincts yielded better results. It was clear that she had burned out her taste buds years ago on those same instincts. As she reached for the ketchup, he laid a restraining hand on her arm.

"You deserve a break. Let's go out."

Jayla's eyes narrowed, and James knew she was trying to decide if this was an insult or an invitation to rekindle the romance. He had been cool toward her, but she had steadfastly borne his slights. A cause as worthy as James merited tenacity, and that was Jayla's specialty. How else could the child of a single, drug-addicted mother on welfare have earned two degrees and risen to the top of a prominent consulting firm?

The storm brewing on Jayla's face passed, and James gave an inward sigh of relief.

"All right," she said, batting her long lashes. "Where are you taking me?"

James thought quickly. Nowhere too romantic, and nowhere with wine bottles decorating the walls.

"I know," Jayla said. "Café Bel Sogno."

A little pricier than he would have liked, but it would do. Besides, he was feeling a bit kinder toward Jayla, knowing he was going out with Felice on Friday. A secret date wasn't a bad substitute for the illicit thrill of sneaking a drink. If Jayla really cared about his sobriety, she should be happy that he had a date with another woman. His circular logic made him smile.

Café Bel Sogno was more crowded than usual, and the few tables for two had just been seated. James was about to suggest they try someplace else, when he felt a tap on his shoulder. He smiled when he saw who it was.

"Bill!"

Bill looked like he was amazed anyone could be so happy to see him. Then again, Bill wasn't stuck on a pseudo-date with his bossy ex-girlfriend.

"We were going to grab a bite, but the wait's too long for two. I just thought I'd say hello. And see how you're doing," Bill said meaningfully.

"Not bad. Hanging in. You know Jayla."

She shook his hand. "Good to see you again."

"And this is Nancy," said Bill, gently maneuvering a petite Asian woman into the conversation.

"Since there's a wait for small tables, why don't we pair up and eat together?" James suggested enthusiastically.

"That would be great," said Bill, looking distinctly relieved. The women were too polite to object, although James could feel the steam rising off Jayla's face. Within minutes, the four of them were tucked away at a cozy four-top in the corner.

They all stared blankly at each other. There was plenty to discuss, at least as far as Bill and James were concerned, but not in company. James suddenly realized that he might have created a situation worse than being alone with Jayla. That was one thing that could be said for alcohol; it relaxed people socially. James ordered a bottle of sparkling water and tried to avoid Jayla's eyes. She was fuming and clearly determined not to participate in the stilted conversation. After they'd covered the weather and the upcoming November elections, Nancy had the good sense to admire Jayla's Prada handbag, her prized possession. It soon transpired that Nancy did something in high fashion. Jayla was forced to relent, and they forged ahead on this common ground.

James knew why he'd suggested they dine together, but he wondered why Bill had been so willing. Presumably, he was on a date because he wanted to be. Bill had never mentioned Nancy to him, but that didn't mean much. All he really knew about Bill was the sad tale of his divorce and children. The meal settled into the kind of detached rhythm that comes from being thrown in with people you have no intention of socializing with ever again. They finished their main course, and Jayla and Nancy retired to the ladies' room, chatting about the resurgence of ponchos.

James and Bill looked at each other and the strained social mask fell away.

Bill let out a long breath. "That's a relief, isn't it?"

James nodded. "No kidding. So, who's Nancy?"

"Blind date. Conchita set me up. Nancy's mom is a friend of hers. I don't know why she thought it would work. The only thing we have in common is that we're both single."

Bill took an overlong sip of water, and James knew he was pretending it was vodka. He often did the same thing.

"But that's Conchita." Bill wiped his mouth slowly with his napkin. "She's determined to save the world. One poor schmuck at a time."

"Lucky for me." James sipped his water and indulged the same alcoholic fantasy. "If she hadn't saved you, you wouldn't be able to save me."

"Yeah, she's a remarkable woman."

"Has she saved anyone else recently?" James asked casually.

Bill tipped an ice cube into his mouth and crunched it. "Well, she's trying. Her current project is a much bigger challenge than I ever was."

"Who is it?"

"I shouldn't say."

"Sure, I get it." James nodded. "Anonymous and all that."

"No, no, it's not an AA person." Bill gave a bemused chuckle. "But it's weird. Way weird."

"Yeah?" said James hopefully.

"Well, there's a guy she works with...I don't know. I shouldn't say."

James felt his pulse quicken. "C'mon, buddy. I'm good. Won't tell a soul."

Bill leaned across the table. "Okay, this guy she works with likes to dress like a woman. And that's not all," he said, warming to his subject. "He wants the operation!"

Suddenly, the women were back. James tried to rearrange his face, but he wasn't quick enough for Jayla. She stared at him.

"What?" she demanded. "What did we miss?"

THIRTY

NIKKI WAS BACK AT HER DESK on Wednesday morning. She didn't even look up when Isobel came in, which was fine, since she knew she couldn't look Nikki in the eye after the message she'd left for Detective Kozinski. It was a testament to how frosty the silence was that Isobel went off in search of warmth and acceptance from Stan and Conchita's quarter. Conchita was nowhere in sight, but Stan's door was ajar, and he was rifling frantically through a desk drawer. He started in surprise when Isobel rapped gently on the door.

"Is Conchita in?" she asked. She had no interest in speaking to Conchita, of course. She only wanted to gauge how much time she might have for a quick chat with Stan.

"She went for coffee."

Isobel noticed that his soft, smooth face was glistening with sweat. "Is something wrong?"

"No...I, uh, can't find something."

"Can I help?"

"It's nothing. Just a personal, um, item. I'm sure it will turn up." He mustered a wan, but unconvincing smile.

Isobel was itching to ask him about being blackmailed by Doreen, but he looked on the verge of nervous collapse as it was. Besides, if Conchita had only gone for coffee, she would likely be back any moment.

"If you tell me what it is, I'd be happy to keep an eye out."

"No, that's not necessary. I'll tell Conchita you're looking for her," he said, turning his back on her to inspect another drawer.

Isobel left, shutting the door behind her. Feeling the need

to procrastinate further, she knocked on Frank's door and entered.

"Anything you need this morning?" she asked.

Frank looked up from his open desk calendar and nodded. "Good timing. Yes. I need you to make a lunch reservation. Two people today, one o'clock at Printemps, under my name. I also need you to file these." He handed her a stack of papers. "And I'll email you some correspondence to print out on letterhead."

She took the papers and headed back to her desk to call the restaurant. For once, she was grateful for the work. It would help her avoid Nikki.

If only she'd been a few moments longer with Frank, she might have missed Nikki altogether.

Detective Kozinski and Detective Harvey were at Nikki's desk, along with two uniformed policemen who held a handcuffed Tom Scaletta between them. An InterBank security guard hovered nearby.

The color had drained from Nikki's face, but it rose scarlet as her eyes landed on Isobel.

"You little bitch!" she spat.

Isobel glanced at Detective Kozinski, horrified that she might have revealed her sources, but an almost imperceptible shake of the policewoman's head telegraphed that she had not. Isobel decided to play dumb. She would show them all what a good actress she was.

"What's...what's going on?"

Detective Kozinski answered crisply, "Nothing that concerns you."

A small crowd was gathering. Conchita appeared next to Felice Edwards, holding two steaming cups of coffee, which severely impeded her ability to cross herself. Frank, Paula and Stan had emerged from their offices, and several others were craning their necks to see across the vast plain of cubicles.

Nikki glowered at Isobel. "This is your fault."

"New York is a tough town, but I didn't know you could

get arrested for bad acting," Isobel said, unable to help herself.

"Terence is a genius, and you're too much of a bird-brained little no-talent to recognize that," Nikki snapped.

"Yeah? Well, how do you explain Justin?" Isobel asked. "Terence thought he gave an Academy Award-winning performance!"

Detective Harvey turned to Detective Kozinski. "Am I missing something?" Detective Kozinski shrugged.

"You weren't interested in Terence's class. You just wanted to mock me. Well, I hope you enjoyed your little joke, you and that trashy blond bitch. This town is going to swallow you both up, like it does every stupid, bright-eyed wannabe. I worked hard to get where I am, and it's clear that you don't have the talent to get there."

"I sure hope that's true," said Isobel sincerely, eyeing the handcuffs that Detective Kozinski was locking around Nikki's wrists.

"Nikki Francis, also known as Annika Franklin, I am placing you under arrest for fraud and suspicion of murder."

The InterBank security guard unplugged Nikki's computer and began packing it up. Nikki looked at the computer and then at Isobel. Her eyes narrowed. Isobel looked away.

"You were snooping yesterday, weren't you?"

The others shifted their attention to Isobel, making no effort to hide the natural distrust of outsiders they'd been nurturing in one way or another since her arrival.

"You had something to do with this." Nikki gestured toward the detectives with her shoulder. "And I thought we were friends. I tried to make it nice for you here, and this is what I get?"

She had, it was true. Isobel didn't know what to say.

"I'll bet you anything, you'll still be temping in ten years' time, you little snot," Nikki said nastily.

That was too much. "You were right about one thing, you know," Isobel said.

"Oh, yeah? What?"

"You were miscast as Alma Winemiller."

Nikki summoned what was left of her dignity and took in her entire audience. "Maybe so, but I was damn good." She tossed her head defiantly, and Detective Kozinski led her away.

Isobel decided to let her have the last word. After all, Nikki was being arrested, and she was not.

THIRTY-ONE

JAMES COULD HAVE DONE WITHOUT the photos. Some of them were so graphic, he had to look away. He couldn't begin to comprehend how any man could go through gender reassignment surgery, as he discovered it was properly called. Then again, it might be the perfect lie to get Jayla off his back. Of course, she'd never believe him—or worse, she would deem him the ultimate challenge.

Bill had to be talking about Stan Henderson. So, was that the attraction? Was Stan the ultimate challenge or, as Isobel had speculated, was Conchita actually in love with him?

He rolled his chair away from his desk, put his feet up, and considered what Felice had told him: Conchita thought Doreen made good people do bad things. Did Conchita believe that Doreen was somehow responsible for Stan's sexual confusion? The marriage had been annulled. Was that because Doreen discovered Stan's orientation or because Stan was so disgusted with Doreen that he turned transvestite? James didn't know much about these things, but he was pretty sure it didn't work that way.

He scanned the web page he was on, which maintained that gender confusion was present from earliest childhood, and that those who change gender don't necessarily alter their sexual orientation. Doreen hadn't turned Stan into a transsexual any more than a bad relationship could make you gay. (He briefly contemplated telling Jayla he was gay, but ruled that out also.) So was this the bad thing Conchita thought Doreen was making Stan do, or was there something else?

He hit a few more keys on his computer, and a pair of "before and after" close-ups appeared.

"Eeeeccchhh," groaned James. He rose from his chair, disgusted, and retreated to the window. He looked down at the tiny, scurrying people below and the cars, which looked like the Matchboxes he'd played with as a kid. He tried to imagine Conchita wielding a pair of deadly scissors. People did all kinds of things in the name of tough love and religious salvation. Maybe she had fallen off the wagon and done it in a blackout.

What he really wanted to know was where things had stood with Stan and Doreen. Why had she gotten him the job at InterBank in the first place? Had she been trying to do something nice for him—or did she want him close by so she could somehow humiliate him for having made a joke of their marriage? Had she ever been able to forgive him for their wedding night when he'd (presumably) revealed his true self? Can any woman forgive a man for shunning her in bed, whatever the reason? And wouldn't a woman like Doreen be more vengeful than most?

The door to his office, which he'd left ajar, creaked open suddenly, and James leaped across the room to his computer. Unfortunately, Ginger was quicker than he was. Worse, his finger hit the wrong key, and instead of closing the window with the graphic "before and after" photos, he enlarged it.

"I was just passing by, and—aaargghh!" Ginger let out a strangled shriek.

James fumbled for the right key and managed to close the window on his computer screen.

"I, uh, that was—it's research."

"I will not have my employees looking at pornography in the office! Do you understand me?" she snapped ferociously.

"It wasn't pornography! I was researching sex-change operations," he blurted out.

Ginger blanched. "I…had…no idea."

"Not for me!" Although, as soon as the words were out of

his mouth, he realized there was no recovery. It only sounded like a cover up. "I have a girlfriend," he added. Shit, he thought. That sounded even worse.

"I don't really need to know...*anything*...about your personal life, Mr. Cooke," Ginger said stiffly. "Now, please return to the work for which you were hired."

"Right."

"And see that you trash your browser cache."

"Yes, ma'am."

It had always been his intention to trash his browser cache. But now, as he did so, he wondered if there was anything he could possibly do or say to set the record straight.

THE MOOD IN PROCUREMENT SUPPORT was even stranger than it had been the day Doreen was killed. With the police gone, everyone was free to gossip about Nikki's arrest. It was the most sociable Isobel had seen the group since she arrived. On her way back from the supply closet for more Post-It notes, she passed Conchita and Paula, who seemed to have shelved their customary wariness.

"I never liked Nikki," Conchita was saying. "Something sneaky about her. And if she can steal, she can kill."

"One should never trust actors as a breed," Paula said. Catching sight of Isobel, they turned their backs and continued in lowered voices, with occasional, not very subtle glances in her direction. Isobel rounded the bend past Frank, Stan and Felice, whose voices followed her.

"She'd done this sort of thing before," Frank said. "Detective Harvey explained her system to me. She was stealing money through a phony vendor, then giving it to Scaletta to invest."

"I had no idea." Felice's voice held more than a hint of defensiveness. "She came to us initially through Temp Zone, but they obviously didn't do a background check."

Isobel moved out of earshot before she was forced to hear

the likely follow-up question: Do you think they ran one on Isobel?

These conversations only made her feel more isolated and vulnerable than ever. Regardless of what Nikki had done, Isobel had lost her only ally, and the others seemed determined to tar her with the same brush. Besides, even though they and the police still suspected Nikki of the murder, Isobel was reasonably certain she was innocent of that charge. Which meant that in all likelihood, she was still working alongside a cold-blooded killer. It was scary how easily she had lost sight of that unnerving detail in the daily grind.

She decided to embrace that dull routine to take the edge off her anxiety, so she made Frank's lunch reservation and set about printing his letters. She wanted to tell Delphi about Nikki's arrest, but Delphi was working a double at the restaurant and couldn't take calls. Besides, Isobel didn't want anybody in the office to think she had an unusual interest in the matter. The argument about Terence's class was suspicious enough.

Just before one o'clock, Audrey Lusardi glided in, looking glamorous in a long floral wrap skirt and a stylish bolero jacket, toting two large shopping bags from Barney's. Isobel was glad she was seated at her desk. Standing next to a statuesque woman of beauty always made Isobel feel mousy. She felt less intimidated sitting down.

"Where's Frank?" Audrey demanded.

"He's in his office. Shall I tell him you're here?"

"No."

Isobel, irked at being dismissed so curtly, scooped up Frank's letters and followed her. She turned the corner just in time to see Audrey disappear into Frank's office. Stan and Paula were standing nearby, and Paula was trying to get Stan's attention. Stan, however, was looking rather pale, and staring blankly at Frank's door.

"Stan? What about that furniture wholesaler?"

"What?"

"You've come over rather queer," Paula said, indulging her wayward British accent to accompany the expression. "Are you all right?"

"Sorry," Stan said. "I'm feeling a little dizzy."

"Never mind. Go and get some water. We can talk about the wholesaler later." She turned to Isobel, whose hand was poised to knock on Frank's door. "I wouldn't go in there if I were you."

Isobel leaned against Conchita's desk and pretended to leaf through Frank's letters. She didn't have to pretend long. Frank and Audrey emerged a few moments later.

"You made the reservation at Printemps?"

"Yes. And I have your letters," Isobel said, holding them out.

"Put them on my desk. I've pulled up a list of files on my computer. While I'm out, please copy them onto a flash drive, then load them onto your computer. They're backups of Nikki's invoices. You can work off them."

"Work off them how?" Isobel asked, confused.

Frank rolled his eyes impatiently. "You'll have to pick up the invoicing and billing for the department until we hire somebody new."

"We don't really need someone in that position anymore," said Stan, who had reappeared looking a bit steadier. "We only ever had Nikki because accounting was short-staffed last summer."

"I'll check with them." Frank turned to Isobel. "But in the meantime, you need to keep up with it."

"Frank!" Audrey pulled him away and knocked into Stan, who had taken a step toward Paula's office.

"Sorry," he muttered. "Nice outfit, by the way."

Audrey paused long enough for a quick smile. "This? Thanks. I have so many clothes, I don't even remember where it came from."

Isobel looked longingly at Audrey's red bolero jacket. Stan was right. It was gorgeous. She watched Frank and Audrey depart. When she turned back, Stan had disappeared into Paula's office, and Conchita was watching Isobel, an undisguised look of mistrust on her face.

"First Doreen, now Nikki." She crossed herself. "Who will be the next to disappear?"

"Me," Isobel said. "Temporarily, at least."

She rounded the corner to the supply closet to get a flash drive. The ladies' room was not far beyond, and she saw that the police tape had finally been removed. They must have taken it down when they arrested Nikki. Isobel poked her head in.

A cleaning woman was wiping down the counter. Fingerprint powder lingered on every surface, giving the room a weird gray shimmer. Isobel smiled at the woman and gingerly pushed open the door to the first stall.

"You wanna use the one down the hall. I still gotta do the toilets."

"That's okay," Isobel said. "I just need to check something."

The woman shrugged and went back to her scouring. Isobel held her breath and looked into the stall. She wasn't sure what she was expecting to find, but it was blessedly empty. An image of Doreen, dead on the toilet, came back to her, and she shut the stall door. It clanged against the frame and swung open again. Isobel caught it and, clearing her mind of the unpleasant memory, went into the stall. She ran her fingers over the lock, then slid the bolt into the hull. It slid right back out. She tried again, and it slid out once more. She gave the bolt a good slam. This time it stayed locked.

"You okay in there?" the cleaner called.

"Fine, thanks. Sorry to bother you."

She pondered the significance of the finicky lock. If Doreen was in a hurry, as presumably she was, and she thought everyone else was about to flee the building for the drill, there was no reason for her to fight with the lock. But beyond that, Isobel could find no further meaning in it.

She passed Conchita, whose hands were clasped in full prayer mode, and entered Frank's office, shutting the door behind her. His desk was cluttered with papers, and she moved aside a stack in the middle to make room for the letters she'd typed, tamping them down with a smoked-glass paperweight.

Frank had left a folder open on his computer, marked "Billing." All the files she had seen on Nikki's computer were also on Frank's, except, of course, for Untitled and Untitled2. She began to copy them onto the blank drive, idly wondering if Conchita had intended her comment about disappearing secretaries as a rhetorical question or a warning.

"Damn," she said, as an error message overtook the screen, instructing her to quit all open applications and restart the computer.

Isobel sighed and clicked on Frank's desktop. His word processor was open, so she brought that up, saved the document he had been working on and exited. She did the same for his email program, and then she pulled up his open web browser.

Isobel inhaled sharply as a photograph of two naked men flashed on the screen. The suddenness of the image was as much of a jolt as its content, but as Isobel's eyes adjusted, she gasped even louder.

It was Justin, the underwear model, wearing no underwear at all this time, his legs twined around another man's taut, tanned body.

It was a few moments before Isobel recovered from the shock of seeing someone she knew on a gay porn site, as the significance of the image on Frank Lusardi's computer began to sink in.

THIRTY-TWO

"DO YOU THINK DOREEN KNEW?" Delphi asked, leaning against the bar.

Isobel took a long sip of red wine before answering. "How could she not have?" She set down her glass. She'd had to pay for her drink this time, but it was worth it. "Doreen made it her business to know everything about everybody. And Frank was her boss."

"Then why wasn't he on her blackmail list?" asked Delphi.

"She had that secretarial devotion thing going. Like Conchita has for Stan. If there was any animosity between Frank and Doreen, I have yet to get wind of it."

Delphi shook her head. "I don't buy it. If she knew, she was blackmailing him. I bet she has another page of names hidden somewhere."

"It does seem impossible that she didn't know," Isobel conceded. "Assistants are, by definition, keepers of the secrets."

"And it seems impossible to me that she knew and wasn't using the information to her advantage," Delphi concluded.

Isobel sipped again thoughtfully. "Maybe it suited her better not to. Maybe she enjoyed being in the driver's seat of that relationship. Doreen would have gotten off on that. Maybe she even helped him arrange trysts or whatever, and he rewarded her with little perks."

"What about the wife?" Delphi asked.

"*Si, si!* What about the wife? Will you be mine?" Carlo had come up behind Delphi and was nuzzling her neck.

She pulled away. "You already have a wife, Carlo."

"Seven years it takes to get a divorce in Italy. Who can wait?"

"You can. I can. Especially because I'm not interested."

Carlo staggered and placed his hand over his heart. "You wound me! That dark boyfriend of yours, where is he?"

"Oh, we, uh, broke up." She shot a look at Isobel, who was intently arranging pretzel twists on a coaster.

"*Grazie a Dio*—there is hope for me!" Carlo gestured melodramatically at the ceiling and left them to greet more diners at the door.

Isobel looked up from her pretzel collage. "He is too much."

"Don't you think he's attractive?"

"We've been through this. No."

"Speaking of attractive, are you sure it was Justin?"

"Positive. He was wearing the same self-satisfied smirk he had after Terence's class. And nothing else."

Delphi sighed. "Well, that's a shame."

But Isobel didn't want to talk about Justin. He was no longer remotely interesting. "Back to Frank," she said. "It explains why Audrey is a shopaholic. She's lonely."

"That doesn't necessarily mean she *knows*," Delphi said shrewdly. "Denial ain't just a river in Egypt."

"There's some mystery around them having, or wanting, a baby," Isobel said. "Frank said it was a sore subject."

"If he's not sleeping with her and she wants kids, I'm sure it is."

"I overheard them discussing *in vitro*. I assumed it was because of infertility, but maybe there's more to it."

"Why doesn't she just divorce him? Is he that great a prize?

"He's good-looking in an empty suit sort of way. Sort of moody, though."

"There are a lot of cute guys out there. Why hang onto him?"

"I have no idea," Isobel said. "But I don't think she knows. She barged her way into Frank's office, and he rushed to hide the photo on his computer. He didn't even take the time to quit the program, he just hid the window on the desktop."

"Then don't you think Doreen was threatening to tell her? There's got to be another blackmail record somewhere. It's the only explanation," Delphi said decisively, cascading a handful of pretzels into her mouth. "My order for table sixteen is probably up by now. We can talk about this more later if you want."

Delphi headed off to the kitchen, and Isobel finished her wine, thinking more about Doreen and Frank. Something didn't add up, and she felt certain that even one more hour in Doreen's presence would have given her additional insight into that relationship. It was hard to believe that Doreen hadn't caught wind of her boss's closet homosexuality, and, as Delphi said, it was even harder to believe that she would let something as juicy as that go unblackmailed.

Knowledge was power, and Isobel was sure that if Doreen had the knowledge, she wouldn't have thought twice about wielding the power.

JAMES FASTENED ANOTHER TEN POUNDS to his barbell and heaved it over his head, grunting with the exertion. He was pushed almost to his limit, but he wasn't quite ready to shower and head off to work. After catching him online, Ginger had spent the rest of the previous afternoon lurking around corners, stealing horrified glances at him. He knew he owed her an explanation, but what credible reason could he possibly have for surfing sex-change websites? As he rested between reps, it occurred to him that he could offer up the truth. But then he'd have to explain why he was spending his time delving into the murder at InterBank Switzerland instead of doing his job.

Maybe if Ginger thought he was a candidate for gender reassignment surgery, she'd be afraid to fire him for fear of a bias suit. It couldn't hurt to have a safety net, in case he fell off the wagon again. He hoisted his barbell. But was it worth having Ginger think that about him? As he bench-pressed his weights, he told himself for the hundredth time that he should call Isobel. She needed to know what he'd found out about Stan and Conchita. It was bordering on irresponsible not to tell her. But then he'd have to apologize for Jayla's outburst on the phone and explain why he'd been in no condition to answer it himself. He set down the barbell and crossed his arms to massage his throbbing biceps. How come he had so much trouble explaining himself? Why did the truth always sound so outrageous coming from his mouth?

After their impromptu double date with Bill and Nancy, Jayla had accused him of avoiding being alone with her, which, of course, was true. She'd insisted that he had a problem with intimacy and that the best way to overcome that deficiency was to spend more time with her, not less. She even went so far as to suggest moving in together.

He hoisted the barbell for one last set of lifts, but after three reps, he let it come crashing to the floor. This had to stop. Jayla was running his life. She was using his weaknesses like a crowbar in a crevice to get what she wanted from him. And if he was sure of anything, it was that he did not want Jayla, although she was right about one thing: he was afraid to go it alone. But he wasn't alone, he reminded himself, he had Bill and AA. Maybe that's what he needed—to express his fears to the group and get support for the insecurities that went beyond drinking. The failures that had dogged him his whole life: his failed football career, his failed college career, his failed relationships.

He showered and called Bill on his way to work.

"Are you going to the lunch meeting at that church tomorrow?" he asked.

"Hadn't planned on it."

"I was thinking I might go. I'd like to speak. You said there's usually time."

"Sorry, I have a conference call at noon tomorrow that I

can't miss. I could ask Conchita. I'm sure she'd go with you."

James wasn't sure he wanted to mix business with self-improvement. "I can go by myself."

Bill paused. "You can, but if you're planning to share, it's good to have someone there with you."

Even if that person might be a murderer? James thought.

Bill continued, "You never know how you're going to feel afterwards. In my experience, it's usually pretty vulnerable. I'm happy to call her, if you want."

On the other hand, it would be a good opportunity to get to know Conchita better. Maybe he could even get some information out of her.

"If you think she wouldn't mind," James said.

"She almost always goes if she can get away. I know she's had some problem with a new secretary or something, but I'm sure if she can, she will."

James tensed at the veiled reference to Isobel. "Thanks. Yeah, sure, check with her. See you Sunday."

He descended the stairs to the subway. There was something unsettling about Bill's confidence in Conchita. Maybe it was because she seemed to be cut from the same cloth as Jayla. When one person wants to save another, there's usually an ulterior motive. Was Conchita trying to save Stan because she feared damnation for his soul or because she wanted him for herself? In the end, it probably made no difference, but along the way, it possibly did. Only one of those motives suggested itself for murder. He had a sudden, wild vision of Jayla going after Isobel with a pair of scissors.

The train screeched into the station and he shook the image from his head. There was no way he was going to let things progress to that point. Not with Jayla, and certainly not with Isobel.

THIRTY-THREE

IF FRANK REALIZED WHAT ISOBEL HAD SEEN on his computer the day before, he gave no indication. Isobel tried her best not to scrutinize him more closely when he handed her a sheaf of papers to file and told her he didn't want to be disturbed under any circumstances. She returned to her little nook and surveyed the three desks.

And then there was one, she thought.

She was about to start Frank's filing when she heard her cell phone ring in her bag. She rooted around for it, grabbing the call just before it went to voice mail. It was Sunil.

"I'm glad I caught you," he said. "The girl they cast as Rachel in *Two by Two* got a non-Equity tour of *Fiddler*."

"How nice for her," Isobel said, unable to keep the envy from coloring her words a middling green.

"The point is, she has to drop out and we open next week. We need to find someone to replace her ASAP."

"Oh!" Isobel sat up in her chair, as her jealousy turned to excitement. "Me?"

"I said you were a friend of mine. They remembered your audition, but they, um, have some questions."

"About my sanity?"

"I wouldn't go that far. But they want to hear you sing more and read from the script. We're having an emergency rehearsal tomorrow night and they want you to come by early and basically audition again."

"Is there anyone else?"

"There's another woman who they called back last time. They'll hear you both and then decide. But you have to be prepared to stay and rehearse if they hire you. What do you think?"

It was a fifty-fifty chance, better than anything she'd had so far.

"I think I owe you!" She wrote down the address of the rehearsal studio. "Thank you so, so much!"

"I really hope you get it. Although you'd be playing my daughter-in-law!"

Isobel hung up the phone and leaped from her chair, taking advantage of the solitude of her little corner to indulge in a spontaneous happy dance. She wished she could do the audition right away. What a different sensation from the jitters that overtook her when she even so much as read an ad in *Backstage*. Knowing that the director wanted to see her, was expecting to see her, and was actively hoping she would be the solution to his problem gave her a feeling of optimism that was missing when she wandered into an audition anonymously.

Isobel hoped she could hang onto this confidence until tomorrow night. She was being given a chance to redeem herself, and she was determined not to let herself or Sunil down. She would blow the other girl out of the water and nab the part. She'd make her New York debut with Sunil in *Two by Two* and get every agent in town to see it. She began to hum quietly to herself, as if the need to warm up her voice was imminent and not thirty-six hours away.

Frank's line rang, and she picked it up.

"Edmund Jeffards for Frank Lusardi."

"I'm sorry, can I take a message?"

"Edmund Jeffards."

"And the message?" Isobel asked. *It's love*, her mind sang.

"EDMUND JEFFARDS."

"Yes, I got that part. Can I take a message?"

There was a pause. "Who the hell is this?"

A warning bell went off in Isobel's brain, and she shut off her internal music player.

Then she remembered. The head of IBS North America. Frank had said to put him through right away if he called.

"Nobody. A temp," she spluttered. "Hang on."

She put Jeffards on hold before he could explode at her and buzzed Frank.

"I told you I don't—" he began.

"You do—it's Mr. Jeffards!" She put the call through, slammed down the phone, and glared at it. Phones were not to be trusted. They could bring happy news, like an audition, but they could also catch you off guard and screw up everything when you least expected it.

She pushed all thoughts of *Two by Two* aside and concentrated on Frank's documents. Maybe someday she'd have a job that paid her to do what she was good at, but until then, she'd better concentrate on keeping this one.

GINGER'S BEHAVIOR HAD REVERSED itself one hundred and eighty degrees from the day before. Instead of tiptoeing around James, she was more attentive and forthcoming than he had ever seen her. By noon, she had "passed by" three times, just to see how he was "feeling."

When she came by for the fourth time, he felt he had to say something.

"Ginger, I know what you're thinking—"

She cut him off with a dramatic gesture. "James! James. I've decided that you're very brave. I'm sure this would be difficult for anyone, but for someone like you...someone who looks like you...it's not that I don't think you'll make a lovely um, woman, it's just that..."

"It'll be a lot of work for somebody?" he finished.

She swallowed self-consciously. "Well, yes."

"You can cross that off your list of things to worry about. I'm not having a sex change operation."

"It's all right. Really! I can be very open-minded when I have to be."

194   JOANNE SYDNEY LESSNER

James stood up, and Ginger, in spite of herself, took a step backwards, tripping over her heel.

James held out his hands as if to steady her and said gently, "I know this is going to sound like I'm lying or covering up, because if I really were having a sex change operation, I'm sure I wouldn't want anyone to know about it. But you have to believe me when I tell you that I'm not. I have a girlfriend!"

Ginger's eyes narrowed suspiciously. "What's her name?"

"Jay—lice."

Damn.

"That's an interesting name."

"It is. Jaylice..." He figured he may as well combine their last names too. "Jaylice Cumwards."

Shit. He couldn't have said Eddings?

"And, uh, is your girlfriend..."

"Jaylice," said James firmly.

"Jaylice. Is she, um, he..."

"*She's* in the consulting business."

Ginger backed up a step further. "It really is best if you keep your personal life personal." She held a carefully manicured finger to her lips. "I won't tell a soul."

It was too much. He slammed his fist on the desk. "I am not a transsexual!"

His booming baritone resounded in the small room, and Ginger gave a little shriek. It struck James suddenly that she was more afraid of him because he was a big black man than because he might be sexually confused. He tried to dial his temper down to simmer.

"Look," he said, as slowly and evenly as he could, "I have a good reason for being on that website. It's work-related."

That caught Ginger's attention. "What do you mean...work-related?"

"It has to do with the murder at InterBank Switzerland." There was nothing left but the truth.

She gave a dismissive wave. "InterBank? Don't worry about them. I told you, we're phasing them out."

"We still have one temp there. Isobel Spice. She's working in the department where that secretary was killed."

Ginger frowned. "I don't understand."

"I found out from…somebody…that one of the men in that department is a cross-dresser. He wants to have the operation. I just wanted to make sure that Isobel was safe."

Ginger wagged a finger at James. "Transsexuals are not inherently dangerous. You should try to be more open-minded."

It was no use pointing out that there were reasons that had nothing to do with the characteristics of cross-dressers that might make Stan, or anyone else in that office, a danger to Isobel. Ginger had her own peculiar way of parsing information.

"I was curious, that's all," he said.

"Well, you don't need to waste any more time researching transsexuals, if that's really what you were doing. They arrested someone for the murder."

James looked up sharply. "What?"

"Very embarrassing. She used to work for me. A woman named Annika Franklin. I had a call from the police, asking for my records." She dropped her voice and added, "As you can imagine, I have no desire to trumpet it around."

James steadied himself against his desk.

Ginger let out a deep breath. "To be honest, I'm glad you're not a transsexual. You're way too tall and not nearly pretty enough." She walked toward the door, and then turned back to him. "And I hate to tell you, but you're not much of a detective, either. The killer was in my files under your nose the whole time, and you didn't find her. You'd better get back to work placing temps. You seem to do all right there."

And with that, Ginger returned to her rounds, leaving James too stunned to try to correct her for the second time in one day.

THIRTY-FOUR

"ISOBEL!"

She flinched at the command and set Frank's papers on the stepstool next to the filing cabinet. "Coming!"

Frank was standing by the window in his office. Innocuous palm trees and ocean vistas faded into one another on his computer screen.

"I know, and I'm sorry," she said immediately.

He looked startled. "I didn't realize you'd grown so attached to me."

It was worse than she thought. She was being fired.

"I like working here, I actually do. I'm so sorry. I didn't mean to be rude."

"No, no. Under the circumstances, I didn't mind at all."

Isobel shook her head. "No, not to you, to Mr. Jeffards. If I'd remembered his name, I would have put him right through. Was he really angry?"

Frank gave her a strange look. "What are you talking about?"

Percival's voice teased in her head: "It's not always about you, Iz."

"He didn't, um, say anything about me on the phone?" she asked cautiously.

"No. Look, I'm flattered that you'll miss me, but I'm sure you and Paula will be fine."

Paula?

"Frank...I'm a bit confused. Are you going somewhere?"

"You said you knew."

"I misunderstood. I thought...never mind."

"I've been promoted to Senior VP of Procurement. Paula is stepping into my role here."

Isobel's mouth flapped open, fishlike. She shut it, then nodded, as if she somehow knew this was coming. "Congratulations!"

Frank gave a dry laugh. "I have to admit, that's closer to the reaction I expected. Stan will be Assistant VP." He shrugged his shoulders apologetically. "I don't know what's going to happen with your position. I'm still waiting to hear back from accounting about who'll cover Nikki, so can you hang on with us a bit longer?"

"Sure," said Isobel. Until it looked like she might lose her job, she hadn't realized how little she relished the idea of adapting to a new office situation. The devil you know versus the devil you don't. Although in a way, Paula was both.

"Tomorrow's my last day here. I have to wrap up some loose ends. They'll move Paula into my office over the weekend, and starting Monday I'll be downstairs in Procurement." He gave a self-satisfied smile.

"It sounds like a good move," Isobel said, although she still hadn't grasped the finer points of differentiation between Procurement and Procurement Support. "And, um, nice for Paula, I suppose."

"She's been waiting a long time for this. Far be it from me to tell her it's not all it's cracked up to be."

"I imagine Stan will be disappointed."

Frank shifted his gaze out the window. "He hasn't been here as long as Paula. Doreen was really pushing for him, though."

"Oh?"

"She had...issues with Paula. She went so far as to bring them to Felice Edwards. Paula found out, and they had a big blow-up."

"When was this?"

"Shortly before Doreen was killed."

"Did you ever wonder if...if Paula could have been the one

to…?" Isobel purposely didn't finish her thought.

Frank glanced beyond her to make sure nobody was lurking in the half-open doorway. He lowered his voice.

"I'll admit, the thought did cross my mind. But now that Nikki's been arrested, we know Paula didn't have anything to do with it. In any case, I'd rather work with her than Stan. That's why I called Mr. Jeffards yesterday and told him I was recommending her." Frank gave a wry laugh. "It took some convincing. He's very conservative in his views about women."

"Prehistoric, you mean?"

"Look, it's probably best not to let on that you know about any of this, if you know what I mean. Tell Stan to come in, will you? I'd better give him the news."

Isobel passed the word to Conchita, who passed it to Stan, then lurked by the supply closet until Stan disappeared into Frank's office, shutting the door behind him. Conchita was watching her with a steely eye, so she rooted around in the closet, picking up an extra phone message pad that she didn't need and some ballpoint pens that she did.

Isobel suddenly understood why Detective Kozinski had charged Nikki with suspicion of murder, even after Isobel had taken pains to explain Nikki's alibi in her phone message. There was a distinct advantage to letting people think the perpetrator had been caught. With a cat in the bag, people were more inclined to let down their guard, as Frank had just done.

So Doreen had actively tried to keep Paula from being promoted. She must really have hated Paula, to go to such lengths. Was it simply because Paula looked down on secretaries, or was there more to it? Paula's name was conspicuously absent from the log. Maybe Doreen knew something about Paula and had tried, unsuccessfully, to blackmail her. To show her she meant business, Doreen had tried to sabotage her promotion, but Paula got wind of it and killed her.

Paula had known about the fire drill in advance, and she'd

stayed on the floor after everyone else left. Isobel didn't recall seeing Stan, and he was the other fire marshal. Even he was gone by the time Paula came back into the women's bathroom. So what was she still doing on the seventeenth floor?

Isobel had ruled out Paula's complicity largely on the evidence of her throwing up when she saw Doreen's body, but now she reconsidered. It was one thing to commit murder in the throes of emotion, and another to return and see your handiwork after the fact. And without question, it had been a disgusting sight.

Isobel turned the corner and found Paula standing by the filing cabinet. Some of Frank's papers were still on the stepstool where Isobel had left them. Paula let the rest tumble to the floor from her hands.

"I wasn't finished yet," Isobel said.

"I noticed."

"Congratulations on your promotion," Isobel said, making an effort to sound sincere.

"Yes. Lovely, isn't it?" Paula slammed the file drawer shut with her foot and pointed to the papers on the floor. Isobel knelt down to pick them up.

When she stood up, she saw Paula at her desk, holding up her copy of *Backstage*. She waved the newspaper at Isobel, gave a phony, saccharine smile, then tore it in half down the middle and dropped it into the wastebasket.

"Now that I'm in charge, things are going to be different around here. You'd best get used to it."

THIRTY-FIVE

THE RHYTHM OF THE SUBWAY USUALLY lulled Isobel into a trance, even when she was being crushed by her fellow riders. But as she rode home from work Thursday night, she found herself replaying her conversation with Frank instead of zoning out.

They'd all been up for promotion: Frank, Paula, Stan and, if Frank was successful, Doreen. So clearly Doreen had a stake in it, although she couldn't have had much influence if her pleas on Stan's behalf ultimately fell flat. But the really interesting question was why Doreen had been pushing for Stan in the first place.

Why, all these years after the annulment of their marriage, would she get him a job at the bank and push for his promotion, while at the same time, she was blackmailing him—and for more money than anyone else? What was he paying her for? Was he trying to keep her quiet, or had she promised Stan something else—something that was worth $5,000 a month to him?

She was still lost in thought as she ambled down Fiftieth Street toward her apartment, although she had strayed from office politics to her audition for *Two by Two*. She was imagining herself saying nothing more than the title of her song, when she practically bumped into the wiry, bespectacled, backpacked frame standing on her stoop.

"You should be more aware walking down the streets of New York!"

As always, Percival was right. Isobel clutched her brother in a fierce hug, which he submitted to patiently. She pulled away and glanced guiltily at her watch. "Am I late? You haven't been waiting here long, have you? I should have left you a key."

"I just got here. My plane was a little early, if you can believe it." He looked up and down the shady, tree-lined street. "Nice block."

"Believe me, it gets more colorful after dark. Come on in."

He followed her up the three flights of stairs. "I wasn't kidding, Iz. You should be more careful walking around. You can't zone out on the street like that."

"I wasn't zoning, I was thinking."

"Same thing." Percival shrugged off his backpack and looked around the apartment. Isobel had stayed up the night before trying to straighten up, but there was only so much one could do with two women's assorted belongings and limited storage space.

"Are you sure this is okay?" Percival asked doubtfully. "I think our bathroom at home is bigger than this."

"Midwest small isn't the same as New York small. That's something I know about New York that you don't," she said playfully. "Delphi's got five sisters. She can deal. And you know I don't mind." She hugged him again. "I really missed you."

Percival squeezed back. "I missed you too. You seem well, though."

"I am," said Isobel, almost surprised at how true it was. "I have a callback tomorrow night from that audition I botched the first time around."

Percival threw back his head and laughed. "Right! Remind me what you did...lectured them about the differences between auditioning and performing, was it?"

"Shut up!" She gave him a good-natured punch on the arm. "At least they're seeing me again."

The key turned in the lock and Delphi shoved open the door, struggling with a heavy bag of groceries. Percival jumped up to help her.

"I got 'em," he said, deftly taking the bag from her. "I'm Percival," he said over his shoulder. "Nice to meet you."

Delphi pushed her curls out of her eyes. "I know. And you don't need to curry favor, I already said you could stay." She turned to Isobel and stage-whispered, "Oh my God, he really does look like Harry Potter."

Percival set the bag down on the counter and cast an approving eye over Delphi. "And you look like Aphrodite."

Delphi laughed. "Ha! What a charmer!"

"Doesn't she, Iz? She has that Greek goddess thing going."

"Yeah, if that's the case, I'll be the first Jewish Greek goddess in history. I'm a real pagan."

"Are you Wiccan?"

"Am I what-an?"

"Wiccan. When people say pagan these days, that's usually what they mean. Contemporary witchcraft. The black arts."

Delphi shrugged off her coat and handed it to Isobel. "Did your brother just call me a witch?"

"I'm sure he meant it in the nicest possible way," Isobel assured her.

Percival began unpacking the groceries. "I really appreciate your making room for me."

"We aren't making any room for you. What you see is what you get, and you're bunking with your sister," said Delphi.

"Ah, pomegranate juice," Percival said, as he pulled a bottle from the bag. "The sacred fruit of the underworld. Excellent antioxidant properties."

"Tell me, do they offer grocery analysis at Columbia?" Delphi asked.

Isobel watched their instinctive sparring with amusement. She could tell that they liked each other already.

"Whole wheat bread, white rice—I sense internal conflict here—eggs, bacon, obviously you're a non-kosher pagan, frozen pizza with everything on it and…diet Coke. Definitely conflicted." He crumpled up the paper bag. "Do you recycle?"

"No, I'm conflicted about that, too," Delphi retorted.

"Yes, we do. Under the sink," Isobel said, laughing.

Percival stowed the bag and turned back to them. "So, Mom and Dad gave me money to take you guys out to a nice dinner tonight. And, being the goody two-shoes that I am, I didn't go and blow it all on illegal drugs on the corner. Only some of it, and I'm not sharing."

"Kidding," Isobel mouthed to Delphi.

"How about Greek food, in honor of the curls on the oracle of Delphi?" he suggested.

"There's a place on Tenth Avenue that looks nice," said Isobel.

Percival waved a hand toward the door. "Lay on, Macduff!"

"He opens doors, unpacks groceries, cites mythological references, and quotes Shakespeare correctly. How old is this kid?" Delphi said as Isobel passed her.

"Too old for you," Isobel said snidely.

Delphi made a face and shut the door behind them.

They chatted amiably on the way to the restaurant and were soon ensconced in a booth in the cozy blue and white interior. After placing their orders, Isobel and Delphi raised their wineglasses, while Percival held up his ginger ale.

"Here's to New York and new friends," said Isobel.

"And smart siblings," Delphi added. "Maybe Percival Popp here can help you solve your office murder."

"What?"

"Percival Popp, 1940s comic strip hero. Percival Popp, the Super Cop? Aha!" Delphi pointed triumphantly at him. "I think I've got you there, whizbang."

But Percival was looking at Isobel, his head cocked questioningly, and she knew she was cornered.

"I know who Percival Popp is," said Percival dismissively, as Delphi wilted. "What office murder?"

Isobel laughed weakly. "Oh. I guess I forgot to tell you about that."

He frowned. "I guess you did."

Isobel sighed. "I knew you'd worry. And I didn't want you to tell Mom and Dad. Anyway, it's not as bad as it sounds. I mean, it is, but it isn't."

Over lemon soup and moussaka, Isobel told Percival the whole story, or as much of it as now made sense to her.

Percival stirred his soup, brooding. "I don't like this, Iz." He looked up. "But you knew I wouldn't."

"Delphi's right. Maybe you can help," she said. "It's all swirling in my brain. I need logical, objective eyes."

"Why?" He gave her a wary look. "Isobel, you're not trying to solve it yourself, are you?"

"I didn't set out to, but I've been learning things about the office and the people, just to get along with everyone and do my job, and it's hard not to ignore some of the things I found out."

"Have you gone to the police?"

"Of course. Everything I know, they know." But as Isobel spoke, she realized there were some discoveries she hadn't bothered to share: Frank's sexuality, Paula's hatred of Doreen, Conchita's religious passion for Stan. "Well, maybe not everything," she said. "But I'm not about to do their job for them. I'm sure they're making inquiries."

Percival looked at her with a mixture of hurt and concern. "I still can't believe you didn't tell me about this."

Delphi threw up her hands in mock annoyance. "Great, now he'll never leave."

"I know. I'm sorry, I should have. Don't be mad at me. Help me," said Isobel. She knew that her brother could no more resist a puzzle than she could, and it wasn't long before he relented.

"Is the entrance to the ladies' room visible from all the desks and cubicles?" he asked.

"It's down the hall beyond Frank, Paula, Stan and Conchita. It's not central, but a person ducking in there would still risk being seen."

Percival pondered this. "Seems likely the killer was a woman. A man would attract attention going into the ladies' room."

"That leaves Paula and Conchita. Paula hated Doreen, and Doreen was doing her damndest to keep Paula from being promoted. Not only does Paula have a motive, she was one of only three people who knew about the fire drill in advance."

"Was Doreen blackmailing Paula?"

"Seems likely, but I don't have evidence."

"What about Conchita?"

"Opposite problem. Doreen *was* blackmailing her, only I don't know why. Also, she's fiercely protective of Stan, who married Doreen right out of high school. The marriage was annulled, but I don't know the reason for that, either."

"Do you know why Doreen was blackmailing Stan?" Percival asked.

"Nope. That one really has me stumped."

"Where's this blackmail log? You said you kept a copy."

Isobel opened her wallet, unfolded the paper and handed it to Percival. He pushed his glasses up the bridge of his nose and peered at the figures scrawled in Doreen's handwriting. After a moment, he was grinning like the Cheshire cat.

"Well, she wasn't," he said.

"Who wasn't what?"

"Doreen wasn't blackmailing Stan." Percival handed the paper back to Isobel, who stared at it blankly. It revealed nothing new.

"Look at the amounts and how they're laid out on the page. $200, $475, $750, $1,275, $2,300, and then, a little farther down, $5,000. Don't you see it?"

"No, I don't," said Isobel. Now she was getting annoyed. Really, sometimes Percival could be too much, even for her.

Percival leaned over and pointed with his fork. "Do the math, Iz. The first five amounts add up to $5,000. Doreen wasn't blackmailing Stan. She was paying him. With the money she got from the others."

THIRTY-SIX

JAMES SPENT THE ENTIRE SUBWAY RIDE home psyching himself up for a confrontation with Jayla. It was time to put an end to this frustrating limbo, once and for all. But when he exited the subway, he found he wasn't quite ready to face her. Not yet. He set off instead toward his buddy Gerald's house. He pressed the buzzer several times, but there was no answer, so he hiked a few blocks north to his friend Michael's house. There was nobody home there, either. James paused on the corner, just outside a deli.

He hadn't seen Michael, Gerald or any of his old buddies in several months. It was too hard to chill with them and not drink. These were the guys he'd played football with in college, but unlike him, they had graduated, and they could hang out in bars without it being a threat to their health and sanity. Since James had started AA, he'd avoided them entirely. Now he was seeking them out again...why? He was forced to ask himself that question, and he didn't like the answer.

He was too much of a coward to face Jayla.

What he really needed was moral support. He wanted desperately for them to tell him that it was time to dump her, that he didn't owe her anything. He was even, he realized, prepared to admit he was in AA, although he wasn't sure what their reaction would be. But even if he ran down the list of all his buddies, he'd still have to have it out with Jayla eventually. There was no point in putting it off any longer.

He ducked into the deli and bought a Coke. He downed it in several strong gulps, crushed the can against his forehead just because he could, and ditched it in a nearby trash can.

Then he turned the corner and headed downtown to Jayla's apartment, ten blocks away. Just as she had a key to his apartment, he had a key to hers, although it had been a long time since he'd used it. That should have told her something. He took a deep breath, sucked in his stomach, walked up the two flights of stairs and let himself in.

For one endless moment, he stood in the foyer wondering why Jayla was sitting naked on her kitchen counter. Then he took in the bottle of chocolate syrup next to her and the mini-fro between her legs.

"What the fuck—?"

Jayla's eyes popped open, and she let out a shriek. Her legs closed reflexively, pinning the man's head between them, and James heard a muffled, "Thassit, baby..." Jayla, returning quickly to her senses, jumped off the counter, knocking the kneeling man headlong into a cabinet.

"Shit!"

Jayla kicked him. "Get up, Michael!"

"Michael?" roared James.

He stood up, rubbing his head, and backed away from James. "Hey, bro'...go easy."

"You sonofabitch! What are you doing eating my girlfriend?"

Michael giggled nervously. "We are in the kitchen, man."

"Get the hell out of here right now!" screamed James. "This is between Jayla and me!"

"He can stay," Jayla said defiantly.

"Don't worry, I'm not gonna hurt you. But I might hurt him," James said, cracking his knuckles into his fist. "So get the fuck out of here!"

Michael bundled his clothes into a ball and ran toward the door. James grabbed a roll of paper towels and threw it after him. "And wipe your mouth! You're all sticky!"

He slammed the door behind Michael and whirled around to face Jayla, who had wrapped herself in a blue silk kimono. She looked at least as angry as he was.

"How long has this been going on?" he demanded.

"You can't have it both ways, James!"

"You can't, either!"

"It's pretty clear that you're not interested in me anymore. Don't you think I'm gonna look elsewhere for satisfaction?"

"If you know I don't want you, then why are you hanging around me all the time?"

Jayla gave a strangled, exasperated howl and threw her hands up toward the ceiling. "Because I love you, you stupid asshole! I care about you, and I want to make sure you stay clean! I'm sick of seeing good black men ruin themselves, and you have everything going for you. I don't care if you dropped out of Columbia—you got there in the first place, didn't you? I don't care if you had to stop playing football—you were a star when you did. You could be again! It's all up to you. You could take back your life or you could piss it away like my father did and wind up a homeless drunk." Angry tears trickled down her face.

James slammed his fist on the counter. "I'm not your father, goddammit!"

Jayla shook her locks and gave a hard laugh. "You didn't hear the very first thing I said, did you?" She grabbed his arm and yanked him toward her. "I love you. You're the one I want."

He pulled his arm away as if she had scalded him. "But you're gonna fix me first, and while I'm still broken, you'll fuck my friends. Then once you've got me how you want me, good-bye to them, hello picket fence?"

"Why do you turn everything around and make me seem like a manipulative bitch?"

"What's so goddamn great about me, huh? Why do you want me in the first place?"

She stared at him. "I don't know," she said, her voice husky. "If I did, maybe I could talk myself out of it. But I don't, so I can't."

James swept the syrup bottle into the sink with a clatter. "I went by Michael's before I came over. It never occurred to me he'd be here."

"I didn't think you guys were still friends," Jayla said.

He whirled on her. "You know damn well there's only one reason I've been staying away from him. And Gerald. And Dewayne and all the rest of them."

"Then why did you go to Michael's place?"

"Because I was too chickenshit to come over here and say what I have to say to you."

"Which is…what?" Jayla asked, her voice trembling.

"Does it matter now?"

"Yeah, it matters."

James sighed heavily. He was suddenly exhausted. He leaned his elbows on the kitchen counter and rested his head in his hands.

"You're too strong for me, Jayla."

"You need somebody strong."

He looked at her, focusing on her beautiful long eyelashes. He would miss those lashes. "No, that's exactly what I don't need. I need to find my own strength. And if I fail, if I wind up on the street even, I have to know that I can get myself out of it."

"You won't be able to get yourself out of your own shitpile if you're drunk," she spat.

"Jesus, Jayla. Don't make me say it!"

"Don't be such a pussy, James. SAY IT!"

"I don't love you!"

After a moment, Jayla said quietly, "In a relationship, there's always one person who loves more than the other. That can be me."

James was taken aback. It was as if she had been waiting for him to make that argument, just so she could counter it.

"Jayla, you're the one who's not listening. You haven't been all along, and, yes, I was too drunk to argue with you the night you found me."

"You'll take my help and then throw me away?"

"I didn't ask for your help, Jayla!" His voice boomed around the small kitchen. "I didn't ask to be saved. Maybe I don't want to be saved!"

"You want to keep drinking?"

"Yes. No. I don't know! But I don't want to be with you anymore, Jayla. I don't want to marry you, and I know that's what you're after."

She looked down at the floor. "It's that white bitch, isn't it?"

"I haven't seen or spoken to her since the night I passed out drunk. She's another one I can do without, believe me. You had that all wrong!"

Jayla shook her head, a rueful smile on her face. "Oh, you may think that, but don't you mess with a woman's intuition. I know how you feel about her better than you do. Asshole."

"I told you, I'm taking out someone else. Her name is Felice Edwards and she's a sister."

"You love her?"

"I hardly know her! But that's the thing, Jayla. This is the part I can't get you to understand. This being sober shit is scary, but it's also like waking up from a long nap. I don't know who I want to be with. I've gotta figure out everything about myself all over again. I've gotta figure out who James Cooke is when he's not drinking. It's scary, and yeah, it's scary to do it alone. If I could do it with someone I knew I loved—and who I knew loved sober James Cooke—I would. But that's not you, baby. I should have been straight with you a long time ago. Believe me, this is not easy for me. But being strong and telling you how I really feel is the first thing I have to do to reclaim my life."

The tears were falling fast down Jayla's face now. James felt sorry for her, sorry for himself. Even sorry for Michael, who was probably standing on the corner trying to wipe chocolate syrup off his face with a dry paper towel.

"I know you think I can't do it without you," he said finally. "But if that's true, then why the hell do you want me in the first place?"

But Jayla just shook her head. He walked back to the foyer, where her keychain was sitting on a small table by the door. He picked it up and worked his apartment key off the ring. Then he slid Jayla's key off his chain and set it on the table.

"Michael's a good guy. Better than me. And you can tell him I said that," he said and shut the door behind him.

He heard her sobs grow louder inside the apartment, but he walked on with newfound resolve. If Jayla thought he couldn't stay sober without her, he was damned if he would prove her right. In fact, he couldn't think of a better incentive to keep him on the wagon than showing Jayla he didn't need her. As he walked, he imagined himself purging his apartment of the random girlfriend paraphernalia she'd left behind. Maybe he'd give her clothes to old Mrs. Dunkirk upstairs. Her wardrobe could use a lift. Maybe he'd sleep on the couch tonight. Not because he had to, but because he could. And right now any decision he made, by himself and for himself, felt good.

Not just good—great.

THIRTY-SEVEN

FRIDAY MORNING REVEALED OCTOBER in New York at its meanest: cold, windy and rainy. Isobel dragged herself out of bed with great reluctance. Her sleep had been fitful, and not just because Percival kept kicking her from his pile of blankets on the floor next to her air mattress. She dreamed that she'd found Conchita and James together and stabbed James. Then she and Conchita went to a Cinco de Mayo festival and drank margaritas until Detective Kozinski arrived and arrested Isobel, not for James's murder, but for Doreen's. Percival was waiting for her in a prison cell, holding stalks of purplish flowers and a giant calculator that was running numbers incessantly.

Now, as she passed her sleeping roommate on the way to the bathroom, she realized the flowers must have been delphiniums. Isobel groaned at her reflection and wondered if there was any way to arrange her hair to hide the dark circles under her eyes. The only solution she could come up with required Scotch tape, so she pulled out her makeup box and applied light dots of rose lipstick to counteract the blue, then layered yellow-based cover-up over that. She stuffed a small cosmetics bag with these and other implements of facial wizardry and prayed she'd look better by seven thirty in the evening. When she emerged from the bathroom, Percival was sitting up against the wall, rubbing his eyes.

"You sleep okay?" she whispered, trying not to wake Delphi.

"More or less." She knew that meant he'd been about as comfortable as she was.

"What time is your Columbia interview?"

"Eleven. Then I'm going to hang around and visit some classes. Can we meet up later?"

Isobel checked to make sure Delphi was still sound asleep, then she leaned closer to Percival. "I haven't told Delphi, but if I get this audition tonight, I'll have to stay and rehearse. I'll call you and let you know."

"Listen, good luck!"

"Yeah, you too. Not that you need it against all those other prospective fifteen-year-old freshmen."

Isobel kissed her brother, grabbed her bag and her sorry excuse for an umbrella, and then, on impulse, snatched up her audition materials, just in case she wasn't able to get home first. She staggered into the pelting rain and almost immediately had to abandon her splayed, torn umbrella in a trash can. By the time she got to the subway, she was drenched.

Where were all the street umbrella vendors when you needed one?

She was in a completely foul mood by the time she arrived at InterBank. To make matters worse, Paula was still reveling in her promotion, and her abrasive cheerfulness worked for her about as well as standup comedy from an undertaker. If she continued to punctuate each sentence with an incongruously girlish chuckle, Isobel would be calling Temp Zone for a new assignment sooner rather than later.

Stan, on the other hand, was slouching around the office, his shoulders buckling under some unseen weight, and whatever color was normally present in his pasty complexion had faded to a sallow, depressive gray. Percival must be right about the blackmail log. It made perfect sense. Stan had talked about the sacrifices Doreen made for him, and even though their marriage hadn't been a success, it was easier to take Doreen getting him a job at face value, rather than try to put some kind of evil spin on it. No, despite his failures, Doreen must have loved poor, plodgy Stan. And he wouldn't have killed her if she was giving him money.

That was another idea that she was having difficulty getting her head around: Doreen helping someone. It seemed so out of character—but then again, maybe it wasn't. For a certain kind of personality, dispensing good will was just another form of power. Doreen must have imagined herself as a latter-day Robin Hood, stealing from the careless to give to the ex-husband. But what on earth did Stan need that kind of money for? Isobel remembered Conchita insisting that she could provide Stan with everything Doreen had. But did she even know what that meant?

Frank, who had been unusually industrious all morning, pitched another stack of files and documents onto Isobel's desk, with instructions to file the old stuff and give the rest to Paula.

Isobel set about sorting the papers, wishing more than ever that she could have given her *Two by Two* audition yesterday, when she and the world were sunnier, not to mention well-rested. The only person who was acting normal was Conchita, who continued to snub Isobel, glower at Paula, ignore Frank, and cross herself every time Stan walked past. As difficult as Conchita could be, at least she was predictable.

Shortly before twelve, Conchita appeared at Isobel's desk.

"I'm going to noontime Mass," she said.

Isobel didn't even bother looking up. "I don't have a working umbrella anymore, so I'm staying in."

"I'll say a prayer for your soul," Conchita said.

Isobel gave a dismissive snort. Noontime Mass. Yeah, right. Conchita's ostentatious piety notwithstanding, Isobel somehow doubted that was really where she was going. She wondered again why Doreen had been blackmailing the sainted Conchita.

Without stopping to think about what she was doing, Isobel suddenly shoved Frank's papers aside and leaped up from her chair. She grabbed her still-soaked raincoat from Nikki's old desk where she had set it to dry and was still struggling to get it on when Frank appeared with another overflowing banker's box.

He set the box on her desk, eyeing her coat. "Didn't Conchita just leave for lunch?"

"I just remembered a super quick errand I have to do," Isobel said hurriedly. "I promise, back in ten!"

Frank wiped his hands together releasing a puff of dust. "Doesn't matter to me. I'm not your boss anymore. Just don't let Paula catch you."

Isobel nodded gratefully and took off down the hall. As she reached the etched glass doors, she saw Conchita disappear into an elevator. Isobel waited until she was gone, then ran out into the hallway and pressed the button repeatedly.

Richie, the IT guy, who was also waiting, shot her a snide glance. "Yeah, that always works for me."

But an elevator did come, almost immediately, and Isobel took it down to the lobby. Conchita was standing just in front of the building, putting up a sturdy-looking, long-handled umbrella, which Isobel immediately coveted. Protected from the deluge, Conchita headed east on Twenty-third Street.

The rain was coming down even harder than before, but Isobel bent her head and plunged into a crowd of slow-moving pedestrians. She was getting soaked, but at least she was able to follow Conchita at a comfortable distance. Isobel trailed her down Park Avenue South and saw her enter a brick building. Isobel drew nearer and read the plaque above the door: Park Avenue Presbyterian Church.

Damn, damn, damn.

So much for her suspicions, and now she was going to get pneumonia.

She sloshed to a deli at the end of the block. "You don't happen to sell umbrellas, do you?" she asked doubtfully.

The man behind the counter pointed to a small pile of black umbrellas on top of the *New York Post*, and Isobel grabbed one with relief. As she fished out five dollars from her wallet, she was struck by a sudden, incongruous thought.

Presbyterians didn't have noonday Mass. She ought to know—she was one.

She grabbed the umbrella and darted back out into the rain and down the block, wrenching open the door to Park Avenue Presbyterian Church.

In the damp wood-paneled hallway, she saw a small blackboard with the day's events posted in white block pin letters. She scanned it eagerly.

Noon: Alcoholics Anonymous.

Isobel let out a long, slow breath. "Well, what do you know?" she murmured. She took a step backwards and her heel dug into a man's foot behind her.

"Hey! Watch it, will you?"

Isobel spun around. It was hard to say who was more surprised, she or James.

THIRTY-EIGHT

IT WAS ISOBEL WHO FINALLY BROKE THE SILENCE.

"I, uh, just came in to get out of the rain. I don't have an umbrella."

James pointed to her hand. "What do you call that?"

Isobel looked down, "Oh. Right. I just bought it. I guess I forgot."

"I know why you're here," James said.

"No!" Isobel shook her head vigorously. "I'm not an alcoholic!" Water from her hair spattered his face, and he coughed gently as he wiped it away.

"You were following Conchita, right?"

Isobel stared, dumbfounded. "How did you—?"

James took her arm and pulled her to her toes to whisper in her ear. "We have to talk. About a lot of things. Come on."

This was Providence, James thought, as he steered Isobel back outside, up Park Avenue South and into the same diner where they had eaten and fought the week before. On his way to the meeting, he had begun to get nervous about revealing his innermost fears to an unfamiliar group, even with Conchita as backup. The decision had been made for him; he would save it for his home group on Sunday, in Bill's comfortable presence. Another decision had been made for him as well: he would set things right with Isobel.

A few moments later, they were squeezed into a corner booth amid the additional layer of commotion that accompanies a rainy lunch hour.

"You haven't said a word," James commented. "That's not like you."

"I'm trying to figure out whether you were following me or Conchita."

"Aren't you overlooking the obvious?" James closed his eyes, opened them and spoke again, holding her gaze steadily. "I'm an alcoholic."

"Oh!" Isobel's eyes widened for a moment, but she quickly tamed them.

"So is Conchita. I came to this group last week and my sponsor introduced me to her."

"So you did come back to follow her!"

"Not exactly. There was something on my mind that I wanted to share. It's kind of complicated, I'd rather not go into it."

Isobel's brow wrinkled with concern. "But you're missing the meeting."

"This is more important."

The time had come to explain and apologize, but somehow that was more daunting than admitting he was an alcoholic.

"Can I take your order?" asked a cheery voice.

"Two grilled cheeses and two Cokes," James said.

Isobel smiled. "You remembered."

"I also remember that you were pretty bitchy to me," he said, and immediately wished he hadn't. But Isobel looked down at her hands and shook her head.

"I know. And I'm really sorry." She looked up at him again. "Especially because you were right about Nikki."

"I know. She was arrested for Doreen's murder."

"How did you find out? It wasn't on the news."

"From Ginger. Remember, Nikki used to work for Temp Zone."

"Well, she was arrested, but not for the murder," Isobel said. "She was embezzling money from the bank and her boyfriend in Equities was investing it."

"So, up to her old tricks," He tried not to let his satisfaction show. "But she didn't kill Doreen?"

Isobel shook her head. "I don't see how she could have. I

saw her going down the stairs during the emergency drill. She might have had time to double back, but she seemed genuinely intent on getting out of there, and I think I'd have seen her when I was running around looking for the bathroom."

Their sodas arrived, and Isobel took a sip before continuing. "There's more. Doreen was blackmailing almost everyone in the office."

Unfortunately, James had also just taken a swig of Coke, and he inhaled sharply, choking and spluttering.

"What?" he croaked out finally.

Isobel handed him a folded piece of paper from her wallet. James opened it and scanned the contents while Isobel talked. "That's why I was following Conchita. Obviously, Doreen knew what Nikki was up to, but I couldn't figure out why she was blackmailing Conchita. When she told me she was going to noonday Mass, I just didn't believe her. I had this hunch that if I followed her, I might figure out what Doreen had on her."

"Looks like you were right," James said, his throat returning to normal.

"I was also having trouble figuring out what she had on Stan, but then my brother looked at the numbers and realized that she was actually paying him that $5,000." Isobel leaned over and pointed. "See how Stan's line is separated out? All the other amounts add up to $5,000." Isobel shook her head. "But what I can't understand is why he needs that kind of money."

James folded the paper carefully along its lines and handed it back to her. "I can help you there. Stan is a transsexual. He's saving up for a sex-change operation."

"Here are your sandwiches. Can I get you anything else?" chirped the waitress. "Miss? Miss? Are you all right?"

James leaned over and patted Isobel's hand. "She's fine."

Isobel shook her head in astonishment. "Wow. Oh, wow. That explains why their marriage didn't work out."

"Must have been a bummer on their wedding night."

"But Doreen must really have cared about him. She got

him the job, she was helping him raise the money for the operation…"

"And Conchita didn't approve of Doreen indulging Stan's baser desires."

"On top of which, Doreen was blackmailing her because she was an alcoholic. For a woman of that age in the Hispanic community, especially one so ostentatiously pious…well, it sort of ruins her image, doesn't it?" Isobel pointed out.

He nodded. "It gives Conchita a double-whammy motive."

Isobel picked up her grilled cheese and set it down again without taking a bite. "It's just too weird, too coincidental that Stan is transsexual. You know, Frank is married and in the closet."

"What?! How on earth did you find that out?"

"He was looking at a gay porn site on his computer." She held up a hand defensively. "I wasn't snooping! He asked me to do some archiving, but he forgot to close his browser." She smiled sheepishly. "I recognized one of the models."

"Excuse me?"

"From acting class!"

James put his hands over his face for a moment, and then looked back at her. "Wait, when did you have time to go to an acting class?"

"I skipped lunch Tuesday and Wednesday to make up for the—" She gasped and jumped up. "I completely forgot! I told Frank I'd only be gone a few minutes. I'm not supposed to take lunch at the same time as Conchita. Paula's in charge now, and she's looking for any reason to cut me loose!"

"Paula's in charge?"

Isobel chattered on as she pulled on her raincoat. "She and Stan were both up for Frank's job, and Doreen was pushing for Stan because she hated Paula and vice versa, but once Nikki got arrested, Frank called up the head guy and recommended Paula, even though the guy's really conservative and doesn't approve of women in management!"

"But Isobel, there's more I have to tell you—about the

woman who answered my phone the other night…"

"Sorry, James, but I've got to go!" She took one last, frantic bite of her sandwich, then grabbed her coat and umbrella. "I'll call you later!"

It was the second time she'd run out on him at this diner. He looked across at the empty chair opposite and spoke the words he had been wanting to say ever since their last lunch together.

"It was all a big mistake. I'm sorry."

"No problem," said the chirpy waitress, who had appeared out of nowhere. "Would you like your check?"

THIRTY-NINE

PAULA WAS SITTING AT ISOBEL'S DESK when Isobel returned, her hand on the receiver and a look of triumph on her face.

"When you've finished sorting through Frank's things, you can start packing your own. We won't be needing you anymore after today."

Isobel pushed her dripping hair out of her face (the umbrella she'd bought at the deli had already given up the ghost) and took a deep breath.

"You can't do that."

"Isn't that funny? I just did," Paula said smugly. "I've informed Felice Edwards that your questionable services are no longer required."

"But Frank said—"

"It doesn't really matter what Frank said, does it? At precisely 5:01 p.m. today, this is no longer his department."

"But I—"

Paula stood up. "You said you'd be gone for ten minutes and it's been," she consulted her watch, "forty-five. You and Conchita cannot be gone at the same time, you know that."

"It was an emergency!"

"Oh, really? What was so urgent?"

What could she possibly say? I had to follow Conchita because I thought she was lying, and sure enough, she was?

"If you must know, I had to give something to my temp agent, and it took a bit longer than I expected."

Paula laughed shrilly. "Whether or not that fool continues to employ you is his folly." She tapped the side of Frank's banker's box. "You've quite a bit left to do in your time remaining with us. You'd best not waste any more of it chatting." She wrinkled her nose in disapproval. "And you've made a puddle. Please clean that up."

Well, that's that, thought Isobel, as she peeled off her sodden coat. She squelched past Conchita's still empty desk and around the corner to the bathroom, where she examined herself in the mirror. She looked like a drowned rat. Thank God her audition was still several hours away, although she was down another umbrella.

She grabbed two large handfuls of paper towels and returned to her desk, where she contemplated her change of fortune as she blotted the excess water from the carpet. All things considered, it was probably for the best. Working for Paula would have been a nightmare of passive-aggressive putdowns. It was time to move on. At least she and James were back on speaking terms. And since he was partly responsible for her being terminated, he owed her one.

James.

He was revealing his secrets slowly, if accidentally. An alcoholic college dropout? Well, the one probably explained the other. Poor guy. Isobel had an uncle who was an alcoholic, and she knew from her father how hellish life had been for his family before he sobered up eighteen years ago. But at least James was in AA. That took courage. She dropped the soggy paper towels into her wastebasket and resolved to be more kindly disposed toward him.

A moment later, Stan appeared in front of her desk, holding a ledger and hovering apologetically.

"Could you make five stapled copies of the twenty pages I've marked? I'd ask Conchita, but she's still out."

Between her mad wet dash back to the office and her spat with Paula, Isobel had completely forgotten James's bombshell about Stan. Now she stared at his soft, doughy cheeks and looked for hints of femininity. They were there, to be sure: long eyelashes, thick hair, full lips, and smooth, fleshy cheeks. He had removed his jacket and was wearing a loose-fitting shirt. Was she imagining the outline of smallish breasts?

"If it's really a problem, I can wait," he said, misinterpreting her silence.

"No, no, that's fine. I'm happy to do it." She took the ledger from him. "Are you feeling all right?"

"I'm a bit tired."

"I can imagine."

"What do you mean?"

"Oh, just that work is probably tiring. And life. And, um, thinking about Doreen and wondering who killed her."

He gaped at her for a moment, then turned and walked away faster than she'd ever seen him move.

Isobel plopped down in her chair with a sigh. I need to just forget about all these crazy people, she thought. They deserve each other, and after today, I'm free of them. She trudged over to the copier with the ledger.

"That's Stan's."

Isobel jumped. She hadn't sensed Conchita's approach and was annoyed at having been caught off guard.

"I know," she said. "He asked me to make copies for him."

"I'll do it."

Conchita grabbed the ledger from Isobel. Isobel resisted the temptation to ask, "How was the AA meeting?" and returned to her desk.

At first, she patiently examined every paper, folder and notebook from Frank's box, separating the items into neat piles: Paula, back to Frank, garbage. After a while, Isobel realized how little it mattered—she would never see these people again—and started tossing more and more stuff into the recycling bin. She hesitated over copies of Nikki's old billing records. The police probably had everything they needed, but it was a good idea to make sure.

She picked up the folder and headed around the corner to Frank's office to double check with him. The door was ajar, and Isobel could hear the soft rumble of his voice as he talked on the phone. She looked around. Stan's door was closed, as was Paula's, and Conchita was nowhere in sight. Probably in with Stan. Isobel couldn't resist. She put her ear to the crack in Frank's door.

"Of course there's nobody else. We've been through this. I thought things might be different with you, but I'm not going to change. And a baby…even if it's in a test tube, it's a terrible idea in more ways than you…"

Isobel stepped away from the door and backed into Conchita's desk.

So his wife does know, she realized with surprise. And not only does she still want him, she wants his child. She walked slowly back to her desk, shaking her head in bewilderment, and tossed the folder with Nikki's records onto Frank's pile. As she did, she resolved never to be the kind of woman who begged to stay with a man who didn't want her.

JAMES WAS FEELING SURPRISINGLY UPBEAT as he settled himself back at his desk after his encounter with Isobel. It had been more restorative than the AA meeting would have been. He hadn't apologized or explained about Jayla, but the breach had been mended, and the path of communication was open once again. That's what counted.

Anna poked her head into his office, and James jumped instinctively.

Anna laughed. "It's just me. Ginger's at lunch with that PR guy. Listen, while you were gone, I took a message for you from Felice Edwards at InterBank Switzerland."

Felice. His date tonight. He'd almost forgotten. "I think I know what that's about."

"I wouldn't worry too much about it. Ginger was just waiting for her to be finished so she could close the account."

"Wait—what?"

"Your temp, Isobel. She's done. You have to file a termination report." Anna pulled his door shut as she retreated.

So, Paula had cut her loose. James felt the loosening of a small knot in his stomach that he didn't even realize had been there. He was relieved to have Isobel safely out of there. He'd better call Felice back and get the official reason. They also had to set the details of their date tonight, although with Jayla out of the picture, the illicit thrill was somewhat diminished.

"Felice? James Cooke here."

"Hey. Sorry about this," said Felice.

"What's the deal?"

"The whole department is breaking apart. Frank Lusardi's moving up to Procurement, and Paula Toule-Withers is replacing him. I'm sure you've heard that Nikki Francis is gone. So there's really not much left for Isobel to do there."

"That's the reason Paula gave?"

Felice hesitated. "Well, not exactly. She said Isobel was taking inappropriate breaks and not completing her assignments. But you have to consider the source," Felice added quickly. "Paula's hard on secretaries, and we never had any complaints from Frank."

"Can you give Isobel a good recommendation? I need to put something down on her form."

"Sure. You can write that we were pleased with her work, but the position has been eliminated."

"Thanks. I appreciate that." James circled the five on the one-to-five performance scale on Isobel's form. "Aren't you surprised that Paula got the job? I thought you said it was unlikely."

"It was. But apparently Frank called Mr. Jeffards—he's the head of IBS North America—and said he definitely didn't think it should be Stan."

"What reason did he give?"

"I don't know, but whatever it was, he must have been pretty persuasive."

"Did Paula put him up to it?"

"I wouldn't put it past her," said Felice, "except that would be begging. Not her style. I'm telling you, it's not going to be easy to find people willing to work for her. To change the subject," Felice dropped her voice half an octave, "we're still on for tonight, aren't we?"

For a moment, he was tempted to lie and say that something had come up, but he figured he might as well go through with it. Especially since she'd given Isobel a good recommendation.

"Yeah, sure."

"Have you been to Xavier's?"

"No. What's Xavier's?"

"Oh, it's *the* hot club! Impossible to get into."

"Doesn't sound like a good bet, then," James said, relieved.

Felice gave a dismissive chuckle. "My buddy Dexter is a bouncer there. He'll let us in. We'll hardly have to wait at all."

James's mind raced. He hadn't been to a club in months. Alcohol was absolutely unavoidable at those places, and Felice had made it clear that she was looking for a good time. That was why his gut had told him to wriggle out of it a moment ago. Now it was too late. He blamed Jayla. Somehow, somewhere, she was behind this: putting him in the way of temptation, knowing he would fail, proving that he needed her.

"Let's go somewhere for a nice dinner, just the two of us without the mob scene," James said, as seductively as he could over his rising panic.

"Xavier's has bar food. And I'll get Dexter to put us in the small room."

"I gotta be honest, it doesn't sound like my scene."

"How do you know if you've never been there?" she teased. "Meet me there at eight thirty. The big thing about Xavier's is that they start hopping early. It's their gimmick. And then if you want to, you can go to one of the other clubs that start later, but nobody ever does. See you tonight!"

Before James could say anything more, she had hung up.

Life on the wagon is a fucking roller coaster of temptation, he thought. I'll never last.

FORTY

NOW THAT ISOBEL KNEW HER HOURS were numbered, InterBank Switzerland suddenly didn't seem so bad. As she continued to slog through Frank's box, she reminded herself how depressed she'd be if she knew she were staying. The afternoon wore on, the rain continued to lash against the windows, and Isobel was surprised to find herself wishing she didn't have to go to an audition. It would be so nice to go home and curl up with Delphi, Percival and some Moo Shu Pork.

Then she remembered she'd never called Percival to find out how his interview went. She took out her cell phone and was surprised when it rang in her hand.

"It's James."

She swallowed. "I suppose you've heard."

"Yeah. Listen, I wanted to tell you not to worry about it. The official reason is that the position was eliminated. Nothing negative is going on your form."

"So I passed my first test?"

"I'll send you out again, if that's what you mean."

"It is. And thank you."

"Sure."

There was an awkward pause, but just as James started to speak, she saw Frank heading toward her with his hat and coat on.

"I've gotta go."

"Listen, I didn't get to tell you this before, but—"

"Sorry," whispered Isobel. "I'll call you back."

She set down her phone and stood up. Frank was wearing

a long, navy raincoat and a slightly wilted Fedora.

"I'm taking off early. Do you have everything in order here?"

Isobel nodded. "I'm almost done. What should I do with your stuff?"

Frank glanced at the pile. "Do you know where Procurement is? One floor down, on sixteen. I'm in the corner office to the left, just as you come onto the floor. I've already moved some stuff in there, so just leave whatever you're keeping for me on the desk."

"Okay."

Frank cleared his throat. "Paula told me you're not coming back."

"Right."

"Well, that's her decision." He leaned forward. "Just between you and I, you're better off."

You and me, thought Isobel. But Frank had been decent to her. More than the others. No reason to embarrass the man.

"Good luck with your acting," he said.

"Thanks. You, too," said Isobel. "I mean, with your new job."

Frank touched his hand to his hat in a strangely old-fashioned gesture and left. Isobel checked the time and was surprised to see it was later than she thought. Almost five, and there were still plenty of papers to sort through. It occurred to her that it might make sense to stay after everyone else had gone and warm up in the ladies' room. Dashing around town during rush hour in punishing rain with no umbrella wasn't the best way to prepare for an audition, and if she went straight from the office, it was only two quick stops on the subway. Besides, she couldn't remember which shift Delphi was working tonight, and Isobel still hadn't told her about the audition. She was glad some instinct had made her bring her music to work. As long as everyone else left on time, she could linger, finish sorting, and have the place more or less to herself.

230 JOANNE SYDNEY LESSNER

At quarter past five, Paula appeared at Isobel's desk, her raincoat slung over her arm.

"I'd like to say it's been a pleasure, but of course, it hasn't." Paula made no attempt to disguise her sneer.

Isobel returned her gaze coldly. "Good luck. I hear it's lonely in the middle."

Without another word, Paula turned on her heel and strode down the hall.

I've never been so happy to see anybody's ass in my life, Isobel thought, casting her mind back to her very first day and the floral skirt Paula had been wearing. It reminded her of the security photo Detective Kozinski had shown her of a woman leaving the building in a floral skirt. As far as Isobel knew, she had never been identified. A wisp of a thought fluttered along the outer edge of her mind, a flash of half-delineated insight that didn't alight long enough for her to grasp it. She closed her eyes and tried to bring it back, but it had vanished.

Down the hall, more people were abandoning their cubicles for the weekend, although the lights were still on in some side offices. Another advantage to staying late was that she'd be able to squeeze out a few extra billable hours on her last day. InterBank Switzerland supports the arts, she thought with some satisfaction. And who knew how long it would be before James sent her out again?

James! She had completely forgotten to call him back.

She grabbed the phone and dialed Temp Zone.

"Hello, this is James Cooke, and you've reached my voice mail…"

Oh well, she thought, replacing the receiver. She'd have to wait until Monday to hear whatever it was he wanted to tell her. There was no way she was going to call his cell phone again. Not after the last time.

By six fifteen, she had reduced the contents of Frank's boxes to two medium-sized piles. As she carried Paula's pile to her office, Isobel realized that this was the first time she'd actually been inside. It was perversely clean. The desk was neatly organized, and every book was lined up precisely one inch from the edge of the bookshelves. Several C-level business magazines, a testament to Paula's not-so-secret ambitions, lay on a small table, fanned out like they might be in a doctor's office before bored or nervous patients had scattered them about. Isobel was struck with the urge to vandalize the room, but she resisted. Paula was her own punishment.

Instead, she tossed her stack of papers sloppily on the desk. She smiled to herself and turned to leave.

Through the half-open doorway, she glimpsed Conchita emerging from Stan's office. She hadn't realized Conchita was still here. In no mood for another snarky good-bye, Isobel lurked behind Paula's door and watched as Conchita shut down her computer, gathered up her things, sent a quick prayer heavenward, then wiped her eyes and headed down the corridor.

Isobel waited another moment before she left Paula's office and returned to her own desk. She could hear the quiet murmur of conversation down the hall, interrupted by a spike of hearty laughter. The office had an oddly homey atmosphere after hours, as if it, too, were relaxing and lightening up for the weekend. She collected Frank's papers and followed Conchita's path toward the glass door and the elevators. Three men were lingering by the cubicles, including the stout, bearded man who had been rude to her on her first day.

"They're finally moving me away from the goddamn traffic," he was saying.

"Good thing, too," Isobel said, as she passed by.

"What the—?"

While she waited for the elevator, she reflected on her time at InterBank. It had certainly been an education, in more ways than one. At least she'd be better prepared for her next assignment.

If signs of life lingered on the seventeenth floor, the sixteenth, home of senior management, was completely deserted. She found Frank's new office easily. It was a spacious room, with recently purchased furniture and an attractive faux-Turkish rug. There were open cartons of books and stacks of papers piled on the floor. Frank had already set his nameplate and college diploma on the desk. Isobel placed her pile next to them and picked up the framed diploma.

Rutgers. Good theater department, she thought.

A door slammed somewhere nearby and Isobel jumped. The diploma flew out of her hands and she lurched forward to keep it from falling. She managed to catch it, knocking over a small carton of books and binders in the process. Her heart was pounding. She hadn't realized how nervous she was, alone on the sixteenth floor. She gingerly returned the diploma to the desk and took a deep breath. Maybe staying late wasn't such a hot idea. After all, someone had been murdered here once.

Okay, stop right there, Isobel counseled herself. Before you let your imagination run away with you, calm down, clean up the mess you just made, and go back upstairs. Even if it's deserted now too, at least it's familiar.

She righted the carton and began replacing its contents. Accounting books, ledgers, a small photo album.

And a small, tapestry-covered Filofax.

Even before Isobel picked it up, she knew whose it was. She held her breath and was suddenly glad there was nobody around. She picked up the Filofax and ran her fingers over the pink leather border. Then, steadying herself against the desk, she snapped open the cover and read the name on the identification page.

Doreen Fink.

Isobel closed the book again. She knew that within its pages were at least some of the dead woman's secrets, maybe even the one that would reveal the truth of her murder. She would call Detective Kozinski immediately without looking any further.

Who was she kidding?

She flipped first to the address section and found the

names and contact information she had been searching for all week: Kim Wong, Susan Hart, Lenny DeCarlo, and of course, Nikki, Conchita and Stan. Frank and Paula were listed too, along with Felice Edwards and many other names, most of which were unfamiliar. The Filofax also had a calendar section with three days per page. Isobel bit her lip and slowly thumbed through the pages to her first day at InterBank Switzerland.

There, in the space for one o'clock, Doreen had written the word "Drill," and right next to it, the letter "S."

FORTY-ONE

CLUTCHING DOREEN'S FILOFAX to her chest, Isobel sat with her back against the door to Frank's office and tried to think.

On the day she was killed, Doreen had planned to meet Stan at one o'clock, during the emergency drill they both knew had been scheduled. The question was, had they met? Had Stan darted into the women's bathroom just before the bell rang, had a brief argument with his ex-wife, and killed her?

Right from the start, Nikki, criminal though she herself turned out to be, had suspected Stan. But why would Stan kill the person who was helping him raise money for his operation?

Maybe she wasn't. Percival was mathematically gifted, true, but maybe the numbers didn't mean what he thought they did. Doreen must have known about Stan's proclivities. It easily explained the annulment of their marriage. But maybe Doreen had seen it as a betrayal and had never forgiven him. Then Stan had told her he'd changed his ways in order to convince her to help him get a job. If Doreen found out that not only did he still like to dress up, he wanted the operation, maybe she'd started blackmailing him.

But according to Frank, Doreen had been pushing Stan for promotion. Why? Because in the end, she hated Paula more than she hated Stan? Or was she just perverse enough to toy with Stan, one day helping him, the next day hurting him?

And speaking of Frank, what was Doreen's Filofax doing in his possession? There was only one explanation for that, and the realization made Isobel groan aloud. Stan and Frank were lovers. Frank had found out somehow that Stan had killed Doreen and was hiding the Filofax to protect him.

If that was the case, then why not destroy it? But Isobel knew the answer to that instantly. If Frank ever needed a hold over Stan, he could literally take a page from Doreen's book.

Isobel's head was spinning. She opened the Filofax again to the calendar page, only this time she noticed something she hadn't before. In the same spot the day before the murder, Doreen had written the letter "P."

Well. That was intriguing. Doreen had met Paula during her lunch hour the day before. If they hated each other so much, what was that meeting about?

Isobel stood up and stretched her cramped legs. Still holding Doreen's Filofax, she paced the room, weaving around the boxes as she worked through her thoughts.

Doreen didn't want Paula to have Frank's job. She was trying as hard as she could to keep her from getting it, but the one thing she hadn't been able to do was blackmail Paula. Yet.

But what if Doreen had finally found something? What if they'd met, and Doreen had laid out blackmail terms? Then, the next day, during the emergency drill—which Paula also knew about beforehand—Paula had waylaid Doreen in the bathroom and killed her before she ever got to meet Stan.

Isobel paused and looked at her watch. Six forty-five! She had completely lost track of the time. She was due at her *Two by Two* audition at seven thirty and she hadn't warmed up, or put on makeup—or anything!

Filofax in hand, Isobel ducked out of Frank's new office and instinctively turned the corner to the ladies' room, which was directly below the one on the seventeenth floor. She was a mess. Her hair was lank, and the dark circles under her eyes had returned. She spun her voice up and down the scale, then sang out a tentative arpeggio. Her voice echoed off the bathroom tile, startling her. She sounded tired, but there was no time to warm up if she wanted to get to the audition. She would just have time to dash back upstairs, quickly refresh her makeup, and then hightail it out of there.

As Isobel turned to go, a sound stopped her. Someone had flushed the toilet in the ladies' room above her, on the seventeenth floor.

She cast her mind back to the group that had been gathered by the glass doors. All men. She had an irrational impulse to bolt, but her things were upstairs: her coat, her bag, her music, her high heels. And she wasn't ever coming back. She had to get them now.

It's probably the cleaning lady I saw the other day, she reasoned. Or maybe it's somebody from one of the other departments on the floor.

Except that they generally used their own bathroom at the other end.

She left the bathroom on the sixteenth floor and made her way quickly and quietly back to the elevators. She exited onto the seventeenth floor, pressed the entrance code into the keypad on the wall and proceeded through the etched glass doors.

There was no one in sight. Someone had turned off her computer. Isobel knelt on the floor to gather her belongings, which she had stowed, as always, under her desk.

A door creaked open. The door to the ladies' room.

Isobel stood up. She knew the smart thing to do would be to stay low, under her desk, just in case it wasn't the cleaning lady. But she didn't. She backed up to the wall next to Nikki's desk and stood flush against it. In this position, Isobel would be able to see who it was without the person seeing her.

She pressed her body against the wall and held her breath. After a moment, a tall, voluptuous woman with auburn curls, wearing alligator pumps, palazzo pants, and a purple silk blouse strode past her. Isobel's eyes grew wide.

It was Stan Henderson. And she was beautiful.

FORTY-TWO

JAMES WAS NERVOUS. He couldn't remember ever going on a first date without the safety net of alcohol. He knew this little outing to Xavier's was going to test him in every way, and he hardly felt up to the challenge. Cranberry and seltzer. That was Bill's recommendation. It looked like a mixed drink and was less likely to provoke comment than, say, a Coke, which, James had to admit, was threatening to replace alcohol as his addiction. On the other hand, he could just come clean and admit his weakness. Why not? He'd admitted it to Isobel and survived. But he was still afraid that an admission like that might start an avalanche. He was full of weaknesses. He was even too weak to talk Felice out of Xavier's.

Out of the frying pan and into a bigger fucking frying pan, he thought. Why do I always wind up with these Mack truck women?

If he wasn't going to drink, he at least had to look like he would beat the crap out of anyone who messed with him. Black silk shirt, thin maroon tie, the silver and garnet cufflinks Jayla had given him for his birthday. He stepped back and checked himself out in the mirror. Not bad. In the bathroom, he splashed cologne on his neck and pushed a small gold hoop through the hole in his ear. Then he sat down on the couch and took out his phone.

"Bill? It's James. I'm checking in."

"Hey, buddy. How did it go at the meeting today?"

"Something came up and I couldn't get there. I'll talk on Sunday at home group."

"Good. You doing okay?"

James flexed his fingers and looked at his gold Columbia ring, which he had also added for the occasion. "Yeah. No. Here's the deal. I've gotten into a situation. I'm going to this club tonight, Xavier's. You know it?"

"I've never been a clubbing kind of guy. Always sounded like fun, though," Bill said wistfully.

"It's some hot new joint. It's a first date, and I'm worried about the scene. I mean, everyone will be drinking."

"Everyone but you," Bill said firmly.

"I need some help here."

"Eat before you go, so if you do slip, you're slipping on a full stomach."

"Thanks for the vote of confidence."

"I'm just being practical. Look, it would be easier if you didn't go, or at least not yet. But let's face it, it's hard to avoid social alcohol completely. And if you can make it through tonight, that'll be a big achievement."

"Give me some things to think. Things to say."

"What can you control?"

"What I drink."

"So what are you going to drink?"

"Cranberry and seltzer."

"And when she says, 'Aw, come on, have something stronger. I don't want to drink alone,' you're going to say…"

James rubbed his forehead wearily. "Here's where it falls apart for me."

"James. You're not a sissy if you don't drink."

"In my world you are. And this chick likes to drink."

"Too much?"

"Yeah, maybe."

"There you go! Couldn't be better. Tell her the truth. Maybe she needs to hear it. Maybe she needs AA. You're Daniel in the lion's den, and you've got a lioness to convert, and you can't do that drunk."

Besides, if I get drunk, that will mean I can't do it without Jayla, James reminded himself. Maybe, in the end, that was the only encouragement he needed.

"Yeah, all right. What are you doing tonight?"

"Going to bed early. I've got the kids tomorrow, and I want to make every minute count."

"Okay. Take it easy, man. And thanks."

"You too. Good luck. You can do it."

I can do it, James repeated silently, as he hung up the phone.

He put on his coat and picked up his umbrella.

"I can do it," he said aloud. Then he shut the door behind him and raced down the stairs, out into the night and toward temptation.

FORTY-THREE

IS OBEL GRABBED HER COAT from Nikki's chair and threw it on.
As she ran down the hall, she tucked the Filofax carefully in
the inside pocket, and struggled to get the strap of her bag over
her shoulder. It weighed a ton. In addition to all the extra stuff
she'd brought along for her audition, she also had the personal
items she had accumulated during her stay at InterBank
Switzerland: two sweaters, a stack of pictures and résumés, a
book of monologues, two pairs of shoes, and a travel coffee
mug. She couldn't understand how she had accumulated so
much junk. And she still didn't have a working umbrella.

At that moment, Isobel caught sight of Conchita's sturdy,
long-handed umbrella, which she had unaccountably left
leaning against the filing cabinet.

"*Muchas gracias, señora!*" she said as she grabbed it.

The lobby seemed overly bright, and there was one lone
security guard on duty.

"Sign out, please," he droned.

She scrawled a squiggle underneath the squiggle Stan had
scrawled just moments before. For the second time today, she
peered out the front door of the building, trying to catch sight
of the person she was trying to follow. Only this time, she had
an umbrella. But it had finally stopped raining, and the
umbrella became one more unwieldy thing to carry. Still, as
she followed Stan toward the subway, keeping a healthy
distance, she knew better than to dump it. Ditching an
umbrella, especially one as nice as this, would only guarantee
another downpour.

She saw Stan descend the subway stairs on the downtown

side and started after him.

Suddenly, she stopped short. What was she doing? She had an audition to go to! She knew she only had a few seconds to make her decision. She could take the uptown train and go to the audition she was already late for, with no makeup on, not warmed up, for people who probably remembered her as a blithering idiot.

Or she could follow her instincts and trail Stan downtown. Gay, straight, male, female, you don't get all decked out like that unless you're meeting someone. And she wanted to know who it was.

Your gut is a better actor than your brain, Delphi had said. And in some cases, your gut is also smarter than your brain, Isobel thought, as she followed Stan into the subway. There would be other chances to perform, in better productions that actually paid something. There wouldn't be another chance to follow Stan Henderson in drag.

The platform was crowded enough for Isobel to observe Stan at a comfortable distance. Strangely, his new look was an improvement. He simply made more sense as a woman. The soft contours, fleshy lips, even his hips. He must have been wearing shapewear of some kind, because he had an actual figure. He even turned a few heads, although Isobel wasn't sure if that was because he looked good or because he was still obviously a man.

A downtown R train arrived, and Isobel let herself be carried on by a crush of people. Stan got on at the opposite end of the same car. Given his relative height and his mass of auburn curls, he stood out enough that Isobel could see him get off at Prince Street.

She followed him outside into a soft, misting rain, glad she hadn't ditched the umbrella, and trailed him west into the heart of SoHo. Isobel hadn't been to this part of the city yet, but even at this relatively early hour in bad weather, it was quite obviously the place to be on a Friday night. The streets were lined with small galleries, boutiques and clubs, and the air vibrated with a sense of impending party. She followed Stan as he headed south to Greene Street. On the corner was a windowless black building with a large blue neon letter "X." The only giveaway that it wasn't an abandoned warehouse was the line of people snaking down the block.

Isobel squinted at the "X" and saw the smaller blue letters underneath spelling out Xavier's. So this was the place Nikki had told her about: the trendy, expensive new club with the chic celebrity, gay and transgender crowd.

The door was guarded by a man who looked like Mr. Clean. He had a headset wired around his bald pate, and he was clearly not to be messed with. Stan shouldered his way to the front of the crowd and approached Mr. Clean, who stared dispassionately at him, apparently unconcerned that his gender was open to interpretation. Mr. Clean pulled the microphone closer to his mouth and spoke for a moment. Then he nodded and let Stan pass by him into the club. As the door opened, the line of hopeful partiers surged forward, collective arms waving like a giant sea anemone. Mr. Clean set his legs in a wider stance and pushed against the people in front, sending the entire line staggering backwards. Nobody seemed to mind. This abuse appeared to be part of the game. The club door closed, swallowing Stan into the murky depths of Xavier's.

Undaunted, Isobel approached Mr. Clean.

"Hi, there. I'm with him. Um, her. The person you just let in."

Mr. Clean stared fixedly at her and pointed to the end of the line.

"No, really! That person—we're together. I'm meeting her here. Him. Her!"

Mr. Clean gave Isobel a slow once-over. "Name?" he said finally.

"Isobel Spice."

He tilted his mouthpiece again. "She-male, red hair, just came in. Ask if she's expecting someone named—"

Isobel's hand shot out and yanked the mouthpiece away from Mr. Clean's mouth. He was so startled that for a brief moment, he forgot to look menacing. "It's a surprise," she stammered. "I mean, she doesn't know—I don't want her to know…"

Mr. Clean glared at her. "Which is it?"

"Can't you just let me in?" Isobel asked, smiling her sweetest.

Mr. Clean pointed again to the end of the line. A girl who was trying not to look like she was freezing in her skimpy tank top and short skirt gave Isobel a shove.

"Come on, bitch! You can't just walk up!"

Isobel retreated to the corner. Great, she thought. I blew off my audition, and I can't even get in to spy on Stan. Now what? She paced up and down Greene Street and peered into the window of a romantic-looking Italian restaurant.

That was what she needed—reinforcements!

Delphi answered her call immediately.

"Where are you?" Isobel asked, without preamble.

"Just leaving work. I had to cover until Gina got in. Why?"

"I need you," Isobel said. Although brevity was not her forte, Isobel explained, as quickly as she could, the events of the afternoon.

"Please, please come down here," she begged. "I need a plan, and I need your help. I can't do this alone."

"Where are you again?"

Isobel gave her the address.

"Let me just run home and change, and I'll be right there."

"No! There isn't time. Just come straight here. Please?"

Isobel heard Delphi's exasperated sigh. "Okay, okay. I'll be there as soon as I can."

Isobel hung up and paced back to the corner. Mr. Clean was still doing his impression of a human fortress, and the line outside Xavier's seemed to have grown longer. There was nothing to do but take her place at the end of it.

As she parked her heavy bag on the ground behind a gay

couple with their hands in each other's back pockets, her phone rang. It was Percival.

"Iz! How was the audition? Where are you? It sounds noisy."

"I didn't go. I'm following Stan."

"What?"

Once more, Isobel summarized the events of the past few hours, finishing with a description of Xavier's and Mr. Clean.

"I'm coming down there," Percival said firmly.

"You are not!" Isobel cried, horrified. "It's a club!"

"Sounds like fun."

"You're underage!"

"Iz, you don't really think I'd come to New York to visit Columbia without a fake ID, do you?"

"Where did you get a fake ID?" Isobel asked, aghast.

"Made it."

Isobel shook her head vigorously, even though he couldn't see it. "Okay—no on about five counts! You may be mature for your age, you may be able to run rings around me intellectually, but you're still only fifteen. And if you get caught—"

"Iz, I don't want you there by yourself."

"Delphi is coming."

"So am I."

"No, you're not! I'm supposed to be watching out for you. Mom and Dad trust me, and I'm not taking you to a club—"

"Fine, then. I'm taking you. Don't you dare go in there without me!" He hung up.

She looked at the silent phone, stamped her foot, and swore.

This is not responsible sibling behavior, she scolded herself, letting him come to a club on the heels of a probable murderer. On the other hand, a male presence wasn't a bad idea.

James. That's who she really wanted with her. It was even worth risking calling his cell.

Isobel scrolled back through the log on her cell phone, but his number had been replaced by all the calls she'd made since the night his girlfriend had told her to get lost. She gave up and shoved her phone back into her coat pocket. At least Percival had an IQ higher than most people's cholesterol. Brains, if not brawn. It was the best she could do in a pinch.

The line didn't seem to be progressing at all, and the longer she waited, the stupider she felt. Finally, she heard a familiar voice call her name. She looked up to see Delphi crossing the street.

"This is crazy!" Delphi gestured to the line. "We'll never get in."

"I know. I don't understand how Stan got in immediately."

"His good looks?"

"You'd be surprised," Isobel said drily.

"Maybe they operate on a quota system?"

Isobel's cell phone rang. "Probably Percival," she said, and answered it without checking the number.

"Where the hell are you?" demanded Sunil.

"Sunil! God, I'm so sorry! Something happened. I couldn't get there."

"You could have called me! I went out on a limb for you, you know. They weren't exactly thrilled about seeing you again. I had to convince them you were worth it."

"I know and I'm really, really sorry. I should have called. Did they give it to the other girl?" She glanced at Delphi, who was eyeing her quizzically.

"What do you think?"

"Listen, Stan Henderson is a cross-dresser, and I followed him to this club, and I think something's going to happen—"

"Whatever. I've got to get back to rehearsal. I'm surprised it happened so quickly."

"What?"

"Putting your survival job before your career."

"It's not that, it's a murder—!"

But he was gone. Isobel stared at her phone.

Sunil was right. In a moment of madness, she had completely lost sight of her priorities. Or had she? The truth was, she had a lot more invested in tracking down the person who killed Doreen Fink than in a mediocre showcase company whose producers had rejected her once already. Despite what Sunil might have said in her favor, that was an awfully bad first impression to have to erase.

Delphi's voice broke into her thoughts. "What was that all about?"

Isobel told Delphi about the *Two by Two* audition.

"You blew off an audition for this? Are you out of your mind?"

"Apparently."

"How come you didn't tell me?"

"I didn't want you to be disappointed."

"That's sweet of you, but that wasn't the part I was going for in the first place." Delphi looked at the swelling number of clubbers around them. "You should have gone. This is getting us nowhere."

"I know," Isobel said gloomily. "And now I've let Sunil down."

A moment later, Percival arrived. "Why are you standing back here?" he asked.

Isobel gestured toward the front of the line. "I tried, but Mr. Clean wasn't having any of me. How was your interview?"

"Piece of cake. How did Stan get past?"

Delphi shrugged. "Mason handshake?"

Isobel gasped. "Oh my God. I know how he got in. But there's no way we could possibly...unless..." She turned to Percival. "Do you have any mad money left?"

"About a hundred bucks."

Isobel took a step off the line and looked down the street. Paradoxically, the line seemed to have gained people in front. Clearly, they were stuck with the losers, and getting past Mr. Clean demanded drastic action. There was only one thing to do.

Isobel closed her eyes. "If we're ever deluded enough to think we want it, we'll have to pay for it ourselves." She opened them and looked at Delphi. "Famous last words."

"What are you talking about?" Percival asked.

But Delphi had caught on and was shaking her head. "No way. That's insane! It'll cost you half your share of the rent!"

"I know," Isobel said, squirming visibly. "But if we use Percival's money, I could put the balance on my credit card and worry about it later, like the rest of the country."

"That's a terrible idea," Percival said.

"I gave up a callback for this. I'm not walking away now."

She grabbed Percival's arm, and with Delphi trailing behind them, protesting, Isobel shoved her way to the front of the line, until she was directly in front of Mr. Clean.

"We'd like bottle service, please."

He looked at her for a moment, then beyond her at Delphi and Percival, who was trying to stand as tall as possible, while at the same time slouching with just the right amount of hipster attitude.

Mr. Clean looked at Isobel again. "Five hundred. Bottle of your choice. Food is extra."

Delphi gasped, but Isobel nodded confidently. Mr. Clean stepped aside, and the door to Xavier's swung open. Behind them, the line heaved and surged, and Isobel, Delphi and Percival rode the human wave through the entrance as the big black door slammed shut behind them.

FORTY-FOUR

JAMES ARRIVED OUTSIDE XAVIER'S at precisely eight thirty. From the length of the line and the look of the people on it, he knew exactly what kind of evening he was in for. Even when he was drinking, he'd avoided places like this. He paced up and down the line looking for Felice, but she hadn't arrived yet. He felt immeasurably older than the coked-up, party-hungry hangers-on who were stupid enough to think that all they had to do was wait long enough to get in. A place as hot as this, it took more than that. It took knowing somebody, being a celebrity, paying off the bouncer, or springing for bottle service.

James eyed the bouncer. He was one tough-looking motherfucker. He wondered what Felice meant when she said they were friends. More reason to tread carefully tonight.

"Hiya, good-looking."

He glanced at the hooker who had sidled up next to him. He was about to retort that he usually got it for free, when he realized to his horror that it was Felice. Her hair was braided around a wide orange scarf shot through with silver thread, and her raspberry-colored, one-shoulder T-shirt featured a sparkling hand strategically placed over her right breast. She had stuffed her plump hips into an impossibly tight leather skirt and her shapely legs into the highest, pointiest boots he'd ever seen. She had glitter around her eyes, and the effect she had created was so clearly the opposite of what she was going for that he almost felt sorry for her.

"Come on. Dexter'll let us in."

James followed her wordlessly to the front of the line,

where the bouncer smacked his lips appreciatively at Felice.

"Can we get into the small room tonight?" she asked.

"For you, baby, anything," Dexter said, eyeing her appreciatively. "Dude." He swung his hand up in a brotherly greeting and when James slapped it, Dexter closed his meaty fingers around James's in a grip that shot down to the soles of his feet.

"Right, man. Thanks," said James, resisting the urge to massage his aching hand. If Dante has a circle in hell reserved for me, it looks a lot like this, he thought as they passed through the portal into the inner sanctum.

The club was dark, with barrel-vaulted ceilings and a distinctly medieval look, and it was already throbbing with scantily clad people of every eye-catching variety. There was a long, curved bar and tables with Moroccan fez-caps shading the candles. The seating was low to the ground, divans and couches everywhere, with embroidered satin cushions and the occasional rug. All that was missing were people smoking hash out of porcelain hookahs.

The wall behind the bar was lined, floor to ceiling, with bottles of every kind of alcohol imaginable, and waiters, dressed surprisingly conservatively in classic black and white, milled about. The place was choked with beautiful women. The men were definitely in the minority, and half of them were there with other men. Women and alcohol everywhere, only James wasn't drinking and his date made a cheap whore look like a debutante. It was all a sick joke.

"Come on, the small room is this way," said Felice, propelling him toward the back.

"What is this place?"

"Used to be a wine cellar, then a fancy French restaurant, and then Xavier Barques bought it."

"Xavier Barques? The movie director?"

"Yeah. The small room is the coolest place in the joint."

James did a quick mental tally of the contents of his wallet. "How much does that go for?"

"For me, nothing. The first time I came here, it cost me. Hoo, baby! But Dexter and I were pretty chummy for a while, and now he looks the other way."

They passed a group of low tables set beside a divider topped with an arrangement of blown glass bottles. James sensed a sudden sharp movement behind him. He paused to look, but all he saw was a skinny kid with glasses who looked too young to be there and a blond woman with a face like a painting, dressed just like the waiters. He hurried to catch up with Felice, who had gotten a few steps ahead of him, when he felt someone grab his arm. He turned around and found himself face to face with Isobel.

"You have no idea how happy I am to see you!" she cried.

"What the hell are you doing here?" gasped James. "Are you following me?"

"No, I'm following Stan! He's here, in drag. And that's not all! I found Doreen's Filofax, and she was supposed to meet Stan at one o'clock the day she was killed. And she met with Paula the day before!"

"Whoa...slow down. Why did you follow Stan here?"

"He's on the make. I have a table," she gestured to the bespectacled boy and the blonde. "I can see him from where we are, but I don't think he's spotted me. He's got a bottle of Amaretto and two glasses, but so far he's alone. Come on!"

Isobel started to pull him toward her table.

He shook her off. "No, wait, you don't understand, I'm here on a—with a—"

"James!"

Felice had come back for him and was staring at Isobel.

Isobel regarded her defiantly. "You told me on the phone that James never wanted to talk to me again. But you were wrong. We're speaking again, and right now I need him to come and sit with me."

Felice turned to James. "What the hell is she talking about?" She peered at Isobel. "Wait. I know you."

Isobel shook her head. "I don't think so."

"Felice, this is Isobel Spice, my temp at InterBank."

"Of course," said Felice, nodding. "Hard to see in this light."

Isobel eyes opened wide. "Felice! Wow, I didn't recognize... I didn't realize that you and James were... Okay, now you *really* have to sit with us."

Felice raised a carefully sculpted eyebrow. "Honey, you don't understand. We're here to be together, just the two of us. I don't mean to be rude—"

"Of course we'll sit with you. Come on," James said, taking Felice's hand.

She wrenched it away. "James!" She whispered through gritted teeth, "This isn't exactly what I had in mind. And I know you didn't either—" Her gaze flicked past him, and she let out an annoyed snort. "What the hell is this, the office Christmas party? What is *he* doing here?"

"That's why you need to sit with us," Isobel said. "I can explain what happened with Doreen, why he's dressed up like that—"

"Dressed up?" scoffed Felice. "That's the same damn suit he wears every day. Man has no imagination."

James and Isobel exchanged a glance, then, as unobtrusively as they could, they turned their heads and followed Felice's gaze.

Frank Lusardi had just come in to Xavier's.

FORTY-FIVE

"MOVE OVER, I CAN'T SEE!" said Felice.

"There's nothing to see." Isobel had an unobstructed view of Stan and Frank from her position at the U-shaped banquette. "They're just talking."

James, who was sandwiched in between Felice and Isobel, craned his neck to look. "That's a guy? That's Stan?

"I think he looks pretty good," Delphi said. "Not everyone can rock curls," she added, plumping her own.

Felice poured some Cabernet from the bottle Isobel had ordered to secure the table. "Anyone else want some?"

"I'll have some," Delphi said. "Isobel?"

"No." As Felice tipped the bottle inquiringly toward her brother, Isobel repeated, more forcefully, "No."

"James?" Felice asked.

Before he could respond, Isobel took the bottle and set it down in front of Felice. "No!"

Felice shrugged. "Whatever. More for me." She took an enormous gulp of wine, then picked up the bottle and topped off her glass.

James flashed Isobel a grateful look. "How did you get this table?"

Isobel winced. "You don't want to know. Suffice it to say, you'd better get me a new temp job soon. Preferably one that pays a lot."

"Do we think this is a first date?" Percival asked.

Isobel shook her head. "I don't know. There were several times when Stan and Frank were closeted together in Frank's office. No pun intended."

"I'll tell you one thing," Delphi said. "From the look on Frank's face when he saw Stan, I'd say this is the first time he's seen Stan in full regalia."

Felice poured herself some more wine. "This is great stuff!"

"It better be, for what we paid for it," muttered Delphi.

James pointed to Felice's glass. "You might want to go easy on that."

Felice cocked her head at him. "My date has turned into a party, one of my employees is a drag queen, and another has the hots for him. Her. I think I'm allowed a drink."

James turned his back on Felice and whispered to Isobel, "So what do you think? Doreen was still in love with Stan, but Stan wanted to be with Frank, so Stan snuffed her to get her off his back?"

"I don't know." Isobel wrung her hands in frustration. "It's not lining up. If Percival is right, and Doreen was funneling money to Stan, why would he kill her?"

James threw up his hands. "Who knows what he was thinking? He doesn't even know which end is up."

"Now that's unfair," Isobel said, her voice rising. "Just because he's a lesbian trapped in a man's body or whatever, doesn't mean he's mentally unstable!"

"Uh hunh!" crowed Felice.

"Maybe Stan's been pining for Frank for a while, only Frank didn't know it," Isobel suggested.

"So Stan whacked Doreen on a chance? Doesn't seem likely," Delphi put in.

"Maybe Stan wants to be sure Frank falls in love with the real him. Her." Isobel looked over at them again.

"What's going on now?" Percival asked.

"They're drinking and talking. Frank looks wary, but Stan's face is in shadow."

They sat in silence for a moment. Then Delphi turned to James. "It's nice to meet you. I've heard a lot about you."

"You have?" James asked, surprised.

"You have?" Felice hiccupped.

Delphi looked at Isobel. "Should I not have said that?"

But Isobel wasn't listening. She was staring at the wine bottle, a deep frown on her face. Something didn't make sense. Why meet in a public place? Why, if Frank and Stan were lovers, didn't Frank want Stan to have the promotion?

"Frank's getting up!" James said suddenly.

They all swiveled their heads quickly and saw Frank say something to Stan. Then he disappeared deeper into the club.

"Bathroom," said James, pointing to a carved sign high on the far back wall, just visible over the throng.

They gave a collective sigh of relief.

"So y'all are spying on Stan, because you think he killed Doreen?" said Felice, whose speech was starting to slur.

"Something like that," Delphi said.

"Why don't you just call the police?"

"We don't have enough evidence," said Percival. "It's all just conjecture at this point."

Felice leaned toward him. "You're cute."

Delphi put a protective arm around Percival. "He's with me."

"Are you a secretary, too?"

"I'm an actress, like Isobel."

Felice turned to Isobel, her eyes shining. "I didn't know you were an actress! You been in any movies?"

"I do musicals."

Felice swung her head back to Delphi and reached for the wine. "What about you? D'you sing?"

"I do, but not like Isobel."

"You wouldn't believe what a big, gorgeous sound Iz can make," Percival said proudly. "It's all in the breathing technique."

Delphi laughed. "You sound like my high school music teacher." She adopted a hooty, Julia Child-like tone. "Inhale deeply now, expand your sides like the skin of a drum. Breathe from the diaphragm. If you're going to sing properly—"

Isobel shrieked so loudly that they all jumped. She leaped

up and wrenched her coat out from under James. He went careening into Felice, who put her arms around his neck in what she intended as an embrace, but looked more like a headlock. "What the hell—?" he began.

"Don't talk to me!" Isobel barked.

Delphi held up her hands in self-defense. "Don't worry!"

But Isobel didn't hear her. She was madly fishing around in her coat for Doreen's Filofax. It felt like there were actual alarm bells going off inside her brain, every bit as loud as the ones that had rung the day Doreen was killed.

If she was right—then she'd had it all wrong.

She opened the Filofax to the front of the calendar section and began to flip over the January pages. There it was: "P." She flipped to February, and there it was again: "P." March had a "P," so did April. She slammed the book shut.

"It's Frank!"

"Where?" James said, looking past her. "Yeah, he's coming out of the bathroom. And Stan is—holy shit!"

"What?" said Percival and Delphi together.

"Stan just poured something into Frank's drink!"

Isobel's face went white.

Percival grabbed her arm. "Iz? What is it?"

"He's trying to kill Frank," she said breathlessly. "He's poisoned his Amaretto! We can't let Frank drink it!"

"Amaretto?" Percival grabbed Delphi's arm and pulled her up. "Jump over the barrier, push, shove, do whatever it takes to get over there and grab Frank's glass off the table."

Delphi blanched. "Why me?"

"Because you're dressed like the waiters. Get the glass, and whatever you do, don't spill it. Go!"

Percival helped her over the divide, and Delphi bowed her head and began to elbow her way through the crowd toward Stan's table.

Isobel turned to James, but he was already on his feet, heading toward Frank. She reached into her coat pocket for her cell phone and scrolled through to Detective Kozinski's number.

Percival looked at Isobel. "You're sure about this?"

She nodded gravely. "Absolutely."

"Whaz all the fuss about?" slurred Felice.

Isobel and Percival looked at each other, then Isobel thrust the bottle at Felice.

"Just finish it," she said.

FORTY-SIX

JAMES HAD NEVER BEEN MORE GRATEFUL to be sober as he barreled his way through the crowd. Frank was moving faster than he seemed from a distance, and as James drew nearer, he realized he had no idea what he was going to do or say once he reached him. He only knew he had to keep Frank from returning to the table. He wasn't sure what it was that Isobel had figured out, but he realized that her brother understood, and he seemed like a pretty smart kid.

There were only a few people separating him from Frank now, and James saw that Frank looked preoccupied.

Well, why not? He was on a date with a woman who was really a man.

Suddenly, James knew exactly what to say to Frank.

"Aw, shit," he groaned. But he had no choice. He wasn't going to let Isobel down again.

A tall woman—or was it a man?—standing between them stepped aside, and James put his hand on Frank's arm.

He cleared his throat. "I was just, er, wondering. Are you here alone?"

Frank turned, surprised, but when he caught James's eye, his face relaxed into a seductive smile.

"For you, I could be."

AFTER WHAT SEEMED LIKE AN ETERNITY, Delphi arrived at Stan's table. Isobel and Percival watched as she smiled and bobbed her head.

Then Delphi grabbed Frank's glass, and as best as she

could in a room growing more crowded by the second, she turned and ran.

After a moment, Stan recovered and shot to his feet, his face creased with panic.

"He's going after her!" Percival cried.

"Felice!" shouted Isobel.

"Forget about her!"

"We need her!"

But Percival was gone, shoving his way toward the mass of people separating Delphi and Stan. Delphi was heading for the front door, and Stan was knocking over patrons in hot pursuit.

Isobel slapped Felice hard on the face.

"Ow!"

"Come on, Felice," Isobel pleaded. "I need you to do something for me. You're drunk on my five-hundred-dollar bottle of Cabernet, so you owe me. I need you to stand on the table. Drunk people stand on tables all the time. Here, I'll help you." Isobel threw her arms under Felice's and tried to maneuver her slack form to her feet.

"Oooh, baby!" purred Felice.

"Come on, climb up!"

Lifting Felice was much harder than she expected. Isobel blew in her face and, in a final act of desperation, tossed the remains of her wineglass at her. Somewhat revived, Felice allowed herself to be pulled up onto the table where she stood, swaying precipitously.

Isobel called up to her. "Come on, wave hello to all your fans! Loud as you can. Ladies and gentlemen, the one and only, the fabulous Felice Edwards!" She put her fingers to her lips and blew a piercing whistle.

Felice did as she was told, and several people nearby pointed at her and laughed. Isobel grabbed a small hand-blown bottle from the arrangement atop the divider and threw it with all her might in Stan's direction. It hit the back of a magenta-haired girl in Goth dress, knocking her down, and several people cried out, startled.

But it did the trick. Stan stopped in his tracks and squinted in their direction. Isobel quickly ducked below the divider, watching him through the remaining bottles. She was banking on the fact that Felice in her club getup would be unrecognizable to Stan, yet somehow familiar. If Stan took a moment to work out who she was, then stopped to absorb the fact that InterBank's director of human resources was standing on a table waving wildly at him, it might be enough to buy Delphi and Percival the time they needed. Isobel watched the play of emotions across Stan's face. He looked confused, shocked, and then terrified.

Percival took a flying leap and landed on Stan's back. He threw an arm around Stan's neck and yanked the wig half off his head. Stan shouted and tried to knock Percival off, but he rode Stan to the floor like a cowboy on a bucking horse. As the commotion grew, the crowd parted, giving Delphi a clear path to the club's entrance. She put on speed, wrenched open the black door through which they had fought so hard to come in, and disappeared into the night.

"This is fuuuuun!" Felice squealed.

Isobel climbed up next to her on the table and looked over the heads of the crowd until she spotted James and Frank. Frank was staring, openmouthed at Felice. His face darkened with anger as he spotted Isobel, and they locked eyes for a moment. Then Frank made a dash to one side, but James was ready for him with a quick right to the jaw, and in a moment, they too were grappling on the ground.

A tall, handsome Latin man was advancing angrily toward them. "Break it up! Or I'll call the police!"

"I already have!" Isobel screamed, but he didn't hear her.

It didn't matter. At that moment, the front door of the club opened again, and in came Dexter, Detective Kozinski, Detective Harvey, and two other police officers.

Behind them trailed Delphi, clutching the small glass of Amaretto to her chest like an Academy Award.

FORTY-SEVEN

DEXTER WAS STILL CLEARING OUT the club as Isobel, James, Percival, and Delphi settled down at their table again next to Felice, who had passed out on the banquette. Percival held an ice pack to the back of his head, while James massaged the hand he had used to punch Frank.

At the next table, Frank and Stan sat in stony silence with Detectives Harvey and Kozinski. Xavier Barques, the club's owner, sat at a third table nearby with one of the other policemen, guarding the glass of Amaretto.

Detective Harvey pulled his chair around and looked sternly at Isobel. "Suppose you tell us what's going on."

Isobel unfolded her well-worn copy of Doreen's blackmail log. "This piece of paper is a list of people that Doreen Fink was blackmailing."

"You gave that to us," Detective Kozinski reminded her. "We've been examining it, and we've spoken to everyone on the list."

"You've spoken to Stan?" Isobel asked, surprised.

"Yes."

"I know what he told you. That is, if he told you the truth." Isobel turned to Stan. "Doreen wasn't blackmailing you at all. She was taking money from all these other people and giving it to you, so you could get the operation you wanted. Is that what you told the police?"

Stan nodded.

"You and Doreen were married once," Isobel continued. "The marriage was annulled when Doreen realized it would never be consummated. But she loved you. She's always loved you, and you stayed in touch all these years. And stayed friends."

Isobel saw tears begin to leak silently through Stan's long-lashed, heavily made-up eyes and down his face, leaving black streaks of mascara in their wake. In full makeup and dress, but without his wig, he was a pathetic sight. Isobel felt suddenly, deeply sad for Stan. She reached over and touched his hand.

"I said I was sorry for your loss, and I meant it. Oh, and Maybelline makes the best waterproof mascara."

"Why are we here if Stan didn't kill Doreen?" asked Detective Harvey impatiently. "Which, by the way, we never thought he did."

"Because he was trying to kill Frank." Isobel pointed to the glass that Xavier Barques was holding. "It's poisoned."

Xavier recoiled from the glass, then leaned his head closer and sniffed. "Smells like Amaretto."

"Test it for prussic acid," Percival said. "They both smell like almonds."

Isobel shook her head sadly at Stan. "Amaretto is a weird thing to order if you're having bottle service. You could never make it through the entire thing in one night, and they won't let you take it home." She shot Xavier a look. "By the way, we have to talk about this crazy bottle service thing."

"All right, but why did Stan want to kill Frank?" asked Detective Kozinski.

Isobel looked at her like she was crazy. "Oh, come on! There's only one possible reason for that. Because Frank killed the only person who ever loved Stan for who he was."

They all looked at Frank.

"Why would I kill Doreen?" he asked indignantly. "She was a very competent secretary. I relied on her. I've been lost without her." He gave Isobel a dirty look. "You haven't been much help, you know."

"You killed Doreen because she was blackmailing you like she was everybody else."

"No she wasn't." Frank gestured at the paper. "My name

isn't anywhere on there."

Isobel shook her head solemnly. "She wasn't blackmailing you for money, she was blackmailing you for sex. Doreen had the hots for you, Frank, and you knew it. She was obsessed with sex, and she wasn't getting any. You weren't interested in her, for all reasons, but she, being the keeper of your secrets, was blackmailing you about being gay."

"It's not a big deal," he said. "My wife knows."

"And she's none too happy about it. But that's not who you were hiding it from. Edmund Jeffards. The man at the top. Archie Conservative, who can't even deal with the idea of women in management. You were afraid that if he knew you were gay, it would be an obstacle to your own promotion."

"Blackmailing me for sex? Where would you get a crazy idea like that?"

Isobel set Doreen's Filofax on the table. Frank's face went pale when he saw it.

"I found this in your new office tonight after you left." She opened it to the date of the murder. "You knew about the emergency drill ahead of time. You told me that Stan and Paula knew in advance because they were fire marshals, but you neglected to mention that Doreen told you also." Isobel flipped to the page with the date of the murder. "You agreed to meet Doreen in the bathroom and have sex with her during the emergency drill."

"That's ridiculous! Who would have sex in an office bathroom during an emergency drill?" Frank scoffed.

"She got the idea from your last temp, who used to do it in Starbucks bathrooms with her boyfriend. And you agreed to it. See? The letter 'S' next to the word 'Drill' in her date book. It stands for sex, and you were the one she wanted it with."

"You don't know that. It could stand for anything. Like Stan!"

Isobel nodded. "That's what I thought at first. But look at what she's written the day before. The letter 'P'."

Isobel looked around at the raft of baffled faces.

"Delphi? Detective Kozinski?" she prodded. "Surely, I can't be the only woman who does this! Well, I'm not. Obviously, Doreen did it too. What do you ladies write? A 'P'? A checkmark? A circle around the date…?"

Delphi shook her head, perplexed, but after a moment she caught on. A second later, Detective Kozinski's lip curled in a knowing smile.

"I thought so," Isobel said. "We all keep track of when our periods start." She riffled back through the pages of Doreen's calendar. "Look. There's a 'P' every month. And sometimes you write down the letter 'S' for sex, so if you skip your period, you can see if there's a chance you might be pregnant. Or you might also jot down the letter to represent a noteworthy and exciting encounter coming up, like in this case."

Delphi sat up suddenly. "No jelly!"

Isobel nodded. "That's what did it. When you were talking about breathing from the diaphragm, I remembered Doreen's."

"I still don't get it," Detective Harvey said.

"Doreen wasn't going to let anything as mundane as her period stop her from her own personal porn flick," Isobel explained. "Office bathroom sex? It's like doing it on an airplane, only better. She must have been fantasizing about it for weeks. She wasn't using her diaphragm for birth control— she was using it for flood control."

Isobel watched, amused, as the men squirmed in their chairs. "That's why you didn't find any jelly in her cosmetics bag," she said to Detective Kozinski. "I thought you were wrong, and she must have been taking her diaphragm out."

"No," said Detective Kozinski, "we were pretty sure she was putting it in. There were no traces of semen or jelly." She gave a wan smile. "I just assumed she hadn't read the accompanying literature thoroughly."

"This is bullshit!" Frank finally exploded. "Maybe you're paranoid enough to write down that kind of stuff, but there's no way of knowing that's what Doreen meant except to ask her."

"It's not bullshit."

It was Stan who spoke, in a miserable voice.

Isobel turned to him and asked gently. "How did you know it was Frank?"

Stan looked down at his fingernails, which Isobel noticed for the first time were painted a lovely plum. "The skirt."

Frank opened his mouth and started to say something, but thought better of it.

"The photo of the person in the skirt leaving the building the day Doreen was…the day of the murder," Stan continued, talking to his hands.

"Go on," Detective Kozinski said.

He looked up and met her eye. "It was my skirt. I keep, um, extra clothes at the office. Sometimes it's just easier, because my roommate…well, he knows, but it freaks him out. So sometimes I go out straight from work, like tonight. Anyway, I had a fairly new wrap skirt in my office, and I went to look for it—I wanted to wear it a few nights ago—and it was gone." He glanced at Isobel. "You asked me what I was looking for. It was the skirt."

Stan cleared his throat and faced Frank. "Your wife came in that same day wearing it. I asked her where she got it, and she said she had so many clothes, she couldn't even remember. I'd stepped in the hem once with my heel, and there was a little rip that I'd never bothered to mend, so I knew it was mine. Then I remembered the security photo. At the time, I never thought it was my skirt, because I knew it wasn't me. But then I put it all together. Frank wore my skirt, and then he took it home where Audrey must have found it."

"And why exactly did I need your skirt?" Frank asked.

"It would have been easy enough for you to sneak into the bathroom during the drill without anyone noticing. But you wore the skirt and a big jacket and a scarf for a little extra protection coming out. You knew Paula and I would be checking the floor, including the bathrooms, and you had to get past us without us realizing it was you. It didn't have to be a complicated disguise, just enough so in all the chaos, we wouldn't remember seeing you. And you probably had to…cover up…blood."

Frank waved his hand dismissively. "As evidence goes, that's pretty flimsy."

Stan's face hardened. "I also knew how Doreen felt about you. She told me what she wanted to do, although I didn't know she'd gone as far as to plan it," Stan said. "I tried to convince her to go after your money, like everybody else. I mean, that's what I really needed. But she thought if you slept with her, you'd give up Audrey—and men—for her. Just like Conchita is always trying to change me. I tried to explain to Doreen that it didn't work that way with you any more than it did with me. And I knew from—"

"Stan," Frank warned.

But Stan went on, undeterred. "I knew from the one night you and I spent together that you were curious about my dressing up. I told you that I kept clothes in my office. Even Doreen didn't know that."

Detective Harvey was fuming. "Why didn't you come to us?"

Tears welled up in Stan's eyes. "Because I wanted to …" He swallowed hard and tried again. "Frank killed the only person who ever loved me for who I am. And he killed my best—my only chance at happiness. Those things Doreen did were all to help me. I didn't know how to help myself." Stan gave a hollow laugh. "I wanted to settle the score for her, even if she would never know I did it. Because if hadn't been for me, none of this would have happened."

Isobel hesitated. Part of her wanted to let Stan's story end there, but she knew there was more to it.

"There's another reason you resolved to poison Frank tonight, isn't there?" she prompted.

Stan gave a weary sigh. Isobel continued.

"When Frank called Mr. Jeffards to push for Paula, he told Jeffards about you. That's why Paula got the promotion."

Stan nodded, and as he spoke, his voice caught. "Given the choice, Jeffards would rather have a real woman in the job than…than someone like me."

The click of Detective Harvey's handcuffs fell into the silence as he locked them around Frank's wrists.

"Frank Lusardi, you are under arrest for the murder of Doreen Fink. You have the right to remain silent…"

Detective Kozinski cuffed Stan, and her reading of the Miranda rights echoed in counterpoint with Detective Harvey's. Stan's tears gave way to sobs of grief, which he was unable to choke back.

At that moment, Felice stirred from her alcoholic stupor and sat up against the banquette.

"Whaz goin' on?"

James, seated next to her, answered quietly, "Frank and Stan are being placed under arrest."

"Oh, yeah?" Felice straightened up for a moment and squinted at the two men, who were being helped to their feet by the police officers. "Well, you're both fired!" She collapsed back onto the bench.

Detective Harvey turned to Xavier Barques. "Can you decant that into a clean empty bottle with a top?" He indicated the glass of Amaretto. "I'll take the glass as well."

"Of course."

"Thank you, Mr. Barques. We're extremely sorry this had to happen here."

"Not at all! But don't be surprised if some of the plot elements in my next movie seem familiar," he said with a wink.

Detective Kozinski picked up the Filofax with a napkin and slipped it into an evidence bag. She looked appraisingly at Isobel. "Maybe your next temp job should be with us."

Isobel turned to James. "Is the NYPD a Temp Zone client?" He shook his head. Isobel smiled at Detective Kozinski. "Sorry. But thanks anyway."

"Too bad," Detective Kozinski said, sounding like she

meant it. She followed Detective Harvey toward the front door, where Dexter and the other two police officers were waiting with Stan and Frank.

Xavier Barques stood up. "Your bottle service tonight is on the house," he said grandly, in his mellifluous, accented voice.

For the first time all evening, the knot in Isobel's stomach relaxed. "Thank you. I know we weren't exactly good for business tonight."

Xavier dipped his head graciously. "On the contrary. You know what they say: there's no such thing as bad publicity."

"You know, I didn't realize you were Xavier Barques," Isobel said.

"I am, indeed."

"I love your movies! Particularly your last one." Isobel reached into her shoulder bag. "Can I give you my picture and résumé?"

FORTY-EIGHT

"So Frank killed Doreen because he couldn't bear the thought of having sex with her?" Sunil asked, setting aside the dessert menu.

"Basically," Isobel said. "And he truly believed he wouldn't get promoted if the head of the company knew he was gay."

"There are laws that protect against that sort of thing," Sunil said.

"But companies don't always follow them," Delphi pointed out.

"And this Jeffards is apparently a little behind the times," Isobel said.

Delphi shook her head. "I feel bad for Stan."

"Did he think Frank would like him better in drag?" Sunil asked.

"It wasn't that," Isobel said. "He wanted to reveal himself in his true form, prepared to do right by Doreen and by himself."

"What I still don't understand, though," Delphi said, "is why Stan didn't just turn Frank in."

"People will do all kinds of weird shit for love," Percival said.

Sunil laughed. "And you know this…how, exactly?"

Delphi patted Sunil's hand. "Best not to ask those questions of Percival. Just accept the fact that his intellect surpasses that of us mere mortals."

"And how is everything over here?" Carlo placed his hand on the back of Delphi's neck. "How is the food and service from this end?"

"Food's fine, service is lousy," Delphi said. "These other girls aren't nearly as good as me."

Carlo grinned. "Just as I thought. Although I haven't tried them all." He winked and moved away toward the next table.

Sunil turned to Isobel. "Well, I forgive you for not calling me. I didn't realize what you were in the middle of. And I'm sorry I made that crack about your survival job being more important than your career."

"No, you were right. For a few moments there, it was." Isobel couldn't suppress a momentary pang. "And the girl who got the part...she's good?"

"Not as good as you would have been, but she'll do."

Isobel looked at her watch and tugged Percival's sleeve. "You'd better skip dessert. You don't want to miss your flight."

"Right." Percival pushed his chair away from the table. "It was great to meet you guys. Thanks for taking such good care of my sister."

"I'd love to introduce you to *my* sister," Delphi said. "All of them."

Isobel followed Percival to the coat check, where he retrieved his jacket and backpack.

"Not a word to Mom and Dad, right?"

"Are you kidding? And tell them I went to a nightclub?"

They both laughed, and Isobel hugged her brother tightly. "I really hope you come to Columbia next year."

"Iz, I just wanted to say that I think he seems like a really interesting guy."

She looked over her shoulder at Sunil, who had inched his chair closer to Delphi's. "He is, but not my type, really. I think Delphi's coming around—"

Percival snorted. "Not Sunil, silly. James. I don't know what the story is with that wino chick, but he's totally into you."

"James? That's crazy!" protested Isobel.

"I was watching him when you were talking to the police. His face was wide open, and it wasn't just admiration I saw.

And don't think I didn't notice you helping him 'just say no.'"

Isobel shook her head in astonishment. "You don't miss a trick, do you?"

"Sorry. Can't help it."

Isobel hugged him again. "I love you. Fly safe."

She took her time returning to the table. It seemed ridiculous, except that Percival was so rarely wrong.

ISOBEL PUSHED OPEN THE DOOR TO Temp Zone and caught the eye of a middle-aged woman with graying hair, who was standing by the copier in the cramped foyer.

"Come on in. Are you looking for temp work?"

Isobel closed the door behind her. "Actually, I'm already signed up with you. My name is Isobel Spice, and I'm here to see—"

The woman's face lit up. "Of course! Our very own temporary detective! You're quite the celebrity around here." She extended her hand. "Anna Brackett. I know Ginger wants to meet you."

"Is she the redhead? I met her the day I came in."

"Ginger? Isobel Spice is here!"

Within moments, Isobel was surrounded by James, Anna, Ginger, and two other reps, who shook Isobel's hand vigorously in turn.

"In all my years in the recruiting industry, I've never had anything like this happen before," said Ginger.

"I'm glad to know office murders are rare," Isobel said.

Ginger peered unapologetically at her. "James tells me you're very clever and a good secretary into the bargain."

Isobel glanced at James, who looked simultaneously amused and embarrassed. "Thanks. In my experience, James usually knows what he's talking about."

"I'm very impressed," Ginger went on. "I hope you'll stay on with us. Not that we have any intention of trading on your notoriety."

From the way she said it, Isobel could tell that Ginger planned to do exactly that, a fact that James confirmed once they were alone together in his office.

"I can already hear her on the phone with the next potential client." He mimicked Ginger's voice. "We've got the girl who solved the case of the skewered secretary, but she costs extra."

Isobel laughed. "And let me guess, neither of us will see any of the extra?"

"You know it."

They smiled at each for a moment, until James cleared his throat and looked away. "There's something I haven't had a chance to tell you," he said.

"What?"

"The woman who answered my phone the night you called…"

"The one who said you never wanted to speak to me again?"

"Yeah. That was Jayla, my girlfriend. I mean my ex-girlfriend. I know you thought it was Felice. The thing is, um, this is a little embarrassing." James picked up his nameplate and ran his sleeve over it. Isobel couldn't help but smile.

"That day we argued in the diner, I was really angry at you," he said. "No, I was angry at myself. I don't know, I was just…it pushed me over the edge and I…" He exhaled forcefully. "Wow, I don't know why this is so hard for me to say."

Isobel was tempted to make a witty response but, in a rare moment of restraint, chose instead to keep silent.

James cleared his throat and continued. "I fell off the wagon that night, big-time. Jayla found me—she has, um, had a key to my place—and right before I passed out, I heard her take your call. I never tried to explain or apologize for what she said, because…well…I didn't want you to know that I fell off the wagon because of what you said."

Isobel's words came out in a rush. "I should have called

you to apologize as soon as I realized you were right about Nikki. But I thought you told the woman on the phone to blow me off, so I didn't."

"I know. It was a big mess."

"No, that's only partly true," Isobel said. "You're being honest with me, so I should be totally honest with you. I didn't want to admit I was wrong. I think I knew from the start you were right about Nikki."

"I tried to tell you the other night about Jayla…"

"But you were on a date with Felice."

"Yeah. But you should know there's nothing going on between Felice and me."

"Why should I know? It isn't any of my business." She hesitated for a split second. "Is it?"

"The point is, she asked me out and I was mad at Jayla, so I said yes. I'm sure you figured out that Felice has a drinking problem. I actually got her to an AA meeting last night."

"Really? What happened?"

"I pretended it was a date just to get her there, and she was pretty pissed at first. But I think it might take." James readjusted his clean nameplate. "When it was my turn to speak, I talked about how I don't want to be dating anyone at all right now. I think she got the message."

"Oh," said Isobel, feeling oddly disappointed in Percival.

"Yeah," said James, sitting back in his chair. "I haven't been sober very long. I need to take some time to figure myself out, you know?"

Isobel caught his eye and held it. Was this part of the confession or was he trying to send her the same message he sent Felice? Either way, it was clear he wasn't interested.

"I understand."

He leaned forward and lowered his voice. "Look, nobody here knows about my being in AA, so you won't mention it, right?"

Isobel nodded solemnly. "Sure. That'll be a hundred bucks a month."

He laughed, which was some consolation.

"I wonder how everything went down at InterBank this morning?" Isobel continued.

"They're doing away with Procurement Support entirely."

Isobel's eyes opened wide. "Seriously?"

"Paula and Conchita were the only ones left, so it wasn't much of a department anymore. Conchita's replacing some other secretary who's taking maternity leave."

"And Paula?"

"I guess they couldn't find a place for her anywhere else. Or maybe they didn't want to. So much for her big promotion."

"Funny," mused Isobel. "Somehow, I don't feel too bad about that."

"What are you going to do now?" James asked.

"You mean, right now?"

"No, I mean for the future. You really want to keep working with me? I mean, with Temp Zone?"

"Of course. Last time I checked, there weren't any Broadway producers breaking down my door."

"If you're half as good an actress as you are a detective, they will be."

She crossed her fingers and waved them. "Here's hoping. In the meantime, do you have anything else for me?"

"Not yet. But the next job that crosses my desk has your name on it."

"Thanks, I appreciate that." Isobel stood up. "Well, I'd better get going."

James rose and came around the desk. Just as she held out her hand to him, he bent down and collected her in a hug that surprised her for its gentleness. They pulled apart and stared at each other awkwardly for a moment. Then they both smiled.

"Here, let me show you out," said James.

"No need," she said. "I can find my own way."

And Isobel realized, as she stepped out onto the bustling

sidewalk, that she could indeed find her own way: around New York, around an office, around a theater, and, perhaps at some point in the future, around James Cooke.

ACKNOWLEDGMENTS

As usual, it takes, if not a village, at least a housing development to write and publish a novel, and I would be remiss if I did not single out a few people who were particularly helpful in shepherding Isobel and company to the page. First, my rapid response team: my agent, Kari Stuart at ICM, the most supportive and energetic cheerleader a writer could hope for; my eagle-eyed editor, Jodie Renner, who caught my logic flaws (and, yes, there were a few); and Linda Pierro of Flint Mine Press, who gave me another terrific cover design.

Rick Hamlin, Helen Faye Rosenblum, Elaine Greenblatt, Marc Acito, and Cornelia Iredell were early readers whose feedback influenced the end result. Liz Sanders shared her experiences from the now defunct Evangeline Residence, and Bill T. gave me insight into the workings of Bill W. Detective John Sweeney and Officer Yolanda Williams of the NYPD set me straight on points procedural, while Elizabeth S. Craig generously advised me on matters publicational. Thanks, too, to Kate Koningisor, who lived it with me and knows where all the bodies are buried. Figuratively speaking, of course.

There will never be enough words, even from me, to thank my parents, Helen and Alford Lessner, my sister, Kathy Lessner Yellen, and my children, Julian and Phoebe Rosenblum. In a category by himself is my husband of twenty-one years, Joshua Rosenblum, whom I like to describe as my rock and my redeemer.

I would also like to thank the directors who didn't cast me and the publishers who, after praising my writing to the skies, passed on this manuscript. I'm not being facetious. As any writer or performer knows, there's nothing like a healthy dose of rejection to clarify one's objectives and harden one's resolve. Without those experiences, our stories would be a lot less interesting.

Bluface Photography

About the Author

Joanne Sydney Lessner is the author of *Pandora's Bottle*, a novel inspired by the true story of the world's most expensive bottle of wine (Flint Mine Press, 2010). *The Temporary Detective* introduces Isobel Spice, aspiring actress and resourceful office temp turned amateur sleuth. No stranger to the theatrical world, Joanne enjoys an active performing career in both musical theater and opera. With her husband, composer/conductor Joshua Rosenblum, she has co-authored several musicals including the cult hit *Fermat's Last Tango* and *Einstein's Dreams*, based on the celebrated novel by Alan Lightman. Her play, *Critical Mass*, received its Off Broadway premiere in October 2010 as the winner of the 2009 Heiress Productions Playwriting Competition. Joanne is a regular contributing writer to *Opera News* and holds a B.A. in music, *summa cum laude*, from Yale University.

Look for the next Isobel Spice novel, *Bad Publicity*, in 2013!

www.joannelessner.com

Made in the USA
Charleston, SC
15 February 2013